the fixer's daughter

A Mystery Novel

HY CONRAD

800
402

ISBN 978-1-7355555-1-5

Library of Congress Control Number: 2020912369

Published by Mason Hill Inc.
Key West, Florida USA

HyConrad.com

ALSO BY HY CONRAD

Toured to Death

Dearly Departed

Death on the Patagonian Express

*Things Your Dog Doesn't Want You to Know
(with Jeff Johnson)*

Mr. Monk Helps Himself

Mr. Monk is Open for Business

Mr. Monk Gets on Board

Mr. Monk and the New Lieutenant

PROLOGUE

THE YOUNG LAWYER had been thrilled – thrilled and, if he had
to be honest, overwhelmed. As a third-year associate, he was
still miles away from making partner. Most of his twelve-hour
workdays were spent managing the expectations of mid-level
clients, or being second chair on someone else's case, or pulling
strings on behalf of the teenage daughter of a politician who
needed to get her shoplifting conviction expunged. This was the
preordained path when you were a small cog in a big firm. And
yet here he was, having leap-frogged somehow to this strange
and challenging opportunity, this singular moment in time.

He had met Keagan Blackburn only once before, in February when he'd found himself seated at the same table as
the CEO of Blackburn Energy at a gala for the Austin Symphony. Blackburn had traded chairs with the lawyer's wife, so
the two men could talk. For the life of him, the younger man
couldn't remember what they'd talked about. But he must have
made an impression, because it was three months later and
Blackburn had hand-picked little David Morganthau to be
lead counsel on a murder charge leveled against the oil baron

himself. At some point, one of the senior partners would take over. It was inevitable. But for now... *This could be the case of the year,* he mused. *The case of the decade. Another O.J.*

Morganthau and Blackburn were seated side by side in brown leather chairs, in an oak-paneled study, gazing across to the legend himself, ex-attorney general of Texas, a man who'd been short-listed for the Supreme Court but had famously told the president, "Hell, no." He was still one of the best-connected men in the state. If anyone could pull this into focus...

"Which one of you sons of bitches is pulling my leg? I would make more of an effort to be polite, except I'm not in a joking mood."

Lawrence "Buddy" McFee was a large man without being fat, in his early seventies, with just enough silver hair to warrant an occasional trim around the edges. An ancient Irish setter, his red-gray head propped on the edge of a tartan-plaid dog bed, was vaguely alert to the possibility of a treat, watching as his master ambled over to the wet bar. It was three in the afternoon, but the consultant chose a cut crystal rocks glass and poured himself four fingers of a mellow, blended whisky. Neat. It was a gift, he told them, from a small-batch Fort Worth distillery, in thanks for services better left unmentioned. He offered none of it to his guests, which was just as well.

"It's no joke," David felt compelled to state. Again. "Mr. Blackburn says he has no idea who the woman was. He has no idea how or where she was killed. He maintains his innocence on all charges." The lawyer coughed nervously. "Actually, it's one charge. Murder in the first. Although the D.A. could alter that, depending on extenuating circumstances."

"But there are no circumstances, are there?" Buddy settled

into his own armchair and the dog returned to his full-napping position. Picking up his yellow legal pad, the consultant made a few more notes. "My old amigo Keagan here refused to tell a highway patrol officer what he was doing in an open field a mile or two from his house. He refused to say why he was dragging the raped and murdered body of a young woman through said field. He refused to say why his Escalade was parked by the side of the road, engine running, with the back open, or why he was in possession of a shovel – a shovel that one can only assume, if the very observant officer had not noticed this little excursion, he was about to use to dig the young woman's grave."

"That's an assumption. Possession of a shovel is not a de facto admission of the intent to…" David Morganthau searched for the right word. "…grave dig."

"Not grave dig?" The sarcasm in Buddy's voice was mixed with disbelief. "Possession of a shovel in a field at night with a dead body. What was his intent, for God's sake?" He was almost shouting. "To paint a still life? 'Woman in a Field with Shovel'? Nah, even that won't work. He didn't have his paint set with him."

The young lawyer refused to raise his voice. "From the moment of his encounter with the officer, Mr. Blackburn has offered no explanation, other than to maintain his innocence. That is perfectly within his rights."

Buddy turned to his old amigo and tilted his head. "How the hell do you say nothing? I've known your ass thirty years. I've seen you lie your way through board meetings and skirt around the S.E.C. with the silver tongue of a snake. Hell, in the old days I prosecuted you and your brother on insider trading, only to have you out-talk me at every turn. And yet you had nothing to say to a green patrolman who probably wanted to believe anything you said, just so he wouldn't have to arrest the mighty Keagan Blackburn."

Blackburn swallowed hard and answered in measured phrases. "I told him that I didn't know her. I had never met her while she was alive. And I didn't kill her. I didn't say a thing about the shovel."

Buddy's half-grin was sympathetic. "Bad luck there. If you didn't happen to be holding a shovel – your own shovel from your own garage, according to the report – you might have said – I don't know – that you just stumbled across her while you were out jogging, and you were in the process of dragging the poor girl out of the field and to the emergency room."

The oil executive bristled. "But I was holding a shovel. Number one rule: don't make up a story that you're going to have change somewhere down the road."

"So, what happened, Keagan boy? Really."

When Blackburn didn't answer, Buddy McFee eased his gaze over to Morganthau and locked eyes with the third-year associate. "Y'all boys got attorney-client. Pay me a buck and it extends to me."

The lawyer wasn't sure if this was something that had to be done immediately. But he opened his wallet, removed the smallest bill he could find, a ten, and pushed it across the antique burlwood desk. He was tempted to ask for change but didn't. "Mr. Blackburn has told me nothing," he said. "I advised him that his statement would be held in strictest confidence. I practically begged him. We all did."

"He won't tell his own lawyers?"

"Buddy, come on." Blackburn chuckled darkly and shook his head. "What did you think when I walked in here with this wet-behind-the-ears jackass and not one of the partners?"

'Hey,' David protested, but the word barely hit the air.

"Yes, I found that curious," Buddy admitted.

"Did you think I was slumming it for fun?" Blackburn's tone grew angry. "With my life hanging in the balance? The firm's had my family business since before I was born. And now, the time when I need them most, they all plead some bullshit about a conflict of schedules. No one was available for me except this…" He waved his hand in the direction of his lawyer. "…Whatever the hell it is."

That wasn't how David recalled the sequence of events. Yes, Mr. Blackburn and the partners had exchanged words. Heated words. But at the end, Jonas Price, senior partner of Price, Evans and White, had agreed to take on the case. Personally. One of their most important clients was in peril. It would have been unconscionable, not to mention stupid, to refuse. By this time, however, Keagan Blackburn had dug his heels in. If the partners had any reservations about his story, or lack of one, then they shouldn't bother. The oil executive would prefer to be represented by someone who trusted him, by someone who wouldn't push him to reveal more than he was willing to, by the young, ambitious lawyer, in fact, who had sat next to him at the symphony gala back in February.

"You want me to talk to Jonas?" Buddy reached for the landline on his desk. "I'll get this straightened out."

"Don't bother," said Blackburn. "It's a matter of pride. Between you, me and the young bumwad, we'll handle it."

"Well, at least you had the sense to call me." Buddy picked

up the ten and brandished it for effect. "So, did you kill her? Just between you, me and the bumwad."

"I did not," Blackburn said emphatically.

"Good. Never thought you could kill. Not a stranger, at least."

"Damn right. Hell, she was a black girl, too?"

"And what does that mean?" Buddy asked.

Blackburn squirmed in his brown leather. "You know. A matter of taste."

"You mean you're fully capable of raping and killing a white girl, but not a black one? Not sure that's your best defense. Okay then, if you didn't kill her, tell me how you got possession of the body?"

"I can't tell you."

Buddy McFee sipped his whisky then hunched forward, elbows planted halfway across the desk. "Are you covering for someone, is that it?" Buddy shook his head. "No, that's not you. Did you do something even worse and would rather take the fall for this? No. What could be worse than rape and murder in the first?"

"No comment," the CEO growled. "Make it go away. That's what you do, isn't it?"

Buddy nodded then turned to the lawyer. "Was there a dash cam?"

"Installed but not operational," Morganthau told him. "They're changing systems."

"That's one thing in our favor. And who's the lead detective?"

"Um." The lawyer was taken by surprise. He fumbled for the papers in his lap and the whole file cascaded onto the floor. He scrambled to pick them up.

"Never mind," said Buddy. "I'll get my own guy in there."

"Someone you trust?" asked Blackburn.

"Trust like family," Buddy answered.

In the alcove of the study, behind the gray painted waves of a Japanese folding screen, sat Gil Morales in a matching leather chair, unmoving, focused on every nuance of the conversation. How the hell was Buddy expected to make a rape/murder go away? That was the bad thing about having this mysterious, sometimes exaggerated reputation. It could come back and bite you in the ass.

With the darkness behind him and the lights angled on the desk, Gil had a gauzy view through the translucent waves. This was a tactic they often used when the clients wanted absolute privacy with the great man. In the old days, they had played it straight, with Gil waiting in the downstairs kitchen, nursing a Lone Star, before Buddy would walk in an hour later and tell him everything, no matter how confidential. But that had been the old days.

The conference went on for another ten minutes, five minutes too long for Gil's taste. He waited until the room was empty. When Buddy had gone outside to usher his new clients to their cars, Gil emerged from his alcove, crossed to the desk and took a sip from the rocks glass, just to make sure that it contained colored water and not whisky, to make sure that Buddy hadn't gone back on his word. It was water, he noted with relief. Good.

The yellow pad lay face-up on the burlwood surface. Gil flipped back to the first page. He'd always been impressed by his boss's mental clarity. Even after eighteen years at his side, Gil was in awe of Buddy's ability to organize seemingly random bits of information. It was what had made him a great attorney general and, after that life-changing fiasco forced him to resign, had allowed him to change gears and become a consultant who made problems disappear, who could apply the right pressure and convince everyone, from the press to the police to the governor, that they and they alone had got the best shake.

It was only when Gil flipped to page four that his satisfied grin faded. He flipped again and found that page five was just more of the same, followed by pages six and half of seven. Whatever had been going through Buddy's mind in those last few minutes, he had managed to keep it secret from the bumwad and the CEO. He had also, Gil realized, been able to keep it secret from his second in command, which was much more worrisome.

Gil downed the last drops from the cut crystal glass, as if it were a soothing shot of whisky and not just brown water. "She'll know how to deal with this," he mumbled in a whisper meant for no one but himself.

CHAPTER 1

THE CEILING TILES were of the beige, drop-in variety, interspersed with glaring fluorescent tubes. The chair in the waiting area was uncomfortable and thinly padded, just one step up from a folding chair. Permeating the office's after-lunch atmosphere was the savory smell of Tex-Mex, along with a familiar, slightly more exotic scent. Hummus, she decided.

From a dozen or so cubicles came the sounds of habitation – soft conversations, or phone calls or the low-volume audio from laptop speakers. Callie couldn't help speculating which of these little cubes would become hers, if she was lucky enough to get the job, which was not quite a sure thing. Almost but not quite. It would depend on the interview.

When you're twenty-six and smart and ambitious, she mused, you expect the future to point up, not sideways, or in this case down. There was no way to sugarcoat her prospects – from being a section editor at the state's largest newspaper down to this, interviewing for the metro beat of a free weekly, handed out on street corners or piled next to the change machine in laundromats.

"Ms. McFee?" The sign on office door announced the titles Publisher/Editor-in-Chief, but the man opening it seemed barely thirty. Tall, dark and angular, he kept his thinning hair short, with some permanent stubble on his chin. Callie assumed it was permanent; he seemed the type. "Sorry to keep you waiting." His accent was surprising – a pure, unapologetic panhandle, in which "wait" becomes "white" and people go into "bidness".

"Callie, please." On the way into his office, they shook hands and Callie reflexively closed the door. "If you're going to be my boss, you should call me…" She stopped short. "I'm jumping ahead. Are you going to be my boss?"

Oliver Chesney's smile was boyish, which she found annoying. Bosses shouldn't be boyish. He lowered his eyes to the résumé on his desk. "If you'll have me. It's my job to convince you."

"How sweet," she said, almost to herself. "Modest and reassuring. But you have questions. Everyone has questions."

"And so do you, I'll bet. We wouldn't be reporters if we didn't."

"You're doing your best to put us on an equal footing, even though we're not. Sorry." Callie clenched her fists, willing herself to halt the running commentary. "Sorry. Being back in Austin does this to me."

"I can imagine," said Oliver, losing the smile.

"I hope not. There should be some private things, even for me."

He gave it a moment's thought. "Have a seat, please. Do you want coffee?"

Callie refused the coffee, then refused the tea and the

water and something else that sounded tea-related. She sat herself on the same type of uncomfortable metal chair.

"First question, if you don't mind. Why did you come back to Austin?"

It almost sounded like an accusation. "Do you think I shouldn't have?"

"That depends on which rumor I believe."

"Well, short story, there were layoffs at the *Dallas Morning News*. My role was combined with someone else's. He had more seniority, and I was let go. I looked around Dallas for a few weeks, but the world has changed. I don't need to tell you. Too many people who think they're journalists, publishing online for free, just to get their names out there."

"That's not journalism."

"Thank you."

"Although we do bear the name *Austin Free Press*, so I'm not sure how superior we can be. I think our biggest demographic, in print at least, are the people who forgot baggies to pick up after their dogs."

Callie faked a chuckle.

"But we pay our staff. And we still have a business model. Last year we did a six-parter on Austin's homeless problem, which really increased our visibility. Shortlisted for a Pulitzer."

"I read it. Online. It was terrific."

"Thanks." Something about his tone told her that he'd written all six parts. "So that's why we need Ms. Callie McFee. The metro section is where we're putting our focus. You know this town. You still have connections. Your last name is legendary, if I may be blunt. And when I called the *Morning News* for a recommendation, Bill Carlisle got on the phone personally and sang your praises. Best new hire in decades, he said. A shame to see her go, but his hands were tied."

"Bill Carlisle? Are you sure?" Callie tried to recall the last time she'd had a conversation, any at all, with the aristocratic publisher.

"I'm sure. And that leads back to my question. Why come home to Austin? Was mine the only offer you received?"

"Pretty much. Yes."

"And in six months, if another offer comes along that can take you away from Austin, would you grab it?"

"My father…" Callie didn't quite know how to put it. "My father and I haven't talked, seriously talked, since he left office. Once or twice he tried. Once or twice I tried. I felt like a coward for running away. And, strangely, that feeling's just gotten stronger over time."

"I get it."

"I didn't knowingly betray my father, certainly not over some family squabble, if that's the rumor you're not believing." She sighed. "I'm telling you things that are none of your business. As for my running away again, I won't. You can take the word of a sixth-generation Texan. Or you can write it into my contract. A yearlong commitment, binding on my part, non-binding on yours." She gave it a moment's thought. "With cause, of course. You can't fire me because you're tired of my face."

Oliver Chesney nodded. "There's a lot of your father in you. Not that I've ever met him."

"That's not a compliment."

"I mean in the way you phrase things. Your cadences. Your humor."

When Oliver offered her coffee again, she assumed it was because he needed some himself and she accepted – milk, no sugar. He got it from the Mr. Coffee on his bookcase, assuring her that it was less than an hour old. She settled into the metal chair and, over their matching cups of stale coffee, they discussed state politics, how it had changed or hadn't changed. They discussed the city's growing tech population and the ever-evolving race relations. The publisher of the *Free Press* seemed to have a genuine concern for his city. This struck Callie as both naïve and kind of wonderful. She had spent many a childhood evening sitting cross-legged on the landing at the top of the stairs, peering down through the balusters into the entry hall, eavesdropping on all the movers and shakers of the great state of Texas as they passed through with their whiskies and wine, casually debating the world of power and favors.

"I'll be interested to see what you come up with," Oliver said. He'd given up on the remnants of his coffee. "There are always oddities in this town. Something curious will show up on the police blotter then disappear by the next morning. There's always some explanation, if you care to believe it. Someone will report statewide corruption and the next day they'll claim it was an accounting error. It's a tight little circle. Only someone with connections on the inside could have any hope of penetrating it."

"Connections on the inside?" Her smile fell and her voice took on an edge. "Is that the reason you're hiring me? As an insider?" She had never considered this.

"What?" Oliver blanched. "Oh, no. God, no. I wasn't thinking."

"You think that I blew the whistle on my father and that I'll do it again. For you and your free readers."

"I think no such thing," he stammered. "Honestly."

Callie got to her feet, almost spilling her stale coffee. "Is that what this is about? Hiring Buddy McFee's daughter to snoop around the State Capital? Use the family connections? Or maybe make up with my dad and spy on what he's doing. And if it's not Buddy himself I rat out... Well, I am the sitting governor's goddaughter. Of course, you knew that." Callie realized, in a dispassionate, nearly out-of-body way, as if she were floating near the ceiling tiles and gazing down, that she was over-reacting. But, dammit, she couldn't help herself. Plus she was kind of enjoying it. It was therapeutic.

Oliver looked genuinely shocked. "Calm down. I don't expect you to spy on your dad. And I'm not saying he ever did anything truly illegal. That's not for me to judge."

"You're a newsman. Of course, you judge. My father was never prosecuted."

Oliver refused to raise his own voice. "That's what I'm saying."

"But you're hiring me because I'm his daughter. That seems clear."

"I'm hiring you because you're you." He turned his chin and rubbed his stubble. "Which includes that you're Buddy McFee's daughter. Look, Callie, at the end of the day, you're a reporter. Is it any surprise that I'm hiring you to be a reporter?"

"You're right," she had to admit. "I apologize." In a conscious effort, she lowered her shoulders, trying to let some of the tension fall away.

"Did you think I was bringing you in to do movie picks or

restaurant reviews? We get those for free, by the way. Everyone and his sister want to write reviews."

"I just don't want to make mistakes, okay? It's going to be hard enough for me coming home."

Oliver nodded. "And I don't want you pulling any punches, even if your Governor godfather happens to be involved." He motioned for her to sit down again, but she didn't. "As for your father, they say he's doing consulting work."

"You know as much as I do."

"They say, and they don't say much, that he helps out on publicity and damage control. Access, too. The McFee's have always had plenty of access."

"There's nothing illegal about damage control or providing access. If I work for you, I'll be using my own access."

"And if there's a case where you feel a conflict of interest, you should feel free to stop. Turn it over to me. I won't ask any questions."

Callie cocked her head. "Except that by knowing there's a conflict of interest, you'll know that my father's involved."

"Or your godfather, or your uncle on your mother's side, or your brother. If you want to be a journalist, you may have picked the wrong town. Or the wrong family."

A deep breath. "True."

"Do you want time to think this over? I can give you a few days."

Callie glanced around the office, at the particle board desk and the stacks of books in the corner and the small window that looked out to the parking lot. "Sure. If you can give me a few days, that would be great."

"Or you can start tomorrow. Whatever you want."

CHAPTER 2

THE PAIR OF reinforced steel doors held a pair of reinforced windows, each about a foot square and situated around eye-level. Callie did her best not to look in, but as she paced the small waiting area, her eyes kept wandering in that direction. Every time she heard the whir of a blade or the scrape of metal on metal, she winced. "Who the hell puts windows in an autopsy room?"

The homicide detective shifted in his chair and glanced up from his phone. "You don't have to stay. I just need to get this prelim, now if not sooner."

"I was hoping we could go for a drink, as long as I'm in town. I dropped by the station and they said you were here." 'Here' was the basement of the medical examiner's office, just a few blocks from the Texas State Capital. "At O'Neil's maybe? You still drink bourbon? We can bring each other up to date. Where's your partner? You still have the same partner? Emily?"

"Emily," he confirmed. "She's in her first trimester."

Callie liked Emily and was genuinely happy for her. "Hey, that's wonderful."

"Yeah, wonderful," State McFee said without enthusiasm. "I'm trying to cut her some slack with the workload."

"A pregnant homicide cop? Sounds like a challenge."

"I'm dealing with it."

"I meant for her."

"She can get reassigned to a desk whenever she wants. Right now she prefers to throw up in my passenger seat."

"Well, she won't be drinking bourbon tonight. How about you?"

"I can't," said State, glancing back to his phone. "Where are you staying?"

"The DoubleTree on 15th. It's fine."

Even to a casual observer, the two would seem unmistakably related. Both had their mother's patrician features, fair skin and blue eyes as well as Buddy's Irish-red curls, before they'd thinned out and turned gray. State kept his relatively short, a younger version of Buddy's hair, while Callie tried hard to turn her curls into waves and wore them a few inches past her shoulders.

"You should stay with us," State offered. "There's a comfy pullout in my study."

"How do you know it's comfy?" Callie's mouth twisted into a smirk. "Have you been using it? How is everything on the home front?"

"I said comfy to entice you. I don't know for a fact. Honestly, you should stay with us."

"I already checked in. Besides, Yolie's not my biggest fan."

State winced. "Please don't call her Yolie."

Callie looked around, just for effect. "She's not here."

"Don't get into the habit. You know she hates it. And she knows that you know that she hates it. It's Yolanda."

"Yolanda," Callie repeated. "Yolanda thinks I'm a bad influence."

"On who? On me?"

"On everyone, I think."

"She doesn't really know you."

"Well, thanks for the offer. If I take the job and come back, then yes, I'd love to stay with you, if it's okay with Yolanda. It'll just be till I move my stuff and find an apartment. If I take the job."

"No problem." State finished his text and pocketed his phone. "How about breakfast tomorrow? Come over to the house. The boys would love to see you."

"I doubt the boys even remember me. How old are they now? Five?"

"That sounds about right."

"You don't know?" It was moments like this that reminded Callie of the obvious, that State was nearly a carbon copy of their dad. Buddy McFee had been a loving, even doting father, when he happened to be around and paying attention. That kind of intense contact, followed by long days of absence from their lives, had made his two children adore him all the more.

"Sorry." State had already turned his focus to the case file on his lap. "I was distracted. You were saying…?"

"Nothing." Her own focus had been distracted by the sound of rushing water and the squeal of a sliding drawer. Was the procedure in the next room almost over? "You said this was a rape and murder?"

"Uh-huh." State scanned the report. "Briana Crawley.

Twenty-one-year-old U.T. student. A junior. African-American, from out of state – Phoenix, to be specific. Her body was found in Westlake, in the middle of an open field."

"Westlake?" She was surprised. It was one of the wealthiest suburbs of Austin, only a few miles from the ranch. "Do you get many murders in Westlake these days?"

"There's evidence the body was moved. So, no, we don't. The highway patrol officer who found her last night has reason to believe…"

"Last night?" Callie glanced toward the steel doors. "I thought you had this chronic backlog for autopsies. Shame of the city. That's what the papers say."

"Are you being a reporter? Because you're sounding like one." There was disapproval in his tone. "Did you already take this free paper gig?"

"I haven't decided. And you didn't answer my question."

State rolled his eyes, a habit they'd both picked up from their mother. "Yes, there is normally a backlog. But this case is getting priority. Front of the line."

"Why?"

"Jesus, Callie," he said, slapping shut the file. "Give it a rest."

"Just curious. 'Front of the line' always means something, especially in Texas." She rattled off the possibilities. "Was the victim important? That would get you to the front. Is her family important? Is this part of a larger, ongoing case? Is there a suspect involved who is rich or influential or controversial?"

"Or maybe it's just time-sensitive."

"Okay." It was surprising how quickly the McFee siblings fell into old habits. State, two years her senior, had always held the secrets to life: the rules for high school; the name of a class-mate who had a puppy-love crush on Callie; what the U.S. senator was doing at the house all evening long, locked away with their father. Callie's role was to keep asking questions until she'd pieced together enough information to quench her curiosity. "So why is this case time-sensitive?"

"That's none of your business."

She wouldn't be deterred. "Do you have a suspect already?"

"Again. None of your business."

"If you've arrested someone, then it is my business. I mean, everyone's business. It's part of the public record." She cocked her curiously. "Why haven't I heard about this on the news?"

"I don't know. I'm not the victim's publicist."

Callie reacted with a faux shiver. "That's a little cold."

"Whether it gets publicity or not, we're on this, okay? We're not sweeping it under the rug."

Callie shrugged. "All the same, a rape and a murder in Westlake."

State inhaled through his nostrils, a sign that he was trying to control his temper. Before he could speak or even exhale, one of the reinforced steel doors eased open and a weary-look-ing, middle-aged woman in blue plastic scrubs and a hairnet walked out. "Detective McFee?" In one hand was a surgi-cal mask, in the other a few sheets from the autopsy room's printer, stapled together.

"Dr. Cummings, thank you." State accepted the sheets before they were offered.

"It's a prelim. But we have an approximate TOD. Two hours or so before the highway patrol arrived on the scene."

"Good," said State. "That's good. And the lividity tests?"

The doctor rattled off the facts. "She'd been moved shortly after death, which was what we assumed going in. Now we know. Pending the toxicology screen, we can hypothesize the COD to be strangulation by a pair of ungloved hands, probably male. There's also a post-mortem tear across the front of the neck, caused by some type of ligature, perhaps a cord, perhaps a necklace that was ripped off. Not the cause of death. No usable prints on the body. We took samples from the neck area for DNA, but I wouldn't hold my breath. That kind of match is always problematic."

"What about DNA from the rape kit?"

"We don't call it a rape kit when it's homicide. But yes, we took samples and we're sending them out. If there are no complications, we should have something in a day. For comparison and elimination. To have it all court-ready will take longer. Much longer if there are complications." She reached behind her neck and, with one fluid pull, removed her mask. "The dear put up a fight, bless her heart, so we're going to find something. Was Ms. Crawley a local girl?"

"From Arizona," State answered. "Her parents are flying in tomorrow. I assume they'll want to come by."

"Yes." The medical examiner swallowed hard. "Thanks for the warning. Someone will be here. Not me. Parents are the part I hate the most. Sorry if that seems callous."

"Not at all." State tucked the pages into his case folder then turned on the McFee charm. "I can't thank you enough. I know this screwed up your whole evening. But Dad always said you were the best. I didn't want to trust it to anyone else."

"No problem." Dr. Cummings eked out a smile. "Please say hello to your father for me."

"I will." The mention of Buddy McFee seemed to remind State of his manners. "Oh, and this is my sister. Jocelyn Cummings. Callie McFee."

"Nice to meet you," said Callie with a nod, resisting the urge to shake the woman's ungloved hand.

"Oh." Dr. Cummings pursed her lips the tiniest bit but otherwise displayed no reaction. Callie was used to this. People would recognize the name. A second later their faces would freeze in place as they did their best to reveal nothing, no disgust or sympathy or anything in-between. "Nice to meet you, too. Your father is a wonderful man."

"Thank you. I know."

"Well." Jocelyn Cummings retreated to the safety of her reinforced door. "We still have some cleaning up to do before my team can call it a day. If you'll excuse me…"

State thanked her again and Callie waited until the door had firmly closed. "I love it when people find out who I am."

State ignored this moment of self-pity. "So, are we on for breakfast? You can't leave town without seeing your nephews."

"I know, I know. I can't believe I let it go so long."

For the first year or so, Callie had made a monthly pilgrimage to see her brother and the few friends who hadn't abandoned her, a three-plus hour drive from Dallas that seemed to take longer each time. For the past year and a half, she hadn't visited at all, blaming it on her workload at the paper, or her social life which, if she had to be honest, didn't really exist. "Are you sure you don't want that drink? My treat."

"I'm actually having drinks with Dad and Gil. At O'Neil's. And I'm late. I'd ask you to join us…"

"No, no, no. Dad and I can't meet in public with drinks in our hands."

"I won't even tell him you're in town. See you around nine a.m.? I'll try to talk Yolanda into waffles." State pushed the file under his arm and headed for the door. There was something about the way he did that, as if he were taking a relay baton and racing off to the next runner.

"Is Dad involved in this?" Callie asked. "I mean, you were in a rush to get the prelim, and now you're in a rush to go have drinks with him."

"No, he's not," State said, perhaps a decibel too emphatically. "Come on. I'll walk you out."

They took the stairs up to the main floor and emerged out onto Sabine Street, where they indulged in one of their usual, awkward hugs. Callie watched her brother half-trot around the corner onto 12th Street, heading toward O'Neil's.

She was still standing by the handicap walkway, hugging herself in the light breeze, wondering about her father and State, when a taxi pulled up and deposited a middle-aged African-American couple at the curb. She watched as the driver retrieved two pieces of luggage from the trunk. Even without this, Callie would have known. It was the grief. Grief almost poured off them as they stood at the curb, clutching each other's hand, looking lost, staring up at the letters on the stone-clad wall: Travis County Medical Examiner.

"Mr. and Mrs. Crawley?" Unlike Dr. Cummings, Callie was glad that she happened to be here for this. Whatever she could do. "We weren't expecting you until tomorrow."

"Thank God." The woman smiled. "I told you someone would be here. I'm so glad."

"The airline found room for us," the man said. He had paid off the driver and was taking the lead up the stairs. "After Helen explained."

"I cried until they bumped some poor people off the flight." Her eyes were still glistening. They probably would be for some time.

They were an attractive couple, middle class, thoroughly ordinary looking, hardly the type, Callie assessed, who would rate, or request, any type of front-of-the-line treatment. "Are you with the police?" asked Mr. Crawley.

"I'm a reporter." It wasn't a stretch. Working or not, that was how Callie defined herself. "Callie McFee."

Helen Crawley allowed herself another smile. "A reporter. Good. She won't be just another dead black girl. I won't let that happen to her. You won't let that happen, will you, Miss McFee? That's why you're here, isn't it?"

"Of course. And the police won't sweep this under the rug. Just so you know." It surprised Callie to hear herself echoing her brother's words.

"She was the brightest, the best…" Briana's mother smiled. "I know every mother says that. Briana was a scholarship student. Already picking out a law school. I want you to tell people that. Make her real, not a statistic."

"Has this been on the TV?" the husband asked.

"I don't think so," Callie said.

"I'm asking because we haven't told her brother. Or anyone else."

"Before we tell them, we need to make sure it's her." Helen Crawley wiped her eyes. "Maybe it's not, you know? The police make mistakes."

Callie didn't know how to respond; to conspire in some small, false hope or to help make it all too real, all too soon? "Maybe."

The door behind them opened and they turned to see Jocelyn Cummings and her two assistants, dressed in street clothes, heading home after a long day. The medical examiner had a set of keys in her hand. With barely a glance, she assessed the lost, vulnerable looking couple standing on her doorstep. "Please come back tomorrow," she said gently enough. "Any time after nine."

"No." Helen Crawley's left hand stayed grasped in her husband's. Her right hand gravitated to her chest, as if to hold her heart in place. "You don't understand. We can't wait. Our daughter's in there."

"I know who you are," the doctor said, taking a step forward but still avoiding eye contact. "I'm very sorry for your loss. But we officially closed two hours ago. I know it's no consolation – actually the opposite of a consolation – but the body has been positively identified. Her driver's license, fingerprints from her records. And her roommate came in this morning. They all say Briana Crawley. I know you want to see her. You want to say your good-byes, to see her face. It's perfectly normal. More than normal." She sighed. "No one listens to me, but I advise against a morgue as a place to say good-bye. In a day or so, when we release your daughter to a funeral home, that would be a good time…"

"We gotta see her," Briana's father insisted. "I know it's going to be the absolute worst. But that's our little girl. We can't leave, not without seeing her. You know?"

"Dr. Cummings?" Callie stepped forward. "Please. It will

just take a few minutes. The Crawleys are old friends of my father's. I'm sure he would appreciate the favor."

"Oh." The doctor finally made eye contact with the couple from Phoenix, who had the good sense not to add or contradict. "I didn't know."

"Dad and State and I are all trying to help."

"You should have explained that before." Reluctantly, the medical examiner dismissed her staff then turned to re-open the door.

A white lie told in a good cause, thought Callie. It was one of her father's favorite sayings.

CHAPTER 3

THE LONG-AGO MEMORY, more like a series of half-connected memories, would come to her like a dream in the foggy twilight. And because it was a memory, it was always the same.

It was night and she would be sprawled in the back of the purring Cadillac, lolling sideways against the smoky leather. She would feel the car make the familiar turn onto the gravel drive then under the leafy canopy of live oaks, their gnarled branches arching over them as they approached the house. She would remember looking forward to this moment – ever since the family had left the movie theater or restaurant or some county fair where their father had put in an appearance, the middle-aged politician showing off his young wife and his perfectly handsome family.

In the youngest memories, she would be asleep through the best part, barely waking up as her mother drew back the gingham covers of her bed and her father placed her in the middle and both of them tucked her in and kissed her good night. In later memories, she would wake up still in the car, too tired to respond to their gentle nudges, and feel the warm strength of his arms lifting her, without so much as a grunt of effort, carrying her through the door from the garage, into the house and up to bed. A cocoon of reassurance.

From then on, young Callie would keep awake, no matter how long the drive home, pretending to be asleep, anticipating the turn onto the gravel and the opening of the car door, then reveling in the intimacy, barely more than a minute or two, but so very important. She had no idea how long the ritual continued. At some point, as she grew, the nudges in the car became more demanding, harder to ignore. "Callie. We're home, honey. Wake up." She felt the effort and heard the grunts. Then the ritual ended. And when State started making fun of her for being a little zonk-out zombie, that's when she stopped trying.

Even as a child, she knew it had to end. But that didn't keep her from considering it a betrayal. In her heart, she felt that part of their unconditional parental care had vanished, through no fault of hers, and each time, late at night, when she was forced to walk through the garage door instead of being carried, she would be reminded of the betrayal.

Swatting away the last of the memory, Callie sat up and was rewarded with a throbbing headache. She switched off the Marpac sound machine on the coffee table, which served now as a bedside table. The pullout sofa in her brother's study was just as comfy as advertised, with a deluxe foam mattress, a cushioned topper and 1000 thread-count sheets. Not that this had done anything to improve her dismal sleep pattern.

After checking the clock and the pill bottles lined up beside it, Callie did the morning calculations. Three glasses of white wine to take the edge off. Then a full dose of Ambien

(10 milligrams) around midnight, plus Xanax (0.5 milligrams), even though she didn't think she really needed it. She did. Another tab of Xanax around 1:30 finally did the trick, knocking her out until she checked the clock at 5:38, after which came the drug-induced, half-awake memories. An average night, no worse and no better than usual. Before she could forget, Callie hid the pill bottles in the space behind the top middle drawer in State's roll-top desk.

From the floor below came the sounds of Yolanda and the twins. On her first morning here, just a few days after her interview, she had tried to help with the family's morning routine. She had only succeeded in antagonizing State's hard-edged wife and somehow making the twins more hyper. Now Callie just listened as they negotiated their way through breakfast then battled their way into jackets and out the door, heading over to the most in-demand private school in Old West Austin.

State was at the kitchen counter, in one of his unassuming, brown detective suits, ready for the day's work, when she walked in. Without asking, he took a mug down from a hook by the window and poured her a cup. Non-fat milk, no sugar. "You sleep okay?"

"Perfect. You're making it almost too comfortable."

"Stay as long as you like."

"Tell Yolanda I'm checking out a few places after work. I promise."

"Are you trying to make me inhospitable?" State bowed at the waist then handed her the steaming cup. "You're my sister. You've been here like three days."

"Sorry. I don't want to overstay."

"You're not overstaying. I barely use the study. And the boys are finally getting to know their aunt. Auntie Callie." He chuckled at the name. "It's all good." State eyed his sister's oversized T-shirt and dirty jeans, her not-quite-ready-for-work outfit. "What are you and the *Free Press* working on? You making yourself indispensable?"

Callie sipped the brown liquid. State always made it too weak. "I'm overseeing a four-part series on charter schools. Not the most exciting. Then we're doing a preview of the new legislative session – which is not technically Metro. But it's a good way to get to know the staff. What about you?"

"Me? Not much."

"Not much? You work homicide. What about the Westlake murder? The student." She tried to make it sound light and casual, simple curiosity, even though her encounter with the Crawleys had made it something more.

"We had a person of interest right off, but he developed an alibi."

"Developed an alibi?"

"He has an alibi. I can't really talk about him, Callie."

"Excuse me. I'm feigning an interest in your work."

State smiled but kept it at a minimum. "There'll be more suspects, don't worry. Turns out our Ms. Briana Crawley was a working girl."

"The U.T. student? Are you serious? A sex worker?" For the Crawleys' sake, she hoped it wasn't true.

"Is that the preferred term? Yep, we found out from her friends. Apparently, it's a thing with college kids. It's called 'sugaring'. They refer to themselves as sugar babies, hooking up with sugar daddies who pay off their student loans or their rent or their credit cards. There are websites and apps to make it easy and more mainstream. Some take to calling it the Sugar Bowl. Makes it sound fun and innocent, huh?"

"Okay. But that's not the same as prostitution." Callie took another sip and thought back to her own college days. "I mean, a boy buys you a nice dinner and a few glasses of wine and… Okay, you don't feel obligated to sleep with him. But it does affect your attitude and, to some small degree, your decision. I mean, I've been on a date or two…"

"You've never done it for money, Callie. I know you."

"Not for money. I haven't even done it for a good story, although I've been tempted."

"Right, right," said State, but he was shaking his head. "They call it transactional sex, to try to justify it. All relationships are transactional, they say. Each party has something the other one wants. Even in marriage, they say. Good sex, security, affection, a family. All a transaction. Except in the case of sugaring, it's always money, and the guy's a lot older and his wife doesn't know. Don't fool yourself. It's prostitution."

His phone dinged. He checked the text then wiped his mouth. "That's Emily. I gotta go."

"Oh. Tell her congratulations for me."

"I already did," State said, but his sister knew better.

CHAPTER 4

WHEN CALLIE GOT into the office, she was surprised to find Briana's parents waiting in her cubicle, crowded into the few feet by her desk. For a second, she didn't recognize them. Their first blush of grief had faded, replaced by a kind of sad determination. The husband's name was Frank. He explained and apologized at the same time, saying how they'd known she was a reporter and had tried to track her down, first with the TV stations, then with the *Austin American-Statesman* and finally – perhaps disappointingly, Callie thought – with the *Austin Free Press*. Callie spent this time moving her piles of clutter off the one visitor's chair and onto the already cluttered floor. Neither one took the chair. "I didn't realize you were still in town."

"We didn't know who else to turn to." Helen almost made it sound like Callie's fault. "The police have been nice enough, but it's an ongoing investigation and they can't give us any information. They say."

"We know someone was arrested the night she died," Frank added. "The officer who called us said as much. Caught trying to bury…" He paused, took a deep breath then pressed on. "…bury our daughter's body in a field. Now they say there's no arrest. No arrest. Not even a suspect."

"Someone was burying the body?" Callie asked. This was a detail her brother had failed to mention. How could he not have mentioned this? "You're sure?"

"That's what they said on the first call," Frank assured her. "Someone taken into custody. And now there's no arrest, like it never happened."

"Well, if there was an arrest, that's easy to check. But being in custody and being arrested are two different things. The police can bring someone in as a person of interest or a material witness, but then not charge them with a crime."

"He was trying to bury her." Helen put a hand on Frank's elbow and he lowered his voice. "He was trying to bury her, for God's sake."

"I understand," Callie said. "But there could have been other details. This morning I spoke to the homicide detective on the case. Someone I trust. He said yes, there'd been a person of interest but he's not currently a suspect."

"So, you're investigating Briana's death," said Helen, her voice brightening. "Thank you, Ms. McFee. Thank you."

"I am, yes." She didn't mention that her entire investigation had occurred this morning, over weak coffee in her brother's kitchen while she was barely awake.

"I had a feeling you would," said Frank. "You were there in the room when we saw her. You know her, in a way. She's real to you."

A good way of putting it, Callie thought. Yes, Briana was real to her.

"What else did your detective tell you?" asked Helen.

Callie thought of State's other piece of new information. She doubted the Crawleys knew about her daughter's sideline. At some point, someone would have to tell them, but not here, not now, not her. "Nothing new, I'm afraid."

Frank was still shaking his head. "How can you not arrest someone who's burying a body?"

"I don't know," Callie said. "I'll look into it."

"We went to see the other news people," Frank said. "They knew about her murder. They reported it. But it's just another dead black girl. I don't think they're doing a damn thing."

Part of Callie was surprised. It was a story any reporter would jump at – an unsolved rape and murder; a person of interest burying the body; a suspicious "no comment" from the police. But part of Callie wasn't surprised. If her father was involved, then a lack of journalistic interest was par for the course. Buddy McFee knew all the strings to pull in this town, even with the media.

"Frank thinks we should hire a detective," Helen said hesitantly. "But we don't have a lot of money. And I'm not sure what a private detective could do."

"That's an option," agreed Callie. "But the Austin P.D. has more resources than any private firm. And they're working hard, even if they aren't sharing the results." She wasn't sure if she believed this, but she trusted her brother and felt a certain responsibility for her father, whatever he might be up to. If there was anything to uncover, she preferred not to have a private detective involved. "Why don't you give me a few days? I have some connections in law enforcement. I'll find out what the deal is."

The Crawleys agreed to postpone their decision, Frank

more reluctantly than Helen, who wasn't eager to create any hard feelings with the police. They exchanged contact information. Then just as they were about to leave, Helen put her purse on the desk, found a slim leather wallet and pulled something out of a plastic sleeve. "For you," she said and handed Callie a wallet-sized portrait of a smiling young woman with a delicate, oval face, a younger, thinner, more hopeful version of Helen, dressed in the maroon gown of a high school graduation. "Keep it, please. I have dozens of them."

"Thank you." She gave the image a moment of reverence that it seemed to deserve. "She was beautiful." Briana's parents stiffened, and Callie imagined it would always be painful for them to hear their daughter spoken of in the past tense.

She walked them out, waited with them for their Uber then came back in. She toyed with the idea of going straight to Oliver and pitching a series, the overlooked murder of a black student and a mysterious, unnamed suspect. It was bound to impress her idealistic, granola-fed boss. Returning to her cubicle, she took a roll of scotch tape from her drawer and taped Briana's photo to the bottom right corner of her laptop. It would be a little cumbersome there, irritating her right wrist as she typed, but that would be a good reminder. Then she started combing through the databases: the APD call logs, the arrest reports, the photo booking base, anything that the state of Texas required to be public information but that most civilians wouldn't have a clue how to access.

With almost no effort, she found the report from highway patrol. There was no audio available, which was a shame, since you could tell a lot from the exact words and the tone of voice and the ambient sound. The officer's transcript gave his ID number and location then reported "a suspected 187", a homicide, but no arrest was listed. Had someone made the arrest disappear? She checked the THP's database, also publicly accessible, and found the trooper's name.

Next came the cross-referencing, with Callie comparing all the APD reports for the rest of the night and the next morning. There was one homicide suspect booked that whole night, a male involved in a domestic dispute turned deadly, in the Johnston Terrace area. She did find multiple tags for the name Briana Crawley – the logging of the case into the police system, the dispatch of the medical examiner's van, the request for an expedited autopsy – but nothing more helpful, not even a record of someone brought in for questioning, at least not in the public access.

Callie created a file – "Briana's Case" – input the little information she had, then closed her laptop, leaned precariously back in her cheap office chair and rubbed her eyes with her fists. Had the Crawleys misunderstood what the trooper said? Maybe. The trauma of the news must have been intense, even disorienting. But what about the person of interest State mentioned? Shouldn't that name be somewhere in the system? Maybe yes, maybe no. The public data bases didn't hold everything, since the APD and the D.A.'s office needed privacy in order to develop cases. Still, she couldn't shake the image of homicide detective State McFee racing off to O'Neil's, with the girl's preliminary autopsy report in hand.

"Anita hated when you rubbed your eyes."

Callie almost fell out of her chair. She recovered and stumbled to her feet. "Uncle Gil." Was her laptop closed? Yes, it was. Good.

The short, serious man, her father's longtime accomplice, stood at the mouth of her cubicle. "Your mother said it would cause premature wrinkling. Not that Anita cared about your wrinkly eyes, but she felt it reflected badly. Austin's premier beauty could not have a daughter who would wind up looking older than her. Wouldn't do."

"I was seventeen when she died. I hardly think I looked older."

"Right. I suppose if she knew she was going to die young, she wouldn't have worried." From anyone else, this might have been a caustic example of black humor. But from Gil Morales, it sounded almost like an accusation. Her father's aide stood his ground, not stepping forward to hug her or to shake her hand. "It's been ages," he said, scratching at his short-cropped gray beard.

"I'm sorry," said Callie, without naming what she was sorry for. She left it for him to choose.

"Forget it. He knows you're here, by the way."

"He probably knew the second I drove over the county line."

"Your father's disappointed you haven't been to see him. You've been here how long, three days?"

"Did he actually say he wanted to see me?"

Gil lifted a single shoulder and made a face. "Not in so many words."

"The last time I was at the ranch, he kicked me out."

"As I recall, you were already stomping out. It was mutual." Gil eased himself onto the corner of her desk. "Calista, come on. He's you dad. You're his baby girl."

"Sorry. I don't want to spend an evening rehashing the past. Or worse, pretending it never happened."

"It doesn't have to be dinner. Just drop by the ranch."

"Are you personally inviting me?" she asked. "You?"

"I act in his best interests. His best interest would be for you to take the first step."

"Maybe I'll give him a call."

"That would be nice, but it should be a visit. And soon." Gil saw her bristle. "I don't make the laws of nature."

"No, you just enforce them." Callie didn't mean it to sound so petulant. And then an idea occurred. "What's the old man working on?"

"Not as much as he used to. But you know him. He likes to feel needed."

"I'm sure he's needed plenty. It's the way Texas works."

"It's the way the world works."

"So, he's got a client? Something in the past week or so?" She had to force herself to look away from the laptop and all the unanswered questions she'd just been asking it.

"He does, as a matter of fact," said Gil. "But he'll make the time to see you."

CHAPTER 5

THE MOMENT SHE turned off Hacienda Road onto the gravel drive, the memory dream came floating back, nibbling at the edges of her mind. Then just as quickly, it was gone.

The old homestead hadn't changed, in the way that rich, well-maintained places have the luxury of always looking the same. The front door was unlocked. It usually was. Callie stepped into the cool of the main hall. "Hello?" The word was barely out of her mouth when a soft, happy yelp and the skittering scratch of paws on wood alerted her. "Angus? How's my Angus?" She clapped her hands. "C'mon, boy."

With his rear end wagging faster than his legs could move, the gray-faced Irish setter clattered his way into the hall. She bent down to greet him, and he nearly fell into her arms. Angus had been her mother's dog. After her death and State's departure for college, he had switched allegiance to Callie. Buddy had never been a dog person, preferring to cultivate loyalty in humans instead. "I've missed you," she said, vigorous scratching the dog's bony rump. His reply was almost a kind of purring. "Are you Daddy's dog now? I'll bet you are Daddy's dog. When did you get to be so old, huh?"

"We're all getting old, honey." It was Sarah, coming from the direction of the kitchen, wiping her hands on the apron draped over her gray and white uniform. "Welcome home. Mr. Buddy will be so glad. He's been talking about nothing else."

"Cursing all the way, I imagine."

"Nah, I can tell when he's excited. C'mon, bring me some sugar." After a long, warm hug, the older woman held out a hand to take Callie's jacket. Callie ignored the gesture and crossed to the coat closet half-hidden in the dark paneling by the staircase. "I made brisket, your favorite. Mr. Buddy already started it on the grill when I got here. I'm finishing it in the oven, which probably goes against Texas state law. But it's just as tasty, between you and me."

"When you got here?" Callie closed the closet door. "What does that mean? You don't live here anymore?"

"Honey, where have you been?" Sarah shook her head. "Nobody lives here. Just your daddy and Mr. Gil. They bring me in now and then for dinners. And, of course, for tonight. Just for you."

"When did this happen?" Callie glanced around the entry hall. It seemed just as neat and polished as ever.

"Maybe a year. Oh, they have a cleaning service twice a week, and a gardener on weekdays, but even he doesn't live on the property. I guess with just the two of them, they thought it might be wasteful."

"What about cooking?"

"I asked Mr. Gil about that. He says they do some cooking

and grilling themselves. And I saw some delivery menus in one of the kitchen drawers. The bachelor's best friend."

Callie had once asked her mother what the difference was between comfortably off, the term that almost everyone in their world used to describe themselves, and rich. "Live-in help," her mother had replied rather proudly. The McFees had always had live-in help; Sarah in the kitchen and a full-time maid, a series of full-time maids, changing out every few years to get married or move back home. There had also been a handyman and a gardener sharing the gatehouse quarters, since her mother never thought it proper for a male servant to live in the main house. Gil wasn't a servant, of course. He had his own suite of rooms facing the pond in the back. "Are there money problems?" she leaned in to ask, her voice lowered to a whisper. "Not that you would know."

"That was my first thought," Sarah whispered back with a hint of scandalous glee. "But your daddy's still buying stuff. He had a whole new patio put in with a built-in grill and lots of fancy stonework. Must have cost fifty thou, maybe a hundred."

Callie's father was halfway down the curving staircase before she saw him. He was dressed for dinner, wearing a red tie and the same style of charcoal gray suit she recalled from all the wonderful and not so wonderful dinners of yore. She was glad that she'd changed her outfit at the last minute, opting for a summery dress, not a skirt, gathered at the waist and coming, when she remembered to pull it down, just an inch above her knees. "Daddy," she said. His emergence from the shadows had taken her by surprise. "Hello."

"Callie, honey," said Buddy McFee casually, as if father

and daughter had last seen each other this morning instead of nearly three years ago. "Did you have a good day? Tell me all about it over cocktails." Before she could even think of a response, he had disappeared through the doorway leading to the rest of the house. Angus abandoned her to follow him.

By the time dinner rolled around, her father had reverted into the man Callie had expected. She didn't know if this was a result of the whisky he'd imbibed during the sacred rite of cocktail hour, or if he'd just decided to take a different tact, but the sarcasm and resentment were now on full display. At least the big subject hadn't come up. It was as if they both realized it was off-limits, their family's electrified third rail, the one topic there would be no walking away from.

"About time you came to see the old man." Buddy was smiling his broad, almost threatening non-smile. "Your brother tells me you're writing for the Pennysaver."

Callie remained poised. "I'm surprised you're so badly informed. That's not like you."

"*Free Press*. Same thing." Buddy stuffed an oversized hunk of brisket into his mouth and let his teeth do the work. It was a habit Anita McFee had labeled disgusting but had been unable to change. "I'm shocked it's still in business," he muttered between chews. "Course you got your used car ads and the cents-off coupons."

"A bit more than that," she replied evenly. "We were short-listed for a Pulitzer."

"Was that for the car ads or the coupons?" Buddy covered his mouth and chortled. The chortle turned into a full-blown choke. It was loud enough to make Angus look up from the dog bed that Sarah had moved in from the study.

The choking fit didn't worry Callie. Gil was right there, looking prepared, ready to provide his boss with a pat on the back or the Heimlich maneuver or perhaps a tracheotomy, to be performed with a wiped-off steak knife. The piece of brisket found its way into a napkin before any of them was needed. Angus snorted softly and lowered his head.

It was just the daughter, the father and Gil, at a mahogany table that could comfortably seat two dozen. She and her brother used to treasure their family dinners, at least the ones that Buddy showed up for, which happened once or twice a week. He would be in an expansive mood, eager to hear about their day and to lead discussions about school subjects or current events. He encouraged his children to express their opinions in complete, coherent sentences, a discipline that had served them well in life. By the time Sarah brought in the peach crumble or apple pie, they would be feeling smarter and magically more confident. Their mother was notably quiet on the evenings Buddy was at the table. Only years later did Callie guess what it must have been like for her, to have to deal with two normal, misbehaving kids day after day, and then to see her husband swoop in and mesmerize them with his concentrated doses of attention.

"Not exactly the career I would have predicted for our golden girl," said Buddy. "What happened up in Dallas, if you don't mind saying?"

"There were cutbacks."

"You want me to talk to someone?" Buddy asked. "Is Bill Carlisle still the big man up there?"

"He is," said Gil between his own mouthfuls. "What do you say, Callie? We can make the call. No problem."

There was something about Gil's tone that made Callie even more resolute. "No, I'm fine. Are you really so anxious for me to move back to Dallas?"

"I really don't care where you are, honey," Buddy said. "I just want you to be fulfilled. I can't control your happiness, Lord knows. That's your own doing. But if I can help you be fulfilled…" He paused, as if realizing he'd gone down the wrong path. "Course, it's none of my business, is it? If it's your ambition to write for tomorrow's trash and mooch off your brother, what can I do?"

"Nothing you can do," Callie agreed. "What about you, Dad? What are your ambitions?"

"My ambitions? Ha! What a word."

"I mean, what are you up to these days?"

Not the smoothest of transitions, she thought, not the one she had rehearsed, but her father's little snap of cruelty had emboldened her. "Are you going to travel?" she asked. "Spend more time on the golf course?"

"Golf course. What are you talking about?"

"Now that you're retired."

"I am not retired," her father growled. "What the hell gave you that idea? I still keep my hand in."

"Sorry," Callie said. "Semi-retired."

"Not semi-retired, either. I work all the time."

Callie remained focused. She even added a touch of condescension. "I understand. Arranging access to the governor, getting people 50-yard-line seats at the Longhorn games. But it's really just a few phone calls, right?"

"Not right." Buddy was almost bellowing. "I still have my

license, no thanks to you. And I work big cases. Just because I'm working behind the scenes doesn't mean…"

"Most of the heavy lifting happens behind the scenes," Gil piped in.

Buddy pointed with his steak knife. "You're talking Buddy McFee, little lady. No one knows the system better than me."

"There's a lot of confidentiality," said Gil, trying to be the voice of reason.

"Stuff you can't talk about. I understand." Callie nodded but looked unconvinced. "Change of subject. Sarah tells me you're into cooking these days."

"Cooking?" Buddy pronounced it like a foreign word. "I do no such thing."

"I think it's great having new hobbies, now that you have the time."

"Jeez. Why the hell are you needling me?"

"Dad," she purred. "Dad, there's nothing wrong with slowing down."

Gil eyed her suspiciously, while Buddy's eyes narrowed to wrinkly little slits. "I'll have you know I have a case right now. And it's life and death, not some lousy traffic violation or football ticket."

"Oh, I see. Is this the case State's helping you with?" Callie let the question dangle.

What's your brother been telling you?" Gil asked. "You must have misunderstood."

"You're fishing." Buddy broke into a wide grin. "Very clever of you. All these years, Callie, and I never knew you enjoyed fishing."

"I wouldn't call it fishing, unless you think of Westlake as a real lake. The murder of the U.T. student? Briana Crawley?"

"Westlake..." Buddy scratched his chin. "Yes, I believe State mentioned it. But why would I be helping the police? They're more than capable." It was one of Buddy's oldest tactics, avoiding the question by changing the question.

"I don't mean helping the police. I mean a client."

"A client?" Buddy repeated. "As far as I know they don't even have a suspect. How can I have a client?"

"What about the person brought in for questioning?"

"But he's no longer a suspect, is he? He was released." It was a rookie mistake, one she hadn't expected her father to make.

"Who was released?" she asked.

"Who what?" Buddy said with feigned befuddlement.

"Who was released? Someone important or well-connected? I hope you two didn't manufacture an alibi for this man. That would be a horrible position to put State in. His own father..."

"We didn't need to manufacture anything. As a matter of fact . . ."

"Lawrence?" Gil placed a firm hand on his boss's arm. "That's enough. She's trying to rattle you. Don't say anything more."

"More?" Buddy was almost mumbling. "There's nothing more to say."

"That's right," Gil said gently. "Nothing more to say — except that an oven-finished brisket is never as good as a grilled one. Correct? I don't care what Sarah tells you."

"Damn straight." Buddy waved away Gil's hand and began

to saw off another chunk. His knife hand shook noticeably. "Your mother would never let that happen."

Callie nodded. "Mom was always a stickler for the rules."

"Damn straight," Buddy agreed. "Anita should know better, letting Sarah finish it in the oven." He looked up from his plate and scanned the mahogany table. His face darkened. "Where the hell is Anita? She should be here."

"She should," Gil interjected, shooting out his hand again to Buddy's arm. "I miss her every day."

"What are you talking about?" Somewhere beneath his belligerence, Buddy seemed genuinely confused. He shifted his eyes to Callie on the other side of the table, as if seeing her for the first time. "Why are you sitting in your mother's chair?"

"Mother's chair?" Callie squirmed. This had always been Anita McFee's place, on Buddy's right side, literally if not always figuratively. That part of their lives had ended nine years ago. In the weeks after Anita's death, Callie had refused to sit there, leaving a yawning, obvious space between her and her father. But Buddy had insisted. And for the last year of high school and all of college, she had eaten most dinners and the occasional breakfast at his side. Was he saying that she was no longer welcome there?

"Yes, your mother's chair." Buddy turned his head toward the kitchen. "Anita?"

Gil increased his pressure on the larger man's arm. "She'll be out here. Soon. Probably making herself pretty."

"Bullshit. Where the hell's Anita?"

Gil spoke slowly and firmly. "Lawrence, calm down. She'll be here when she's here." Then his eyes connected with Callie's. "We need to talk," he whispered. "After dinner."

Gil's hand remained in place, comforting and controlling, as the room fell into silence, punctuated only by the sound of Buddy McFee's chewing and his occasional grunt as his anxiety began to cool one degree at a time.

CHAPTER 6

CALLIE WAS IN the oak-paneled study, waiting in one of leather chairs. She didn't get up when Gil came down and joined her. He poured them both two fingers of whisky, no ice, and placed hers within reach on a side table. It was Gil who broke the silence. "He's okay. Settled in for the night. Thank you for asking."

She ignored the sarcasm. "Is it Alzheimer's? Does my father have Alzheimer's?"

"Probably," Gil said. "You know Dr. Oppenheimer. Roger Oppenheimer? Used to be surgeon general? He did a neurological exam – mood tests, blood work. He wants to do brain imaging to make sure. I'm not worried about Roger's mouth. He's safe. But with brain imaging there's going to be paperwork, so I said no for now."

"So, it's a secret?"

"Just me and Roger. And now you. And Buddy on a good day."

"What about State?"

"We've managed to keep it from State. He's not as observant." Gil toasted, his mouth hinting at a smile.

Callie toasted back and took a sip. She took a second sip and made a face. "It's water."

Gil took his own sip then chuckled. "Sorry about that. We keep this on hand for guests."

"For guests?"

"For him to drink in front of guests. To preserve the Buddy McFee illusion."

"Did that include tonight at cocktails? You were preserving the Buddy McFee illusion? For me?"

"We were," Gil admitted without shame or apology, as he took their glasses to the wet bar, rinsed them out and poured a fresh two-fingers apiece from a bottle of Buchanan's at the back of the cabinet above the bar. "When it's just the two of us, we use the real stuff – in moderation. Roger says alcohol's not bad. Makes him a little harder to control. But he'd be even harder to control without drinking. It's a delicate balance."

Callie nodded then took her first taste of the real stuff, welcoming the sweet smokiness, tracking it as it went down. This was a lot to take in, the prospect of her father, the seemingly indestructible force of nature, fading into a fog of dementia. Unthinkable. And yet it perfectly explained their newfound isolation, the firing of Sarah and the rest of the live-in help. "What about me?" Callie asked. "Why did you ask me to come? You must have known I'd figure it out."

"Well, it didn't take much figuring tonight." Gil took his own first taste and smacked his lips. "Your daddy kept asking about you. I thought it might keep him more grounded. And he loves you. I thought it worth the risk."

"Bullshit." She didn't believe it for a second. "You wanted me to find out. I know how your mind works. Having no one to share this with, no woman to help out, no member of the family to bounce things off of or to sign papers when they need signing . . . When you heard I was back in Austin, you must have been thrilled."

"Not thrilled." Gil had always been careful with words. "Grateful perhaps."

"Why didn't you just tell me?"

"Because Buddy made me promise. I've never broken a promise to that man and I don't intend to start."

There were times, every now and then, Callie thought, when she and Gil understood each other, even appreciated each other, although neither ever let it boil over into actually liking each other. "I'm sorry, Uncle Gil. How bad is he?"

"More good days than bad." He used his thumb to stroke the side of his little gray beard. "He was excited all day to see you. Agitated. A little exhausted. And then that glass of red wine with dinner. Most of the time it's no problem."

"You mean no problem covering it up."

"Exactly."

"What about his work? Dealing with clients?"

Gil tilted his head and made a sour face. "We've had a few scares. Two months ago, we were consulting on an extortion case, dealing with intellectual property, and somehow your daddy started rambling on about Cocker and Missy Bess. Did the client want to go out to the stables and see Cocker and Missy Bess?"

"You mean the horses?"

"I mean his favorite palominos that've been dead and gone

for going on ten years. The client, some internet upstart from out of state, actually wanted to see them – until I mentioned the mange."

"The mange?"

Gil chuckled. "Oh, yeah. Cocker's got a real bad case of mange. Not to worry, I told him. Not too infectious. That was enough to cool the boy's curiosity, although your dad was pretty riled that I hadn't told him about the mange. See what I gotta put up with?"

"What about your new client. Aren't you worried?"

"Oh." Gil looked like a guilty little boy. "There isn't any new client."

"But he said…" Callie pointed an accusing finger. "You said yourself, when you came to my office… Dad was talking about the girl's murder, the one in Westlake."

"I believe you're the one who brought up Westlake. Buddy just went with the flow. State brought up the case, but just as conversation. If there's one thing Buddy hates, it's being left out."

"That's true," she admitted. In the shock of hearing about her father's condition, she hadn't thought about the impact it would have on his mind. Not his mind, she corrected herself. That impact was obvious and distressing. But his spirits. His view of himself in the world. His reason for living. If Lawrence "Buddy" McFee was no longer the man in the middle of everything, then what was he? What was left? For the first time since she'd discovered the truth, Callie felt sorrow, a deep pang of sorrow for the larger-than-life man who was now fighting just to stay himself.

"Is your paper interested in Westlake?" asked Gil.

Callie had to force herself back into the moment. "What?"

"The girl in the field."

Callie took another sip of her whisky then placed it down on a coaster. That was part of the family training, always use a coaster. "Yes, we are interested. We're also interested in the fact that no one else seems interested."

"Probably because there's nothing to report."

"Gil!" The voice boomed down the stairs and into the study. "Gilbert!"

Guillermo Morales smiled and shrugged a shoulder. "He's taking to calling me Gilbert."

"Coming, boss! There in a sec!" Gil excused himself and made Callie promise not to leave until he came back down for a proper good-bye.

Her father's study had always been her favorite room. It had been his domain for as long as she could remember and the richly polished oak spoke of a subtle power. It was hard to imagine that the world of this room would be ending, that it could ever end. After Buddy was gone, State, the next in line, would move his family in. The study would become a TV room or a home office, and decades of deals and crisis-management, of quiet disappointments and loud celebrations would fade and disappear – like her father's own memories. Callie listened intently, her ear tuned to catch his voice. But an upstairs door had been closed and the only sounds she could make out were the muffled clangs of Sarah cleaning up in the kitchen.

On her second or third stroll around the room, she noticed the yellow legal pad on the burlwood desk, nearly hidden under the old-fashioned leather blotter, with just its bottom edge sticking out. She might not have been curious about it. It was just a pad, after all. But she recalled all the times she'd seen her father in the middle of meetings, listening to a prosecutor or a state senator and jotting down page after page of notes in his flowing, easy-to-read longhand on a pad just like this.

Callie glanced to the empty doorway, a reflexive move, then lifted the corner of the blotter and pulled out the pad. The handwriting was unmistakably his, and the first words sent a chill down her spine. "Keagan Blackburn w. raped/ strangled girl, April 12, 10:21 p.m. Westlake. Empty field. T.H.P. Dash cam not working. Arrest record expungable? Talk to D.A."

In under a minute she had retrieved her phone from the pocket of her jacket in the coat closet, returned to the study and switched on the desk lamp. Then she took photos, several of each page. There were seven pages of notes in total, although pages four through seven were covered more in undecipherable squiggles than in words, growing larger and more frantic with each line.

CHAPTER 7

"OF THE OVER 500 charter schools in Texas, approximately 100 of them are located in Austin.'" Callie read the rest of the paragraph silently, then skimmed the next two. With a soft grunt, she turned from her monitor to the reporter hovering over her desk. "All right, I'm three paragraphs in and I still don't get your point."

"My point?"

"Why you want me to read it."

The younger woman's soft brown eyes blinked in confusion. "Because you asked to see it before I submitted it to Oliver."

"No. I mean 'me' the reader. What's your POV? Why am I interested?"

"I'm starting with the facts." Jennie Larson was straight out of college, only a few years younger than Callie, cute, fresh-faced and strikingly unimaginative. "Oliver said he didn't want the first installment too political, so I thought we should ease into…"

"Not too political. But you still need a point of view.

Otherwise it's like a Wikipedia page. No one's going to read any further."

"I'm not sure…" Jennie was going into her helpless routine, the one that had probably gotten lovesick high school boys to do her homework. She widened her eyes into a charmingly perplexed expression. "If you could maybe just get me started . . . Please. Oliver really loves your style."

Callie decided to meet her halfway. "Okay, I'll rewrite paragraph one. After that, you're on your own. Oliver needs need the whole thing by end of day."

"You mean five o'clock? Today? Um… I don't think that's enough time."

"No, the day ends at midnight. Get it to his inbox any time before midnight. Actually, you have until four or five a.m. if you need it. I don't think he gets up before six. And copy me on it."

"Tonight? But I have plans. My boyfriend…" Jennie stopped herself then bit her lower lip. "Okay, you're right. Before midnight. Thanks for helping. I appreciate it."

"You're welcome." And with that, she gently motioned Jennie out of her cubicle.

It took her half an hour to rewrite and send off the first four paragraphs, starting with the story of a local family affected by the changing budget at their high school, an anecdote Jennie had buried halfway through the article. Callie added a few notes, outlining a more focused approach to the four-part series, an angle that she knew Oliver would love. Thinking about charter schools was a nice break. It kept her from fixating on the graduation photo that she'd taped to the bottom right corner of her laptop or the pages of her father's handwritten notes stored somewhere inside her phone.

Since she needed Oliver's full attention for this, she waited until after lunch. When she walked in, he was folding his brown paper bag and disposing of it in the blue recycling bin next to his desk. The apple core went into a green composting bin. The non-recyclables went into a standard trash can. Callie recycled, too, but there was something about the way he did it that she found annoying. "Callie, good. We haven't had much time to chat." He sat down and leaned back. "I hope you're liking it here, fitting in. I know it's not what you're used to."

"I'm liking it fine. Do you mind if I close the door?" In the open, egalitarian atmosphere of the *Free Press*, closing the door was the equivalent of "we need to talk."

Oliver noticed. "What's up?"

She could still back out. She could make up any number of excuses for closing the door. But once she started, once someone else knew, someone not dedicated to Keagan Blackburn or Buddy McFee, some impartial journalist, dedicated to unearthing the truth . . . "There's an unsolved murder I'd like to spend some time on."

"A murder?" Oliver couldn't hide his surprise. "Do you have any experience with murders?"

"None," she had to admit. "But I've done some investigative reporting. I imagine it's similar."

Oliver looked dubious. "Not really. For one thing, you'd have the police to deal with."

"I've dealt with the police."

"Not on that level. Is it a cold case?"

"No, it's very warm."

"Okay. Well, that's a problem for a weekly. How do we stay ahead of the pack in something as fast-moving as an active murder investigation?"

"I don't think we'll have competition. Everyone else is ignoring it or trying to cover it up."

"Cover it up?" Oliver reacted with a start, or perhaps just a closed-mouth burp left over from lunch. "That's pretty harsh. Who's covering up what? Can you prove this?"

He was more nervous than she'd anticipated, so she chose her words carefully. "Let's just say I have an unimpeachable source. And my source claims that Keagan Blackburn is involved, either as the killer or as a material witness."

"Keagan Blackburn?" Oliver could barely pronounce the name. "The Keagan Blackburn? Holy Moly. Are you sure?" He glanced out through his glass wall into the bullpen. "Callie, sit down. Try to look comfortable."

Callie sat. "Blackburn was arrested then released and the arrest record expunged. It's the Briana Crawley case, the woman found in the field in Westlake, just a mile or two from his estate."

"I haven't been following it."

"No one has. U.T. student. Raped and murdered."

"And you're saying Keagan Blackburn raped and murdered…?"

"I don't know. All I know…"

"Jesus!" Oliver leaned back in his chair and made quick, little back-and-forth swivels, a sure sign that he was excited. "This is big. I mean, if it's true and the police are trying to cover it up… I mean, this is national."

Callie had been unprepared for this much enthusiasm. "Hold on, cowboy. You're jumping ahead."

"Right." Oliver stopped swiveling and did his best to focus. "And that's not the point, is it?"

"No, it's not."

"The point is a girl was murdered and there may be some conspiracy to get away with it. I apologize. All right, what do you know?"

Callie stayed pretty much on script, outlining what the highway patrol officer had found and how the investigation seemed to stall when Blackburn, one of the most powerful men in the state, developed an unspecified but ironclad alibi. She included her brother's information about Briana's "sugaring" sideline but did not mention her own father's involvement. She was determined not to mention that.

"My brother State is a detective working the case, that's how I know."

"So, your brother is your source?"

More or less. One of them. "Yes."

"And his name is State?" He spelled it out.

"Yes. State is a nickname."

"I should hope so."

"His full name is States Rights. States Rights McFee."

"You're joshing." He could tell she wasn't. "And I thought 'Oliver' was bad. How did this happen? I take it there's a story. How could there not be?"

Callie's mouth curled at the edges. Of course there was. "State had the bad luck to be born when Dad was president pro tem of the Texas Senate. I'm sure you don't remember, but the legislature was trying to pass a bill to reject Federal Highway funds because the Texas Department of Transportation was refusing to regulate..." She stopped for breath. "I don't want to make the story any longer, but it wound up as basically a game of chicken between Texas and the U.S. government."

"A states' rights issue."

"Obviously. Dad was still out wrangling votes when Mom went into labor. He had the House votes, but he was a vote short in the Senate. No one was thrilled with the idea of losing federal money in order to prove a point. The day after the birth, when State's name hit the papers and TV, there was this up-swell in public support. State pride. Buddy McFee had shown his permanent, steadfast commitment. Anyway, the bill passed by five votes. Two days later the U.S. government blinked, possibly as a result of the name thing, which by then was national news. Texas won and my brother has had to live with the consequences."

"Was your mother on board with this?"

"Dad filled out the birth certificate while she was recovering from the epidural. Luckily, there were no pressing matters up for vote at the time I came along. I could have been Right to Life McFee, or Second Amendment McFee."

Oliver chuckled. "How does State feel about it?"

"He's used to it, maybe even proud. He's not the first Texan with that name. And everyone calls him State, which isn't so bad by comparison."

"If you don't mind my saying, that's a very Buddy McFee story."

"I got a million of them." Callie pulled at an eyebrow, a nervous habit when discussing her father's shenanigans. "Anyway, where were we?"

"Rape and murder of a U.T. student."

"Oh, my God, yes. Sorry." Callie straightened up and refocused. "State is working the case, which is how I heard about it. Also how I met Briana's parents. They're very sweet. Devastated, of course, and trying to make someone pay attention. I told them we would help. Was I telling them the truth? Is the *Free Press* in on this?"

"Well, if your brother says Blackburn has an alibi…"

"State's an honest cop. But you know how things work. So, are we in?"

"Um, are we in?" She had been hoping for a more rousing response, but she could see his dilemma. Journalists talk a lot about fearlessly following stories. But there are always considerations: the allocation of resources, possible advertising losses, legal exposure, blowback from the rich and powerful. And, worst case, what if you were wrong? "I guess we're in. Absolutely." His tone did not say absolutely.

"Thanks. I know it's a big deal."

"It is." Oliver cleared his throat. "What's the next step? Think you can get something more from your brother? An unnamed police source?"

"My brother's not saying anything. I found out this much by accident. Like it or not, I'm going to have to become an investigative journalist."

"Not you. We."

"As in 'you and me'?" She smiled. "You want to work on this?"

"Well, you can't do a story this big alone. And I won't bring any other staffers in, not at this point. You know, I began as a crime reporter." He winced. "Not my favorite assignment."

"Well, I appreciate not being out on that limb alone." Not

quite true. She had mixed feelings about letting Oliver get too close to whatever family shitstorm was about to break. But she knew she had to move the case forward, which included letting Oliver get some skin in the game. Callie reached out across the desk and they shook. A solemn bargain. "Thanks. Again. I'll probably be saying that a lot."

"No problem. And don't worry. Your name will be first on the byline."

"I may not want it there at all."

"We'll see." Oliver wrinkled his nose and rubbed his three-day stubble. "Keagan Blackburn. I don't think we should approach the man, not until we know more about his alibi, which could be genuine."

"He was dragging a body through a field, with a shovel." She remembered the thin walls and lowered her voice. "At the very least that's failure to report a crime, withholding evidence, being an accessory after the fact. A prosecutor could probably think up more."

"If we can verify any of this. Otherwise, we're looking at a hell of a lawsuit."

"We'll talk to the state trooper. See if we can get him to say the magic words 'Keagan Blackburn'. Then we can print it."

Oliver didn't agree. "Two things wrong with that. One." He raised a finger. "I'm sure Blackburn and his people have already gotten to him."

"So? We'll get to him, too. Appeal to his sense of justice."

"Maybe. But these people have already appealed to his sense of keeping his career and not having his life ruined."

"It's worth a try."

Oliver raised a second finger. "Two. If we approach the

trooper, then he'll tell his superiors and Blackburn will know we're onto him. I don't know what he can do to shut us down, but I'd like to have a little more ammo before we get to that point. Let's not poke the bear. Not yet." He scooted his chair out from behind his desk so that they were sitting almost knee to knee. "Why don't we follow the sugaring angle. If we can find Briana's sugar daddy and it turns out to be Keagan Blackburn…"

Callie saw his logic. "That would give us a motive – and some leverage in asking him a few questions. I'm sure he wouldn't want his social life going public." She got to her feet. "I can start with Briana's roommate."

"You know where she lives?"

"Her parents told me."

"Yes, of course. And I'll try to clear your workload without raising any suspicions. How's the charter school piece coming?"

She tried not to make a face. "You should have something by tomorrow morning. Jennie may need a little hand-holding."

"Got it." Oliver watched her turn and waited until she was almost at the door. "Callie? Is there any chance your father is involved?"

She turned, poker face intact. "I wouldn't think so. Why do you ask?"

"It's just… Well, it has all the earmarks – money, influence, well-kept secrets. All very professionally done."

"Are you saying my father would manufacture an alibi for murder?" Callie couldn't honestly tell how much of her outrage was feigned. Probably most of it.

"Not at all. I didn't mean…" Oliver held up his hands, palms out. "Sorry. But if I were Keagan Blackburn, I have to tell you, Buddy McFee would be the first person I'd turn to."

"Makes sense," she said, dialing back her outrage a notch. "But Dad would never do this."

"I know you feel that way." Oliver kept his hands raised. "But if you found out he was involved… Would you be honest with me? It could be off the record, not for publication. I get that."

"You would actually keep his name out of it?"

"If I could, yes."

"Why?"

"I can understand you not wanting to hurt him again. But I need your word. If we're going to work together, I need to be able to trust you."

Okay, this was a bad idea, Callie thought. *I should be staying a mile away from whatever my addled father is up to. He's not my responsibility. I should throw away the graduation photo. Briana Crawley is not my responsibility. I can live with not knowing the truth. I can live with a rapist and killer running free. It happens all the time.* These were the lies she said to herself.

"Oliver, you can trust me." This was the lie she said out loud.

CHAPTER 8

CALLIE HAD NEVER lived in university housing. For better or worse, she'd spent her four years at U.T. living at the ranch, doing homework at the alcove desk off the second living room, the less formal one. She regretted not having developed the friendships that campus living might have provided – or the independence, or being part of a culturally diverse world. But with State already out of the house, she hadn't felt able to abandon their father, not so soon after their mother's death. Those four extra years had been important. And, if she was being perfectly honest, the idea of tiny, noisy, overcrowded student housing had never appealed. Although… Callie locked her car and glanced up at the clean lines of the six-story complex, with its limestone exterior and spacious balconies nestled among the trendy coffee shops and bustling bookstores. If she'd known that it could be this nice, she just might have made the other choice.

Sherry Ann Cooper was waiting in the hallway, halfway between the elevators and the open door to the apartment. She was in pre-torn capri jeans and a T-shirt, her golden hair falling to her shoulders. On her face was the sad half-smile of a mourner meeting a fellow mourner. "Callie?" She extended her arms and they hugged. "I don't know what I can tell you, but Mrs. Crawley said you wanted to talk. This has been so hard for them. I swear, they look ten years older." Callie hadn't realized that Helen and Frank were so well acquainted with Sherry Ann, but of course they would be. It was Briana's apartment, too. "C'mon in." And she ushered Callie inside.

"There's something you need to know," Sherry Ann finally said in a soft, confidential purr. They were sitting at either end of a roomy, well-cushioned window seat, overlooking a leafy central courtyard. Sherry Ann, a Texas belle, had made tea and they had exhausted the usual small talk. "Not that I'm being all judgey here." Sherry Ann blew across the top of her cup. "And you shouldn't print any of this, not that I'm telling you what to do."

"I already know. Briana had…" How to put this. "An older boyfriend who paid her bills." Sherry Ann delivered one of those mildly condescending looks, the kind you give your grandparents when they ask about the World Wide Web. "Okay," Callie added, "she was into sugaring. I know."

"You know about sugaring?" Sherry Ann relaxed a little and leaned in. "Maybe a third of the girls I know do it. A sugar daddy is this sort of status symbol. It can be anything from a couple of dinners that wind up in a classy shoe store to a full-out mistress arrangement with an apartment and an allowance. The websites have these big disclaimers reminding you that prostitution is illegal. As if anybody cares."

"So they're like dating sites…" Again the condescending

look. "Okay, not dating. For rich guys and hot girls who know what they're getting into."

"Right. There's also rich women seeking younger guys. Sugar Mommas. And gay stuff. Half of my gay friends are into it. I guess there are enough people out there who want to spoil you rotten. The alternative is grungy college bros who still want sex but want to split the check at the Burger Bar. That gets old." Sherry Ann must have sensed where Callie's mind was going because she shook her golden halo. "No, no. Not me. And not just because my parents are generous. Plenty of rich girls do it. They show off their new shoes and jewelry on Instagram, like a competition. And they invent little code names for their daddies. Bri didn't use a code name. She just called him 'my gentleman.'"

"And where was she on the sugar spectrum? Did she do it for shoes?"

"Bri?" The roommate waved a manicured hand around the apartment. "Does this look like the place a scholarship student can afford? As soon as Bri moved in, she made it clear that this 'gentleman' was paying the bills."

"The police should be able to find him," Callie said. "If he's paying her rent and her bills…"

"She gave me the rent in cash every month. As for the other things, I'm sure the cops are trying. She never mentioned his name or showed me any pictures."

"He probably told her not to."

Sherry Ann nodded. "He was older, of course, she mentioned that, but not grossly old."

"Was he white or African American? Or Asian or something else?"

"She didn't say. I think it made her uncomfortable, you know, talking about him, since I know her folks and all."

"Do you know what website she used to make contact?"

"That I do. It was MySugar.com." Sherry's cheeks reddened. "I checked it out once or twice, just being curious. Just curious."

"I'll take a look." Callie wrote down the name. "Do you know what kind of security they use to keep the site safe?"

"I don't think they have security, just photos and self-written descriptions of the daddies, same for the babies." Sherry Ann's gaze lifted from her teacup to Callie's face. "By the way, one of the detectives who came over had red hair just like yours and these adorable blue eyes." She squinted into Callie's. "Just like yours." She frowned. "What are the odds?"

"The odds are genetic. He's my brother, State. I know, stupid name. He's also happily married and twenty-eight years old." Callie's sly little grin faded. "He didn't come onto you, did he? I'll kill him."

"No, no," Sherry Ann stammered. "I mean, he was very sweet. But, no. Plus there was a pregnant cop with him, so the subject didn't come up. He's really your brother?"

"Detective third grade, State McFee. I'd ask him all the questions I'm asking you, but he's not allowed to discuss an ongoing investigation even with me, except for press releases and press conferences."

"Am I not supposed to be talking to you?"

"Did he say you weren't supposed to?"

"No."

"Then you're okay. What else did my brother ask?"

Sherry Ann paused to think, setting her porcelain cup on

a side table. "He asked when I last saw Bri. I told him she left the apartment a few minutes to seven."

"Was she dressed for a date?"

"No. She was barely wearing make-up and looked pretty casual. Nothing date-worthy. She may have just gone out for a bite to eat."

"On her own?"

"She often did that. A slice of pizza or a salad. Do you think I was the last person to see her alive – other than, you know… ?"

"Probably not."

Sherry Ann sighed. "I'd hate to think I was. I know someone had to be the last, but it's still pretty creepy."

"Did Briana have a car?"

"She didn't. A lot of kids get around without cars."

"Then other people must have seen her."

"Good. I'm glad. Oh, he also asked if there had been any change in Bri's behavior or mood in the days just before… you know…"

"Of course." Callie mentally kicked herself. She hadn't even thought of this most basic of detective questions. "And was there any change?"

"There was," Sherry Ann confirmed. "She'd been depressed for about week, maybe longer. To be honest, I didn't always pay attention. At least a week. Toward the end, it kind of changed from depressed to something else. I don't know. Kind of desperate maybe. Angry?"

"Angry at her sugar daddy?"

"I didn't ask. She didn't go out much for the last week or so. And she borrowed two hundred dollars from me the day before she died. Some kind of cash flow thing. Please don't mention that to the Crawleys. They have enough on their minds."

"It sounds like the sugar daddy may have dumped her."

"That's what your brother said."

"Of course." Callie rolled her eyes. "What else did my brother say?"

"He asked about her other friends and her social media. He also wanted a list of her professors, which I didn't have."

Callie suddenly felt out of her depth. Was this how investigative reporters did their jobs, trying to second-guess the police but with less access and fewer resources? "Is there any question my brother didn't ask? Something maybe he should have asked but didn't?"

Sherry Ann tried not to laugh, but it came out anyway, more of a snort than a laugh. "He asked me that, too. 'Is there any question I didn't ask that you think might be relevant.' I've been thinking, and I honestly can't think of one. Sorry. Sorry about laughing. It was inappropriate."

"No problem."

Callie stayed on her side of the window seat as their tea cooled, politely listening as Sherry Ann free-associated on the concept of roommates and friendships and how easy it is to feel you know someone and yet not really know much about them.

"Are you Facebook friends with Briana?" Callie asked. "I'm sure my brother already checked it out."

"I'm sure he has." Sherry Ann eased herself out of the window seat. "He took her laptop. Do you want to see her Facebook page?"

"I'd love to see it."

Sherry Ann led the way into her bedroom, another bright and airy space, this one with a tiny balcony. Callie brought out her notebook and pen and waited until Briana's roommate had called up the blue-bordered site, tapped Briana's name into the search window and offered the use of her French provincial chair at her French provincial desk. "Here you go."

Callie was disappointed at how ordinary Briana's page was. Scrolling back over six months, she could find little more than inspirational sayings, the usual reposting of social and political articles and only a handful of images from the victim's life, all smiling selfies and party photos with half a dozen girls posing with pouty duck mouths and hand signs. A click on the "Friends" icon revealed 283 tiny portraits, including those of Helen Crawley and a few other young to middle-aged Crawleys. Neither one of them heard the door open or the sound of footsteps.

Sherry Ann got up to greet the new arrival. "Hi, there!" She plastered on a fresh smile and walked into the living room.

"Hello. Oh, Callie. Good to see you." It was Helen Crawley, carrying a pair of Whole Foods bags. "I noticed you were a little low on essentials. Hope you don't mind."

"Mind? Nooo," Sherry Ann drawled. "How absolutely sweet of you."

Callie had no idea why Briana's mother had a key or why she was taking an interest in essentials. She followed them into the kitchen. "Where is Frank?"

"Frank?" Helen pulled a milk carton out of the refrigerator and poured the contents into the sink. "Your milk is about to turn, so I got a new one. I know it's wasteful but..."

She took a deep breath. "Frank went home to Phoenix. This morning. They would have given him more time off, but I think it was better for him to go. It's good for one of us to go back and deal with family."

"Mrs. Crawley…" Sherry Ann corrected herself. "Helen. Helen is taking Briana's room. The rent is paid up through the month and it's ridiculous for her to keep paying for a hotel."

"Sherry Ann is very kind. I don't know how long I'll stay or what use I can be, but at least I'm here."

"The police will catch him," Sherry Ann said. It was a statement based on nothing but optimism, but still it felt comforting. "Oh, Helen, about the necklace. I looked all over. Sorry."

"That's okay," Helen said, but according to her frown, it wasn't. "Maybe she lost it or threw it out."

"Threw it out? Are you kidding me? Bri wore it all the time."

"What necklace?" Callie asked.

Helen reached for her phone and, after several swipes, brought up the image. It was a close shot of Briana, smiling full-blown into the camera, one hand reaching up to touch a braided leather necklace with a strand of gold woven throughout. It was elegant in an earthy way and looked vaguely African. "I gave it to her on her last birthday. She said she loved it."

"She loved it," Sherry Ann insisted. "She wore it all the time."

Callie thought back to medical examiner's report and the abrasion across the front of Briana's neck. "Was she wearing it the night… on that last night?"

Sherry Ann shrugged and frowned. "I think so. I'm not sure."

"You think he took it?" Helen asked, her hand going to her throat. "You think he stole her necklace?" It seemed like the last, most perverse indignity, stealing a dead girl's birthday gift.

"I'll mention it to my brother," Callie said. "Can you email me that? Here. May I?" She borrowed Helen's phone and, in a few seconds, had sent the photo to her own phone. "Thanks."

"Thank you." Helen displayed a half-smile. "Callie, can I talk to you?"

Helen led the young reporter into the second bedroom, a slightly smaller version of the first, complete with balcony. Helen gently closed the door then spent a moment looking around the room, at the jewelry box lying open on the bureau, at the closet brimming with clothes and the rows of shoes lined neatly against the closet's inner wall. "You know about Briana, don't you?"

"Know what?" As soon as the words came out, she felt like a coward.

Helen pointed to the closet. "Prada. Hermes. Jimmy Choo. There's a Cartier watch and some tiny bottles of French cosmetics I never heard of in the bathroom. Frank doesn't notice those things. Even if he did... That's why I talked him into going home. He wouldn't be able to handle it. His little angel. I appreciate them trying to keep it from us, but if you've done any investigating at all..."

"Briana had a sugar daddy," Callie admitted. "My

brother told me. He says a lot of college girls do it. It's not like prostitution."

Helen swallowed hard, accepting what until now had been just a possibility. "It was thinking either that or drugs. Her brother has friends who sell drugs. I'm glad it wasn't drugs."

"It wasn't drugs," Callie emphasized. "And it's very common. The girls hook up with older, wealthy men. An arrangement."

"I don't think Frank would appreciate the distinction. He still wants to hire a private detective but I say no. I don't want some grubby detective poking around, sitting us down and telling us the sordid details of her life."

"It will probably still come out."

"I can deal with the police about it, not get Frank involved. And you... If you have to write something, Callie... I hope you don't, but if... I hope you can do it kindly."

It was moments like this that reminded Callie that mothers were often the strongest, most resilient members of the family. "I can call him a boyfriend, if I need to mention him at all," Callie promised. "I mean, if he turns out to be connected to her death."

"Do the police know who he is? Is it the man who was dragging her body?"

"I'm sure they're looking into that."

'Why in God's name did she do it?" Helen demanded. "She had a full scholarship, plus a stipend. We sent her money whenever we could."

"It's the pressure of college." This was Callie's educated guess. "In high school it's not as much. Everyone knows your life. You can't pretend. But when you get to college, the need for status, to fit in with the cool, rich kids..."

"That wasn't Briana. She was down-to-earth. We talked every day. We texted. I don't understand."

Helen sat on the bed, hands in her lap. Callie sat by her side and forced herself not to say anything comforting and banal. She knew from her mother's death how meaningless that could be. Instead, she just listened as Helen told a few childhood stories about the girl who'd been raped and murdered and dragged through a field. Then Helen said she was tired and wanted to take a nap.

Sherry Ann was in the kitchen, emptying the dishwasher. "Did you tell her?"

"She knew something was up. I was stupid enough to confirm it."

"Well, she had to find out."

"Bri did her best to keep it from her." Callie felt exhausted. "There wasn't a hint of a boyfriend on her Facebook page."

"That's normal. I mean, my nanna's on Facebook. I don't put anything there."

"Makes sense."

Callie gathered her things – her phone, notebook, pen – dropped them into her bag and shared one last mourner's hug with Sherry Ann. She was halfway to the door, wondering about where to go out for a solo dinner, when a thought struck – actually, a series of connected thoughts, starting with the idea of where to eat. "Was Bri on Instagram?"

Sherry Ann had finished with the dishwasher and was wiping down the kitchen island. "Instagram? Sure."

Callie joined her at the island, glanced at the closed bedroom door and lowered her voice. "You were talking about how sugar babies love showing off on Instagram."

"True. But how does that help? We can already see everything he bought her. It's all in her bedroom."

"How about what she ate?" Sherry Ann stared blankly back at her. "In restaurants."

"You think she took pictures of food?"

"It's pretty common. An over-the-top meal in a great restaurant."

"I know the phenomenon, not that I understand. Why would I be interested in your food?" The debutante cocked her head. "Why are you interested in her food?"

"Well, if she posted a food photo and we can identify the restaurant, then maybe they'll remember her and her sugar daddy. Maybe they'll have a name or a credit card receipt."

"Wow." Sherry Ann ran both hands through her hair, pushing it away from her face. "That's good. Are you going to tell your brother about this?"

"No." Callie was surprised at how forcefully the word came out. "He's a cop. He can find out on his own."

CHAPTER 9

THE BARTENDER, RODRIGO according to his shirt pocket, looked busy, in the way that bartenders always look busy. It must be part of their training, Callie thought, to appear overworked and make you consider it a privilege to get a drink. She nursed her depleted vodka/tonic, waiting until Rodrigo finished an order at the pick-up station – two cosmos, a beer and a red wine – before raising her glass in his direction. He still managed to ignore her.

Among all the artfully posed Instagram shots showing off her newest clothing and jewelry and shoes, Briana had posted one restaurant photo, a close-up of a square white plate of linguine, topped with scallops in a brown sauce.

Identifying the restaurant had been simple. Callie remembered the scallop dish fondly. And just to seal the deal, on the wall behind Briana's plate, in soft focus, was the mural painted on white tile, a kitschy depiction of the Bay of Naples with the slopes of Mount Vesuvius in the background, suspended between blue water and sky of exactly the same blue. All through her childhood, Callie had stared, mesmerized at the mural. Anthony's Trattoria was a surprisingly expensive and exclusive spot, a favored hangout of every local celebrity from the first George Bush onward. It was no longer so exclusive but, as Callie could see from the menu, prices had gone up rather than down. Oh, well. She'd needed to eat anyway, eat and drink and ask questions, three birds with one stone.

She didn't mind eating alone. In college there'd always been a few friends to share meals with, but on most evenings she came home to Sarah's wonderful Southern dishes. For variety, she would go out with her boyfriend, Nathan, an argumentative liberal, a true commie by Buddy's standards. Nathan had been her act of rebellion, and they managed to last a remarkable three years. After college, she'd had Nicole, her friend at the TV station as a dining companion. And, of course, Buddy and Gil at the ranch. It was only after her move to Dallas that she'd grown used to eating alone. Except for the rare and awkward date, her meals for the last three years had toggled between take-out meals eaten at the kitchen counter and solo appearances in restaurants like this.

"Want me to repair that?" Rodrigo shouted down the length of the bar. Callie pretended not to hear him over the noise bouncing off the pressed tin ceiling. "Stoly and tonic, right?"

She waited, making him come to her, then pulled out a twenty-dollar bill and held it on the bar. Was this the appropriate amount? In the old movies it was usually a five, but given inflation, she figured twenty would be about right, although the very idea of offering money made it seem shady and underhanded. She held onto the bill, making sure he noticed it.

"Your scallops are out soon," Rodrigo told her. "How is

your drink?" His accent was Spanish sounding, but something a little softer. Portuguese, maybe.

"Another one, please. Lighter on the vodka," she added. All the insomnia articles advised against drinking too much in the evening, which seemed counterintuitive to Callie, since alcohol always made her sleepy. But she was willing to try.

"Light vodka," said Rodrigo. "I make it now."

"Rodrigo…" She caught him before he could turn away. "Quick question." With one hand, she held out her phone, aiming into his line of vision a photo that she'd just downloaded. With her other hand, she tapped the twenty-dollar bill on the bar. "Do you know this man?"

Rodrigo studied the image of Keagan Blackburn, a publicity shot from his corporate website. "No, I think not. Is he famous?"

"Only if you were raised around here. Are you sure?"

"I am sure I don't know him. That was the question, yes?"

"Yes. Okay. How about her?" With a swipe of the screen, Callie revealed a second photo – the birthday shot, Briana smiling and touching the leather braided necklace. Again, Rodrigo examined it. With this one, he took his time.

"I do know her, yes."

"Really?" It was something she'd had to do, to follow up on her only lead, but it seemed such a longshot, like one of those cop show moments when they show a photo to a bartender and he remembers every single customer from the past two months. "Are you sure?"

"Sure, yes." His eyes narrowed. "I remember the necklace, yes. I also remember deadbeat people who run out without paying."

"She did what?" Callie was surprised.

"Maybe weeks ago." Rodrigo's brows furrowed. "She was here alone, right where you are. She tells me she is waiting for boyfriend. She wants to run a tab, since boyfriend will be here to pay. She says they come here before, so I say okay."

Callie tried to keep her excitement under control. "What did the boyfriend look like?"

"No boyfriend," said Rodrigo. "She waits for him. Two glasses of white wine. Maybe an hour. No one comes. She is upset. Then bar gets busy and just like that, she goes. It comes out of my pocket, you know, the money." His eyes narrowed. "The girl is friend of yours?"

"She actually did that?"

"Yes, she did. Now I ask you a question. What is her name? You tell this girl to come back and pay me, okay?"

"It's Briana," Callie said and instantly regretted it.

"Briana," he repeated. "Send me the photo. I will put it behind the bar here."

"No, don't," Callie blurted out. "I'll pay for her." Taking out another twenty, she slapped it on top of the first. "Does that cover it?"

"Maybe it does." Rodrigo snatched up both bills, stuffing them in his apron. "Why do you do this for her? Pay for her like this?"

"She'll pay me back," Callie explained. "I don't want to get her in trouble."

"You are good friend. Thank you." He was warming to her now, his suspicion fading.

"So, this boyfriend she had... Did they come in here before?"

Rodrigo shrugged. "Who can remember? I only remember your friend because…"

"Yes." It was almost a sigh. "Briana the deadbeat. Maybe one of the waiters…" Callie glanced toward the rest of the restaurant and caught a glimpse of an imposing young man with short red hair walking through the front double doors. State McFee scanned the main dining room then the bar and saw her before she could turn away.

"State!" She plastered on a smile and headed in his direction. "What a coincidence. Remember the scallops Mom used to order? They still make them. Can you believe it?"

Her brother met her halfway, between two reserved but empty tables. He resembled their father right now, on those days when he signed their report cards – his rigid stance, the disappointment in his eyes. "I can't friggin' believe it."

"No, really. I ordered them at the bar. What are you doing here?"

"We found the Instagram pic. Emily did. She didn't have our upbringing, so it took her a while to track this place down. You, of course, knew. How did you even see it? Her account is set to private."

"I… " It was time to rip off the band-aid. "I got in through Briana's roommate."

"You went to see…" His disappointment was morphing into outrage. "I should've known you were sniffing around. I'm so dumb. All those questions about what I was working on. Is this what it's going to be like, having you back in town?"

"No." She reconsidered. "I don't know."

"You're living under my roof and spying for some trashy free rag. When did this start? That day at the M.E.s? When you offered to buy me a drink? You come back after all this time and right away, on your first day back…"

"It wasn't like that." She lowered her voice. People were starting to look. "I was still there when Briana's parents showed up. I mentioned I was a reporter and… State, they want answers."

State followed her cue and also lowered his voice. "You know, it's damn unusual for the media to be second-guessing the police on a hot case."

"It doesn't seem very hot."

"I'm here, aren't I? What the hell do you think you can do that we can't?"

Callie had asked herself this precise question. "I just want to make sure she's not forgotten."

"She's not. Meanwhile, you shouldn't forget there's a killer out there. Have you ever fired a gun? And I'm not counting shotguns, or the photo-ops with Dad on the gun range when you were ten."

"Not counting those? No."

"Have you told your publisher what you're up to?"

"Yes, and he's on board."

"Lovely."

State started to approach the bar, but Callie led him away to a high top that a young server was just wiping down. She turned to the server. "Hi. I have a vodka tonic waiting at the bar. If you could bring it over, that would be great. Anything for you?"

"A club soda," State said. He waited until the server had walked away. "Does this mean I have to change the password on my computer?"

"No, no. I would never snoop on family." Callie pushed out of her mind the snooping she'd already done. "According to Rodrigo at the bar…"

"Is Rodrigo the one I should talk to?"

"He's the one I talked to. He remembers Briana." Callie leaned in. "He doesn't remember Keagan Blackburn."

State pulled in his chin, like a boxer pulling back from a swing. "What? Are you just throwing out up random names? Mr. Keagan Blackburn has nothing to do with this." He stared into his sister's eyes, the eyes he had known almost his entire life. Then he flinched. "All right. Goddamn it, how did you know? Damn, I am going to have to change my password."

"No," Callie protested. "It wasn't you. Dad accidentally let it slip." Not technically true, but close enough. "Dad's consulting with him on this. Trying to hush it up."

"There's nothing illegal with that. This whole thing about the public's right to know, it's not really a right. Not in a case like…" State stopped and bit his lip. "Dad let a name like that slip? Damn."

"He'd had a drink. I'm not even sure he was aware."

"The doer is not Blackb…" State couldn't even say the name. "It's not him. The man has an alibi for the time of her death."

"But not an alibi for dragging her body. That one he can't get out of."

"You got me there." The server was on her way and he waited until she'd delivered the two glasses and left. "Callie, this is off the record… And I never thought I'd be saying 'off the record' to my own sister."

"Off the record. I promise."

"The department is not satisfied with the level of Mr. Blackburn's cooperation. DNA traces were found in the back of his Escalade, her DNA, so we know he transported the body."

"What about his DNA?"

"Mr. Blackburn volunteered his fingerprints and a DNA swab when he was brought into the station."

"Did he do it voluntarily or was it part of an actual arrest?"

State gave her their mother's patented stink eye. "Mr. Blackburn is not under arrest. He's lawyered up with Price, Evans and White, so we're not going to get more than they're willing to give."

"What's his alibi for the time of death?"

He laughed. "Why should I tell you? So you can go off and annoy a man like that and try to pick his story apart? It's a good, iron-clad alibi."

Callie took her first sip of her second drink and regretted having ordered a weaker one. *Was there some other approach?* she wondered, some angle that State might actually talk about? She settled into a high top chair. "Where did Briana go when she left her apartment? Or is that a secret, too? A State secret." It was an old pun from their childhood, one of a dozen or more involving the word state. "Come on."

State took his own sip. Then he removed a notepad from his jacket and flipped it open. It reminded his sister just how 'old school' he could be. "According to your friend Sherry Ann, Ms. Crawley left a little before seven. She didn't have a car or a bike. She didn't call an Uber or a Lyft, although she may have hailed a taxi on the street. We're checking into that. Otherwise, she took public transportation or she walked."

"Sherry Ann said she may have gone out for something to eat."

"None of the local places remember her. The ones that have cameras didn't show her. If she was going out for food, she never got there."

"She was found without her cellphone. Can you track it?"

"It hasn't been used since. And, contrary to urban mythology, we can't track a phone that's not powered up. No such technology. Any more bright ideas?"

"Briana borrowed some money not long before her murder. If she had this sugar daddy, why did she need to borrow?"

"Something else Sherry Ann told you?"

"Correct. She thinks you're cute, by the way."

"I am cute. And we always check finances. Finances and boyfriends. The first things we check."

Callie waited. "And…?"

"Do you have a specific question, Ms. Reporter? If you have a specific question, I may be able to answer it."

"Okay." She thought about how to phrase this. "Briana was here two weeks ago, waiting at the bar for her boyfriend who didn't show. He stood her up. I think maybe he was ending the relationship."

"No more sugar daddy?" State took another sip of his club soda. "That would explain her change in mood."

"That was 12 days before her death. My question is, wouldn't she have some money in the bank, instead of having to borrow from her roommate?" State didn't respond. He stayed frozen, glass in hand, gazing into space over his sister's shoulder. "You just said you checked her finances. What's up with her finances?" Callie resisted the urge to press him further, letting the silence between them do the work.

State sighed. "I shouldn't be telling you this."

"Good. I like those words."

He flipped a few more pages in his notepad. "We checked with her bank. Ms. Crawley, or someone using her passcode, emptied her checking account – 12,475 bucks – and transferred it to a new account, under the name Dylan Dane." He spelled out the name. "Within hours of the transfer clearing, Mr. Dane, or someone using his passcode, withdrew the funds and closed the account. He went to her branch and took the cash, so the money trail ends there."

"Interesting." Callie mulled over the new information. "I take it there is no one named Dylan Dane."

"Not that we've been able to track down, no. We're working with the bank, so we'll see what they can provide."

"And there's no connection to Keagan Blackburn? In any of this?"

Her brother slapped his notepad shut. "For the hundredth time, no."

"And yet he was trying to bury the body."

"I am aware of that." State glanced over at the bar. "Did you get anything more from your bartender?"

"Not as much as you'll be able to get with your badge."

"Good. I'll get to him after I talk to the wait staff." He stood up. "Fun talking to you – off the record. Enjoy your dinner."

Callie turned to see Rodrigo looking her way, showing off a white square plate of scallops on a bed of linguine. State was already walking to the maître d's station when Callie caught him by the sleeve. "Um, I may have told the bartender a few white lies. About Briana and me."

"Can't wait to hear them."

CHAPTER 10

THAT NIGHT SHE turned the sound machine on high, took her Ambien, plus one and a half tabs of Xanax, which unfortunately had become the norm, and promised herself to stay in bed till noon. Her plan was to ignore the early morning cacophony as Yolanda and State forced the twins into their Sunday best then carted them off to St. Mary Cathedral where generations of McFees had gone to see and be seen. But as soon as the house was quiet, Callie was up.

She filched the last of the coffee from the Krups and perused the front page of the *American-Statesman*. By ten she was dressed and out the door. So much for promises.

Buddy had stopped going to church shortly after Anita's funeral. Sunday mornings became a time for lounging on the veranda or in the sunroom, reading the Texas papers, sometimes to himself and sometimes aloud, railing against the stupidity of the state government and "that man in the White House", whoever it happened to be. Callie never thought she would miss those mornings, but she had thought about them last night, all through her fitful sleep, and now found herself driving the familiar route over the Redbud Trail Bridge, toward Westlake Drive.

Somewhere along the way, she changed her mind. Callie eased onto the shoulder, looked up an address on her phone and turned on her GPS. A little detour, she told herself, for curiosity's sake.

She had been to Keagan Blackburn's estate several times during her adult life, usually for parties and fundraisers. She vividly recalled one Saturday evening, being cornered in the butler's pantry by Ingrid, Blackburn's third wife, who insisted on spilling out the intimate details of her life. Ingrid was a Norwegian beauty who had traded in her country's values of modesty and self-reliance for the values of a trophy wife. It was not a match made in heaven, said Ingrid, but what could she do? Eventually, Ingrid did find something to do. According to the gossip columns, just this past fall, the third Mrs. Blackburn ran off with her riding instructor, a virile, polo-playing Argentinian, leaving Keagan Blackburn a bachelor for all practical purposes.

Callie turned off onto a dirt road and stopped in front of the closed, wrought-iron gates. The Blackburn manse was a solid brick and timber structure, relatively old and relatively modest. It sat on an artful but artificial hill, its own huge pitcher's mound. The grounds were protected by a wall that overlooked large, scrubby lots on both sides. Callie assumed that someone in the Blackburn family had bought the lots ages ago, intent on preserving their privacy. On an impulse – what could she lose? – she lowered the window of her pickup, a silver GMC Yukon, proudly assembled in Texas, that Buddy had given her on her twenty-first birthday.

Through the gates, she could see the yellow sports car centered on the curving drive in front of the house. Callie had done her research. The CEO of Blackburn Energy and his favorite toy, a top-of-the-line Lamborghini – or was it a Ferrari? – had been on the cover of the local glossies more than once. She had taken this little detour with the vague plan of pushing the intercom button, but now decided against it. What would be the point? What would she even talk to Keagan Blackburn about? Whatever the pretense, he would consider it an odd sort of visit, a definite poking of the bear, as Oliver had warned her against.

Callie was in the process of rolling up her window when she became aware of a security camera, just inside the gates, pointed directly at her.

*

In contrast, the McFee ranch had no gate. There were stone pillars where a gate had once hung, and a two-storied residence in the French style, built by a pretentious great grandmother as a carriage house. This was the same great grandmother who had imported the live oaks from Louisiana in an attempt to give the ranch a more southern plantation look.

Now the carriage house was a gatehouse with no gate. The main house had a line of Italian poplars beyond the pond instead of a backyard fence because Anita McFee had thought a fence looked too suburban. In her childhood memories, Callie didn't recall any locked doors or alarms. But then there had always been a servant or a gardener on the premises to keep an eye out.

When she wandered around to the back veranda, her

father was there, but his Sunday collection of papers was gone. In its place was an iPad in a lime green cover, resting in his huge hands. Angus came over to greet her, tailbone wagging.

"Callie girl," Buddy said. "What a treat!"

"Don't flatter yourself. I came to see Angus."

Buddy snickered. "You redheads stick together. You thirsty for a lemonade? If you are, go help yourself. You know where it is. I'm not getting up."

Callie grinned. "Would you like a lemonade, Dad?"

"That would be sweet. Thank you." It was one of the games he liked to play, being the attentive host while making someone else do the work. Callie leaned in, kissed him on the cheek and retreated into the kitchen. She emerged with two tall tumblers of lemonade with crushed ice and a garnish of mint from the one of the pots above the sink. She placed both on the side table then settled into the other rattan.

"Just thought I'd drop by. And how are you?" Callie's question was quite heartfelt. Just how was Buddy McFee? Was he with her here in the moment or lost in the shadows?

"Well enough. Surprised?" he said, holding up the iPad. "Gil said I was killing too many trees. Must admit I'm getting used to the damned thing, although I do miss throwing the newsprint around. How's everything over at State's place? Boys not driving you crazy?"

"They're angels." She realized how ridiculous that sounded. "As much as two McFee males can be, which is a pretty low bar. Is that a cigar? Dad!" She had just noticed a fat Cohiba with a half-inch ash leaning into a pristinely clean ashtray.

Buddy's morning cigar had been the subject of a legendary war. Early in Callie's life, Anita had persuaded her husband to reduce his consumption to two of the illegal Cubans a day, one in the morning, the other right before bed. In the year or so before her death, she had gotten him down to one, in the morning with his coffee and papers. And on her deathbed, as the cancer ate away at her stomach, she had made him promise to give them up completely. "It is a cigar," Buddy told his daughter. "Why don't you try a puff?"

There was something about his tone. Callie bent over to examine the Cohiba and its half-inch of ash. When she touched it, the ash stayed stubbornly in place. "It's wood. Why are you smoking a wooden cigar?"

"Because I promised your mother. But I like the feel of it. And the occasional puff of wood never hurt anyone." The cylindrical sculpture was remarkable true-to-life, from the ash to the cigar band to the faux chew marks on the head. There was even a narrow hole drilled down the center. "Nice huh? Some artist in Travis Heights made a few of them for me."

Callie handed him the cigar and watched as he took a deep, harmless draw. He grinned up at her as they fell into silence.

With all the most important subjects off-limits – Callie's work, Buddy's work, the last few years of estrangement – their conversation, when it started again, drifted into small talk. "Did you see the grill?" Buddy pointed down the length of his cigar to a stack stone wall at the end of the patio. "It's a Kalamazoo Hybrid. Runs on anything you got – gas, charcoal, wood pellets. Probably nuclear fission, too. Top of the line."

"Pretty spiffy," she agreed.

"Damn right. Keagan Blackburn bought one, so naturally I had to get the same. Keeping up with a goddamn oil tycoon."

Callie gave it a polite glance. It looked like any other

shiny, big, built-in grill. "Have you been seeing much of Keagan Blackburn?"

"I don't remember when he mentioned the grill to me. Probably at some charity thing. Seem to be more and more of those damn things."

"Charity thing?" She couldn't resist. "Are you sure it wasn't when he came over to see you? Part of the non-retirement work you were telling me about?"

He reacted calmly, almost amiably. "Keagan asks my advice now and then. Is that the reason you're here to visit your old dad on a lazy Sunday morning? I'm hurt."

"You're the one who brought him up."

Buddy's smile faded. "Keagan doesn't own a Kalamazoo. I just wanted to see if you'd latch onto his name. State told me you were asking around."

It had been a typical Buddy McFee trap. "Okay. I know he's been consulting you about the body in the field."

"And how do you know that?"

"I'm my father's daughter. I find things out. I also know he has an alibi."

"So that's the reason for your Sunday visit? I'm hurt, darling. I'm hurt."

"You are not hurt."

"Don't tell me what I am," he barked. "My only girl shows up on the Lord's day… Was that your plan coming here? To get your old dad to say something? Something you can use later on? You didn't get me disbarred last time. Maybe this time."

"It was an accident, Dad, please."

"And maybe this will be another accident. If you don't have the brains to avoid a goddamn accident, you shouldn't…"

"Why is his alibi a secret?" She sensed that most of his outrage was fake and she wasn't about to back down. "You think his alibi will get you disbarred?"

"You want to know his alibi?" Buddy calmed himself with a draw on his cigar, like a deep breath. "Keagan Blackburn was at home in his favorite chair, on a video conference – several calls back to back, between seven-thirty and nine-thirty p.m."

Callie almost laughed. "He was Skyping? That's his alibi?"

"Don't interrupt. The M.E. puts her death at between eight and nine. The less time between time of death and a preliminary autopsy, the more accurate these things are, that's what they tell me. But let's give Dr. Cummings a half-hour either direction. That puts the poor girl's death between seven-thirty and nine-thirty, which is pretty much the exact time as Keagan's calls."

"That's a nice coincidence."

"Coincidence or not, it's real. Cummings will testify to it."

"Could she be wrong about the time?"

"If someone wants to hire their own medical examiner and review the findings, that's their right."

Callie remained skeptical. "Who in the world has a conference call at that time of night? For two hours?"

"Someone who is working out the details of his company's petroleum leases with his partners in Anchorage, where it was five-thirty in the afternoon, and his customers in Shanghai, where it was nine-thirty the next morning. Between the lot of them, they confirm Keagan's presence in his living room, where they said he looked relaxed and was not in the process of killing anyone." Buddy reported all of this without notes or hesitation, a reminder of the man he still was, when he was still himself. "And in case you're wondering, the call was not a hurried thing set up at the last minute. It had been scheduled for weeks."

"And less than an hour later, he was driving her body to an open field…"

"I'm well aware of what he did less than an hour later. It's what happened in-between that is…" Buddy cleared his throat, taking his time to find the word. "…problematic. And for the record, I have no idea."

"And off the record?"

"I have no idea."

"Dad, at some point it's going to come out, and if you're involved in covering up a murder…"

"You're wrong." Buddy interrupted. "These things don't always come out. Remember when you and State were kids and the Governor and that movie star, what's his name, came to the house? What's his name? The blond curly hair? I recall you had a crush on his sorry ass. You had a poster of him in your room. I think he came up and signed it. Kissed you on the cheek."

"No." She would have covered her ears, but there was a drink in her hand. "I don't want to know. Was it something illegal?"

"Not per se, no. But it would have ended his career. My point is it's been twenty years and no one knows. In this case, Keagan Blackburn is betting the young lady's killer is never caught. His lawyers are talking to the D.A., doing everything to see he doesn't get prosecuted. My guess is they'll go for 'failure to report a felony', which is a Class A misdemeanor, punishable by a four thousand dollar fine. He may also be faced with illegally disposing of a body, but I think we can make that go away."

Callie couldn't believe it. "That's it? A stupid fine? How about failure to cooperate in a murder investigation?"

Buddy did his non-smile smile. "Did you just make that up?"

"That's not against the law?"

"It's not. In the good old U.S.A., you are not required to assist the police, as long as you don't lie to them, or act to hide evidence or hinder the investigation through positive action. Keegan has done none of that. So, unless they can show that he did anything more than find a dead girl and try to bury her…"

"Then why won't he say anything?"

"That's his constitutional right. And I doubt the D.A. will make waves."

"Because he's Keegan Blackburn."

"Not to put too fine a point on it…" Buddy McFee cleared his throat. "Blackburn Energy is the only major oil and gas company headquartered in Austin. A fluke. I think the city fathers are aware that, given the right impetus, or the wrong one, Blackburn could pick up and move shop to Houston and be with all the other players."

"Is that your doing, Dad? Encouraging them to look the other way?"

"No, darling. My job is to keep the case quiet. Keagan is hoping everything is dropped and his name never comes up. I'm not sure if I can make that happen or not."

An exasperated groan escaped her lips. "So, what do you think really happened? Be honest."

"Honest? Okay, baby girl, you got it." Buddy settled back in his rattan. "Here comes honest. It's been my experience that people keep secrets like this for three reasons. One: for money, which makes sense only if the stakes are super-high, like Keagan losing his company. Two: to protect someone or something. It's hard to imagine Keagan being so touchy-feely, since his third wife left and he isn't that close to anyone, although he could be protecting something we don't know about. Three: out of fear, the fear of a worse consequence if he tells the truth."

Callie found this last possibility interesting. "What kind of worse consequence?"

Buddy gave his lemonade a thoughtful sip. "Could be blackmail, for instance. Or a death threat."

"Someone forcing him to stay quiet about what happened?"

"It's possible. Or he could be complicit without being the killer. Or he could be protecting some juicy secret of his own, one that would come to light if he told us what actually went down. Again, I don't know."

She mulled over the options. "Well, he must know who killed her."

"Can you prove that?"

Callie tried not to let her exasperation show. "Promise me you're not breaking any laws. That's all I ask."

Buddy stared at her stone-faced for ten seconds or so then smiled. "Good having you back."

"Lawrence!" came a shout from around the side of the house.

After Anita's death, Gil was the only person left to call Buddy McFee by his Christian name, and only rarely, most often when he was annoyed. The short, energetic man rounded the corner, his cell phone coming off his ear and going into his pocket. "Callie." He didn't break his stride, although his voice did betray the slightest hitch. "I didn't know you were visiting us."

"What's the matter?" said Buddy. "Can't my little girl drop by and accuse her old man of a felony? What's this world coming to?"

Buddy's assistant regarded him with a practiced eye. "That was Felix Gibson on the phone," he said, pointing to his pocket. "He says he called the office line this morning and you talked to him."

"That I did. Felix and I used to confer all the time, about redistricting or the party slush fund or whichever senator couldn't keep it in his pants. Now I think the only reason he calls is to brag about his kids. How low have we sunk, eh?"

Gil wasn't amused. "He didn't call to brag about kids."

Buddy's eyes twinkled. "Maybe not."

"I don't care why he called. That line doesn't ring in your office anymore. It rings in mine, which means you were in my office, sir, answering my phone."

Buddy shrugged. "It was ringing."

"Am I going to need to keep my apartment locked? Is that it?"

"What?"

"I'm sorry, Boss."

"What did you just say?" Buddy met Gil's eyes with one of those stares no one in Texas politics ever wanted to be on the receiving end of. "Keep your apartment locked? Don't you use that condescending tone with me."

Gil pulled back, but not very far. "Sorry, boss. I am. But we have certain things put in place now. Rules we agreed on. For safety's sake. Your safety."

"I don't give a flying shit. You don't use that tone. I am still Buddy Goddamn McFee." And to show emphasis, he chucked the only thing in his hand, the iPad, in the direction of Gil Morales' head. The device crashed onto the flagstones, its lime green flap still open. Angus let out a little yelp and slunk back into the shade of the willow. "It's your fault for ducking. Get me a new one. Today." And, without another word, Buddy pushed himself up and lumbered into the house.

Gil stood there staring after the retreating figure, wordless, motionless, muscles tensed. The only sound he made were the rapid, deep whooshes of air forced in and out through his nostrils, like a quiet hyperventilation. It took a full minute for the breaths to return to normal.

Callie picked up the iPad and checked the broken screen. "How are you going to get a new one on a Sunday?"

"I bought a couple back-ups," Gil informed her calmly, as if the previous few minutes had meant nothing. "Fully loaded. Don't tell your father that. It would spoil his fun."

"What exactly did you mean 'for safety's sake'? Is my father in danger?"

"Not at the moment, no." Gil paused, as if waiting for her to parse and rephrase the question. Then, quite uncharacteristically, he answered her in full. "Over the years, your father has heard the secrets of a lot of powerful people."

"You mean like Felix Gibson?"

"Like him, yes. Documents can be destroyed, but the details are all locked away in the boss's brain. I've been around for only eighteen years of those secrets and even then not the total depth, especially in my early years. So, if the rumor gets out that the lock is broken, that the great Lawrence Buddy McFee is apt to have a bad day and think he's in the past… If Buddy spouts off something incriminating to the wrong person…"

Callie shifted uncomfortably. "No. These men are his friends. They would never…"

"The best friendships are the ones never put to the test. At least they're the safest. I'm doing this for his own good."

"At some point, people are going to find out."

"I know that," he almost shouted. "You don't think I know that?" Gil took the iPad from Callie's hands and slipped it under his arm. "If you have any suggestions, I'll be glad to hear them. If there's anything you think I should be doing differently, tell me. I'm dying to find some long-term solution, I really am. Your dad needs to be Buddy. And the men who run Texas need that, too."

"Yes, I understand," she said, taking his point seriously. "Let me think on it."

"Will you really think on it, Callie, hon?" He was almost turning human, almost turning vulnerable. "Cause I could really use some help."

"I will." She resented being in this position. At the same time, she hated herself for resenting it. She was his daughter, after all, returning home as if by fate. The fact that she had no idea what to do, or that his job and her job might put them on opposing sides of a murder, didn't change that. They were family, in a world where family meant everything.

When they walked back into the house, Buddy was

nowhere to be seen, not in the kitchen or the dining room or the living room or the second living room or the front day room where they used to keep their toys, or the downstairs study. "I think the dragon's retreated up into his lair," Gil whispered as he walked her into the front hall by the curving oak staircase. "He'll be all right, if you want to leave. I'll say your good-byes."

"Are you sure?"

"Nothing I haven't dealt with a hundred times."

They had never been allies, Callie and Gil. He had been the outsider, the consigliere who always put Buddy and politics first. It was unusual, almost unheard of, for the two of them to hug. But after Gil walked her to her truck, they shared a short, embarrassed embrace.

Callie drove slowly under the shade of the oaks toward Hacienda Road. A glint of yellow up ahead caught her eye, drawing her gaze to a wide, low-slung vehicle near the end of a dirt path just twenty yards to the right of the McFee driveway. If it hadn't been for the glint of sunlight bouncing off the hood, she might have missed it, shielded as it was by the dappled shade of the buttonwood trees flanking the path.

She wasn't a car fan, but she couldn't help concluding that this must be the same Lamborghini/Ferrari she'd seen behind the gated drive at Keagan Blackburn's house. What the hell was Blackburn doing parked in the shadows in front of the ranch?

He must be here to visit her father, she deduced, but he didn't want to show up while there was some unfamiliar silver pickup out front. Part of her wanted to stick around and see what happened, but a larger part of her didn't. Callie turned left onto Hacienda and kept driving.

It wasn't until ten minutes later, as she was turning onto Barton Springs Road, that she noticed the yellow sports car, two vehicles behind her, changing lanes when she changed lanes and flipping on its turn signal two seconds after she'd flipped on her own.

CHAPTER 11

TOMMY ON THE Lake was one of the new spots in town, new in that Callie didn't remember it from before her exile. The casual eatery was open for brunch and had outdoor decks overlooking Lady Bird Lake, which no one really considered a lake, just a wider, dammed-up section of the Colorado River. But the real appeal of Tommy on the Lake for her on this Sunday afternoon was that it was situated within sight of the highway exit. Callie risked her life by crossing two lanes, barely slowing down at the bottom of the off-ramp and making two quick rights until she came to Tommy's parking lot, which was not quite full.

Pulling into a spot between two other pickups, she sat in her truck, ignition off, slouched down, trying to see if any yellow sports car might be turning into the lot. When she was satisfied that she had lost the Lamborghini-Ferrari, she ducked out of her door and sprinted up to the canopied entrance.

It was a seat-yourself establishment with a table for two that had just become available at the very end of a deck. She weaved her way through the usual Sunday crowd: young couples with strollers and child seats, groups of girlfriends catching up on the past week, buddies in Longhorn caps swigging from longneck bottles. There were clumps of techies in logoed polo shirts announcing their affiliations to Apple and Indeed plus several tech companies that she'd never heard of.

After just three years away, she could see that Austin had changed or, more precisely, had continued to change. It was a younger city now, growing younger, with fewer Texas twangs to be heard on the ever-more-crowded streets. The new Indie bands advertised on the downtown bar fronts seemed even hipper than before, which just made her feel older and more out of touch. Austin, the town she'd grown up in, the seat of power, her father's Austin, was fading. But it was still there. As long as the city remained the center of state business, Austin would still be Texas, and people like Buddy McFee would still have a place. And what would Callie McFee's place be in this scheme of things? She couldn't help but feel a little trapped, caught between the world of old boy deal-making, the world she'd spied on as an awestruck girl, and this new, simpler world. Everybody else's world.

The shade umbrellas, celebrating Heineken and Tito's Handmade, rippled in the breeze coming off the water. Within a minute, she had ordered a Bloody Mary. Just ordering it helped calm her nerves. It was a nice place, she decided, probably the perfect spot for an after-work drink, watching the sun set over the lake. The idea of after-work drinks made her think of Nicole, a friend dating back to her last year of college when they both worked as news interns at KXAN. They had grown instantly close, but she hadn't seen Nicole in years. *I should call her*, she thought. *It might help make life a little more normal.*

As soon as the waiter brought her the Bloody Mary, she took a sip then took out her phone. "Oliver?" she whispered. "It's Callie. Sorry to bother you."

"Callie?" She could detect his panhandle in just the one word. "What's the matter? What's wrong?"

"Why do you assume something's wrong?"

"Because you're whispering, first off, and you're apologizing, which you wouldn't do if this was good news. What's up?"

Callie didn't feel like arguing, partly because he was right. "I think I may have poked the bear."

It took Oliver a few seconds to remember his own metaphor. "You confronted Blackburn?" His voice was shaky. "Didn't I tell you? Why would you do that?"

"I didn't do it intentionally." Callie proceeded to review her Sunday morning – the detour to Blackburn's gates, visiting the ranch, seeing his Lamborghini/Ferrari, then finding the same yellow Lamborghini/Ferrari tailing her.

"It's a Lamborghini," Oliver said. "Why would he tail you in a car like that?"

"Quickly accessible? It was the only thing in his driveway."

"So, he's at home on a Sunday," Oliver hypothesized, piecing it together. "He sees an unknown pickup stopping by his gates and he follows it, probably feeling pretty paranoid ever since that night."

"I'm guessing it was him behind the wheel."

"Do you think you lost him?"

"I'm pretty sure, yes."

"Does he know it was you? I mean, there was a security camera. Would Blackburn know your face? When did you last see him?"

Callie glanced up from her phone then back down again. "Oh, Jesus! He knows it was me. Oliver…" Instantly she regretted mentioning his name. Damn. "I'm going to have to call you back."

"Oliver?" The man standing by her table waited until Callie put down the phone. "That wouldn't happen to be Oliver Chesney, would it? Your daddy happened to mention your new job last time we spoke. Congratulations."

She had always been a bit nervous around Keagan Blackburn, based on nothing very definable. Not a large man like her father, he was of medium height and medium build with a comb-over of light brown hair, the shade chemically enhanced, by Callie's guess. His overly white teeth were perfectly even, straight across, and also looked enhanced. "You came to pay me a call, so I thought I'd return the favor."

"You were following me?"

"Not the whole time. Leaving my place, you were a little far ahead. But I figured you might be on your way to the ranch. Damn if I wasn't right."

"How did you know it was me?"

"My gate has a motion alarm, so I was alerted as soon as you pulled up. I was intrigued to see your face, but then you drove off, so I thought it might be a good time to take my Italian friend out for a spin. Don't drive her nearly as much as she needs."

"So, you just sat in front of the ranch, waiting for me?"

"It's a nice day. Why not?"

She tried to ignore his smile. "What else did my father tell you? Did he tell you what I'm doing?"

"He told me you were back, working for some free, liberal

piece of shit. But I'm good at addition. Your brother is on the case. Your dad is a man I confide in. Then you, a reporter, show up. I regret that you find me so off-putting that you couldn't even ring my buzzer."

"I changed my mind."

"I know Buddy didn't tell you anything. I'd trust that man with my life. I can only assume your brother must have let something slip. I'm going to have to have a talk with him."

"State didn't say anything, I swear."

"Well, as a gentleman, I'll believe you." Blackburn borrowed a chair from a neighboring table and settled in across from her. "So, as long as I'm here – any questions? Something you've been dying to ask? Off the record."

"Nothing the police haven't asked a dozen times." Callie reached for her phone.

"Oh, no. You are not recording this."

"I'm not." Callie touched the screen a few times, enlarged the image and handed it to Blackburn. "Here."

He squinted at the image and pursed his lips. "I assume this is her. The young woman. I never got much of a look, it being night and her being dead."

"She had a name," Callie informed him. "Briana Crawley."

"Sorry. My snot-nosed lawyer won't tell me much. Says we have to maintain some kind of firewall between her death and my case." He kept staring at the young woman in her leather necklace. "Does she have a husband or a boyfriend?"

"She has parents."

"Yes, of course. No parent should have to go through that. I've been having nightmares myself. Not that it's comparable in any way."

"Do your nightmares include burying her?"

A hint of anger flashed in his eyes. Then it was gone. "For the record, I have no idea what you're talking about."

"The Crawleys need to know what happened to their daughter."

"I wish I could help them. I really do."

"If you told the police what you do know…"

"That wouldn't help. I've gone over it in my mind a hundred times. Nothing I tell them would help find her killer."

"Did you just find her body somewhere? Why didn't you call the police?"

"It's more complicated than you can imagine." He handed back her phone. "Thank you for letting me see her. Briana," he added, as if to imprint the name in his mind.

Callie took a breath – a deep, cleansing breath, in through the nostrils and out through the mouth. It didn't work. Why did he have to seem so normal, so almost human? "I'm doing a story on one of Austin's forgotten victims. And, full disclosure, I'm going to have to write about your arrest."

The oil executive didn't flinch. "What arrest? I don't believe you'll find an arrest record anywhere."

Callie had thought about this. "Maybe not. But I'm going to talk to that state trooper – see what he has to say about that night." The very second those words passed her lips, she regretted them. Why, oh why had she said it?

Blackburn displayed no reaction, not the bat of an eyelash, which was probably the most chilling reaction possible. "Do you know the officer's name?" She tried not to move a muscle. "Of course you do."

"And he knows yours."

"No comment."

The waiter, a boy looking barely old enough to legally serve alcohol, was on his way to their table, but Blackburn caught his eye, waved him away then stood up.

"Leaving already?" Callie asked with more bravado than she felt.

Blackburn leaned across her Bloody Mary. "You can go down whatever rabbit hole you want, young lady. I'm not going to tell you how to do your job."

"I appreciate it."

"Just remember who you're dealing with." He wrinkled the left side of his face into a wink. "A word to the wise." Then he walked away.

Callie pretended not to be upset or in a rush to leave. She continued to sip her Bloody Mary through the eco-friendly bamboo straw and even managed a few bites of her celery stick. What in the world had made her think she was up to this? Trading jabs with a man like Blackburn. Pitting herself not only against him but against her father. Was it just the hubris of a stupid beginner? Was it a combination of her meds and alcohol and sleep deprivation? Or had she just been following the script of a hundred half-remembered suspense films where the hero and villain face off with thinly veiled threats?

As soon as she heard the heavy roar of the Lamborghini revving in the parking lot, Callie was back on her phone to Oliver, bringing him up to date, an apology gracing almost every sentence.

"I don't know what got into me," she moaned. "I could have said nothing. I could have played dumb." She laughed. "Well, I did play dumb, but in totally the wrong way. I'm sorry."

"That's okay," he said. She could tell from his voice that it wasn't. "What's the trooper's name? As long as we're out in the open, we may as well make the most of it."

She had already looked it up from the notepad on her phone. "Josiah Jackson."

"Unusual name. That's good." She could hear Oliver at his keyboard.

"Are you looking him up on the THP database? I'm not sure how much info they have about officers."

"No, I'm doing a much more sophisticated search. Facebook. Oh, look. There he is."

CHAPTER 12

CALLIE WAS SHOCKED. Even without friending people, you could learn an awful lot about them on Facebook and they wouldn't have a clue. It was a frightening revelation, both the things you could discover and the things you could infer. With Josiah Jackson, for example, she discovered what he looked like – early twenties, white, with a military-style crew cut – that he had a snarky grin and that his Texas Highway Patrol uniform was growing a little snug around the midriff.

His photos showed that he liked to take selfies with a woman named Crystal, who seemed fond of tank tops and whose hair varied in shade between blonde and extra blonde. A comment on one of their selfies was from a Tiffany Shields who referred to Crystal as "Sis". The word sis could refer to many relationships, Callie knew, but another quick Facebook search resulted in a profile for a Crystal Shields, a hairstylist at a salon in Travis Heights, who perfectly matched the woman in Josiah's selfies.

By making a few reasonable guesses, Callie and Oliver pieced together further details of Josiah Jackson's life. The murder had occurred on April 12. On April 13, the highway patrol officer changed his profile picture to a selfie of him alone, smiling broadly and holding a coconut, its top pierced by a straw, with palm trees waving in the background. Definitely not Austin. The comments ran from the usual envy to surprise – "Where the hell are you?" – to more than one inquiry about Crystal. "Where's Crystal, man?" Josiah – Joss to his friends – had not responded to any of them, not even stating where he was or why he was drinking from coconuts.

A similar search of Crystal's page did not show any coconuts or palm trees, just a recently posted quote from Kahlil Gibran, musing about love and disappointment.

Callie and Oliver came to the same conclusion. They, Blackburn's people, had got Josiah time off and paid for him to go away until they could be sure that no one was sniffing around. Maybe a week. Maybe two. They had probably advised him not to say where he was, just in case. But they had not prevented him from posting selfies. And they had not arranged for Crystal to get time off or to pay for her to join him. That may have been a mistake on their part, although, Callie knew, Buddy McFee rarely made mistakes.

Oliver was the one who crafted the Facebook message to Crystal. "You don't know me, but I have news about Joss, if you're interested. Let me know." Callie wasn't sure about the wording. Did he really need to say, "You don't know me"? Oliver explained that it was better to acknowledge the intrusion than not, making the message sound less ominous than a straight, "I have news about Joss."

Callie was still voicing her second thoughts when the reply came. "Who are you? What do you know?" Oliver asked

Crystal to switch over to texts, for privacy, and supplied his cell number. It was an agonizing five minutes before Crystal's text arrived. Twelve more texts, six from each side, led the way to one long phone call and the promise of a meeting.

Crystal told them that she had not heard from Joss and hadn't even been aware of his departure from town. His phone now went instantly into voicemail and his only communication was a message in which he assured her that he was fine and that his absence was somehow work-related. He would explain later, he said, if he was allowed to. She just had to trust him.

Crystal's mind had gone in a number of far flung directions. Was Joss in trouble? Was he working on a special case, maybe with the FBI, which had always been his dream job? Was he lying to her, placating her with some nonsense about work while he had just run off on vacation, perhaps with the Mexican waitress at the Cantina Grille who was always flirting with him?

Oliver was honest with Crystal, up to a point. He identified himself as the publisher of the *Austin Free Press* – Crystal knew the paper; she liked the crossword; she seemed impressed – and while he hadn't personally been in touch with Joss, Oliver did have some information that he felt Crystal deserved to know.

It was still Sunday afternoon, just a few hours after Callie had ordered her Bloody Mary. On the phone, Crystal volunteered to come into the *Free Press* offices on Monday morning. Callie shook her head and Oliver agreed. This was urgent, he told Crystal, and couldn't wait until tomorrow.

They settled on Crystal's apartment in SoCo, the South

Congress neighborhood. Oliver said he would bring along a female co-worker, just to put Crystal at ease, and he encouraged her to have a friend join her as well. Callie shook her head and Oliver replied with a helplessly raised eyebrow. What else could he say? They were both relieved when Crystal said that it wouldn't be necessary. Whatever they had to tell her, she would prefer to hear it alone.

Crystal Shields lived on the ground floor of a long, three-story building with a fake brick exterior and parking spaces in front of a narrow, neglected scrap of a lawn. Angry, big-dog barks greeted them as they walked up the broken concrete path. Callie let Oliver take the lead.

They heard Crystal's voice before they saw her. "Brutus, no! Bad boy. Stop it." Surprisingly enough, Brutus did stop. "Don't worry. He's harmless." When the door opened, they found a large brown Doberman with docked ears, sitting obedient and attentive, directly behind Crystal. "Sorry about that. I'm not really a dog person, but Joss bought him and trained him. Said I needed the protection, so I guess I'm kind of stuck, now that Joss is being such an ass. Do you know anyone who wants a trained Doberman? That would serve him right, wouldn't it? Just give him away."

She was softer than Callie had imagined from the highly posed selfies. More open and vulnerable, with a warm, wide smile. "Oh, I'm so sorry. The first thing you hear out of my mouth. What you must think. Y'all come in. And don't worry about Brutus. He's a sweetheart."

She offered them sweet tea, which Oliver refused but Callie accepted, having been taught to accept hospitality. It was the polite thing. As Crystal went into the kitchen and poured out two glasses from a gallon jug of Milo's, added ice, came back and settled into a chair across from the sectional sofa, the three of them made small talk – the weather and dogs and hair. She asked if Callie's red hair was natural, then offered up some suggestions of what she could do with it.

When a conversational lull arrived, Oliver took out his iPhone and asked Crystal if he could record their conversation. At first, she was reluctant, but after all, as they explained, they were reporters and might use whatever she told them and it wouldn't it be better to have her words recorded so that they couldn't make things up? Also, she could tell them to stop at any time if it got uncomfortable. So, okay. Sure. She even felt a little flattered.

Oliver opened his voice memo app, pressed record and placed the phone on a side table, close enough to Crystal but out of her line of sight. It was his experience that after the first few minutes, people often forgot they were being recorded. He started right in. "Do you know why Josiah left town? Without telling you or anyone else?"

"Shitty bastard," Crystal said then covered her mouth. "Sorry."

"That's okay," Callie said. "He probably deserves it."

"He didn't even tell the guys at work. Just took some personal days and they let him. He didn't even tell his mother, but maybe he did. That bitch lies to me all the time."

"We think we know what happened," Oliver said. "Josiah left on Thursday, April 13. When did you last see him?"

"The night before." She had obviously given this some thought. "Joss's shift ended at midnight. He knows I don't get to bed until late, so sometimes he drops by."

"And he dropped by that night?" Oliver waited and watched as the big dog settled down on the rug beside his owner. Crystal scratched him behind the ears and nodded yes. "Did he talk about what happened at work?"

"You mean the dead girl?"

"Yes, the dead girl," Callie said, trying not to lean toward the phone. "Her name was Briana Crawley."

"Yeah, of course, he talked about it. It was all he could talk about. I mean it's not every day, right?"

Callie suppressed her excitement. There had always been a chance that, in the small window between the event and the containment, that Trooper Jackson had told someone, someone outside the department. "What did he say?"

From all her years listening to politicians, Callie knew that certain people like to have conversations and certain ones like to tell stories. Crystal was a storyteller. They let her start at the beginning – from her long, difficult day at work where one client had insisted on an after-dinner appointment and then was never happy, to her attempt to get to bed early, to her trying to ignore Joss when he banged on her door and wouldn't go away. She hadn't given him a key because he'd never ever asked for one and she considered that to be a telling sign about their relationship, etc., etc. Callie hoped there was enough room on Oliver's phone.

Neither one wanted to interrupt Crystal's flow, to accidentally remind her that this was an interview, not a story. It finally paid off when Crystal described Joss describing the man in the field with the dead girl and the shovel. Joss was used to traffic stops and the occasional car chase, but he'd never seen anything like this.

"Apparently, he's some very rich, important guy. Joss recognized the name right away. But he couldn't have been that important."

Callie asked, "Why not?"

Crystal snorted. "Because I never saw him on the news. If he was someone important getting arrested, he'd be all over the news, right?"

"Did Joss tell you his name?" asked Oliver. It was the million-dollar question.

"Sure, he told me. But I didn't recognize it."

Oliver managed to keep an even tone. "Do you remember the name?"

Crystal gave it a moment's thought. "No. Sorry." If he was really famous, I would have heard of him, right? Some big businessman."

"Do you remember what kind of business?"

"Sorry. Is his name supposed to be a secret? Is Joss going to get in trouble for telling me?"

"No, not at all," said Callie. She leaned across the coffee table. "If I mention the man's name, do you think you'd remember it?"

"I might," Crystal allowed. "It was an odd name, I think."

"Good. Was his name... Hey!"

Oliver had grabbed her by the sleeve and was leaning her away from the phone. "Can I talk to you?" he whispered.

"In a minute," Callie said, not wanting to lose her momentum. "We're so close."

But before she could turn back to Crystal, she was being dragged her to her feet and led into the kitchen. "Sorry. We'll be back in a sec. Keep trying to think of that name." Oliver had already maneuvered her around the little island and back to the far corner. "What?" she snarled.

"You can't give her the name," Oliver snarled back.

"I'm trying to help her remember."

"We can't plant the name. His lawyers will ask for the tape. They'll have a field day."

"We can edit it, make it look like she remembered."

"Are you crazy?" He was nearly apoplectic. "We can't edit it. They'll ask for the original. Besides, it's not right. Besides, they'll interview her and she'll tell the truth."

"So, we give her a choice of four or five names. She can pick out his name, like a line-up."

"That doesn't sound right either."

"Why not? It's like a police line-up. Look, we both know he's the guy."

Their discussion was interrupted by a chirpy ringtone from the other room. Callie knew it wasn't hers. "Is that yours?" Oliver listened, but the chirp had already stopped.

By the time they got back, Crystal was on her phone. "Joss, baby!" At the sound of the name, Brutus perked up his ears. "Where the hell are you? – No, I'm not mad. Well, I should be. How could you just disappear like that?" She covered the phone and mouthed, "It's Joss," then stepped away toward the front door. Callie could barely make out a male voice doing most of the talking.

"Uh-huh. – Uh-huh. – Oh, wow. – You're kidding." Nearly a minute passed. "That's amazing. No, you had no choice. I just wish you could have told me then. I was worried sick. And mad, too." Crystal continued to listen. "Uh-huh."

Callie was inching forward now and was unprepared for

Crystal's raucous scream of delight. "Ahhh! Yeah, of course I wanna come. A free trip to Mexico? Are you kidding? – Oh, Marie can take my clients. Or I'll just cancel. Who cares?" She covered the phone again. "Joss wants me to come to Mexico. He misses me. Isn't that sweet? Do you want to talk to him? I'm sure he remembers the name."

Before Callie could think of anything to say, Joss was speaking. "Yeah, I have company," Crystal answered. "You jealous? No, no, don't be." She tittered. "It's just a couple reporters. – Yes, I said reporters. Two of them. About that murder."

She listened again and lost her smile. "Okay. Okay. Well, how was I to know? – No, I didn't say. I don't even know who that is. – Who? – Okay. Jeez. Whatever you say." She lowered the phone. "Joss says you have to go. I'm so sorry. He says I can't talk to you. It's all classified."

"No, no." Oliver clasped his hands together, pleading his case. "Crystal, a girl was murdered. And someone's covering it up."

She laughed. "Oh, no. I know it looks that way, but it only looks that way. You don't know the story. If you knew… Unfortunately, I can't tell you. Joss can't either."

"Crystal!" The voice on the other end was finally audible. "Crystal! Kick them out now!" Brutus' ears perked up again and he let out a little yelp. "Is that Brutus?" Brutus answered with a bigger yelp, wagging his stump of a tail. "Hey, boy. Good boy."

"Crystal, he's lying to you." Callie kept her voice low. "The man's name is Keagan Blackburn. He's a bad guy, believe me. If he didn't kill her, he certainly knows who did."

"Crystal!" They could all hear Josiah's voice. "Put me on speaker." Crystal did as she was told. "Who the hell are you?"

Oliver raised his voice. "Officer Jackson, hello. That girl you found in the field. We're trying to find her killer. I'm sure you want to find her killer, too."

"That man is not her killer," said the voice on the speaker.

"Then who was he?" Callie asked. "Help us out."

"Crystal, don't say another thing. Kick them out now." Crystal looked confused, apparently torn between not saying a thing and kicking them out. "Brutus!" The Doberman heard his name again and got to his feet. "Brutus, alert!"

The animal obeyed, tensing every muscle, baring his teeth and showing them to the two strangers standing halfway across the room. There was a low, almost inaudible growl in his throat.

"He's doing it," Crystal informed her boyfriend then turned to her guests. "I'm so sorry, guys. But you're going to have to go."

"Get the hell out," shouted Trooper Josiah Jackson from somewhere in Mexico. "Or I'll say the word. I will. You have three seconds to leave. One…"

"Don't forget that," Crystal said, pointing to Oliver's iPhone on the side table. Callie picked it up but didn't turn it off.

"Two."

Callie and Oliver were safely outside with the door slammed shut by the time Joss got to three. The word for "attack" never came.

Halfway down the concrete path, Oliver looked back to see Callie kneeling below the living room window, holding his phone up. "Jeez." Oliver rushed back in a hunched-over waddle, grabbed her arm and pulled her away.

"They're still on speaker," Callie whispered.

Oliver kept pulling. "What do you want? You want her to open the door and let the dog out?"

Callie resisted. "She's not paying attention to the window. If they start talking about Blackburn... If they mention his name..."

"What's wrong with you?" He pulled harder, leading her slowly back to the car. "First off, you can't record someone without their permission."

"In Texas you can, if you're one of the parties in the conversation." After years of listening to her father, Callie knew a few things.

"We're not a party in the conversation." Oliver clicked his key ring and kept pulling.

"We were a few seconds ago. It's the same conversation, right?"

Oliver let go of her arm. "You know, you're more like him than you're willing to admit."

"More like who?"

"You know who."

The comparison was enough to make Callie abandon her plan. Storming around to the passenger side, she yanked open the door. "That's a horrible thing to say."

CHAPTER 13

At some point on Monday morning, Callie had the presence of mind to call in sick – a stomach thing, she said. She didn't talk to Oliver but left a message, saying she didn't want to infect anyone and would try to get a little work done from home.

During her stay at State and Yolanda's, she had made a point of never joining the family for dinner. She figured it would be an imposition since she didn't cook, not even scrambled eggs, and didn't want to impose. But yesterday, after the debacle with Crystal, she arrived home just in time for the traditional Sunday dinner and finally allowed State to persuade her to join them. It felt like a better choice than being alone.

Nothing big went wrong, but almost everything small did. Her five-year-old nephews were at their brattiest, carping about the food, vying loudly for attention and throwing peas at each other when they thought no one was watching. This combination forced Callie to make a few under-the-breath comments, apparently within earshot of Yolanda, who responded with several of her own about Callie's self-destructive life. Callie's way of coping was to pour herself yet another glass of Chardonnay – a mistake, but a necessary one – which only gave Yolanda more to mumble about.

The meal was over by 7:30, late for the children but early for Callie, who then retreated to her room, where she found a romantic comedy that she'd probably already seen and unearthed a hidden bottle of warm Chablis packed in her luggage. The rom-com was fun but predictable and she found herself trying not to think about Oliver.

Had she been right or had he? Getting Crystal to say Blackburn's name on tape would have been huge. They could have told the truth in print, that Crystal had recognized the name, one gleaned from an unnamed source. It wasn't great journalism, but she doubted they could be sued for it. That possibility had been taken away by her boss's squeamish response at just the wrong moment. Part of the blame was hers, she realized, for having alerted Blackburn in the first place. And a big portion had to be reserved for Gil and her father, who must have swooped in as soon as they realized Trooper Jackson might have a loose end that needed tying up.

Another serving of Chablis wound up in her toothbrush glass. Callie vaguely remembered spending her last moments of consciousness sneaking the empty wine bottle into the bottom of the recycling bin in the garage then unfolding the sofa bed and measuring out her pills.

For once, she slept through the night but woke with a cotton-filled mouth and a throbbing head. The house was mercifully empty. For the next hour, the only intrusion was a call from Oliver, which she had no intention of answering or returning.

With the trooper angle sidelined, Callie promised herself

to spend the rest of the day working on the MySugar connection. But first… She wondered if there might be an open bottle of white wine in the fridge, maybe on a high shelf, out of reach of the kids. Indeed, there was. She poured the remains into a tall water glass, then disposed of the bottle in the bottom of the recycling bin in the garage, next to the one from last night.

Now, what was it she'd just promised herself? Oh, yes. MySugar. It was something she'd been putting off. Several times she'd gone to the website, which displayed cheery photos of young female models laughing alongside middle-aged male models who were cuter than any middle-aged men she'd ever met. But there was precious little you could see without inputting your own information and she'd always chickened out. What if someone she knew were to see it? And what kind of spam or other untold dangers was she opening herself up to? Just the idea that her photo, even an artfully obscured photo, would be stored here for who knows how long, with her information, even artfully misleading information… And yet there was no way to get further into the site. There was no way of seeing what Briana might have written about herself, what might have attracted the man who might have murdered her. Callie wondered if her brother had already done this. Had States Rights McFee signed up as a sugar daddy? Had his pregnant partner signed up? Both ideas made her giggle.

Callie brought her laptop into the kitchen and set it up on the marble island. State was at work, the kids in school and Yolanda out doing whatever she did for half the day. She took another sip from her water glass, went to the MySugar site and when she got to the registration window, suddenly remembered an email address from years ago. She had once tried to cancel this address, but it was still active. Every month or so she would check it, erase a mountain of spam and occasionally, maybe once every other month, find a message from someone she hadn't talked to in ages.

This little deception, using an unused email, gave her just enough confidence to start filling in the fields. She decided on a suitable screen name, Heather111, and a suitable age, twenty-one. The site asked for a headline and she wrote, "College girl open to new experiences. First time." She spent the next few minutes pulling back her distinctive hair into a bun – it was a stringy mess today, anyway – and taking a suitable selfie, something alluring, she hoped, something that realistically took off five years, with her face strategically in the shadows. The site was free for sugar babies, which made sense since the girls were the ones without the money, so there was no need for her to divulge a credit card number.

MySugar required a personal description as well as an outline of what Callie was looking for. She tried to mimic what Briana might have said – an out-of-state student, a little lonely here in Austin, looking for mature companionship as a way to defray expenses and even become spoiled. On her daddy request, she tried to keep things open. She didn't mind a married man, she wrote. And she was attracted to all races. Callie had no illusion of actually finding Briana's daddy. And how would she know if she did? But she had to do something.

Without stopping to think, she pressed "JOIN", and was almost relieved when it didn't go through. A line of red letters popped up. "Please designate your SUGAR PREFERENCE." After all that, she had neglected to choose between wanting a "sugar momma" or a "sugar daddy". She clicked the "daddy" button then instantly had misgivings. What could she possibly have to learn from joining? And what if her father found out? Or worse, Yolanda.

Callie was still mulling it over, her finger poised over the mouse – join or not – when the doorbell rang. Thankful for the diversion, she walked into the entry hall and didn't bother to check the peephole.

It took her a few seconds to recognize the young, fleshy woman standing on the porch. "Nicole?" Back in their intern days, Nicole had dyed her hair red. It had come out a dark auburn, not the same shade as Callie's. That had never been the intent, but it was flattering just the same, both to Callie's ego and Nicole's skin tone. Since then, Nicole had let her hair revert to its natural, mousy brown and had it cut shorter, framing her face. "Hi. Wow!" Callie was taken aback. "I've been meaning to call. How did you know I was in town?"

Nicole seemed puzzled by the question. "Last night." Callie didn't react. "You called me in the middle of the night. We talked for like an hour. What are you saying? You don't remember?"

"I called you? Really?" Callie laughed. "I have absolutely no memory. It must have been the Ambien."

"We talked like forever. About your dad. About us. How much you missed the two of us working at the station. Were you drunk, Callie, is that it?"

"No." She pronounced it like a three-syllable word. "But I may have been asleep. I know that sounds crazy, but you hear about people taking Ambien and then walking around or getting into conversations. God, in the middle of the night? I am not taking that again. Nicole, I'm so sorry. Come on in." She moved aside and ushered her friend inside.

"You asked me to come over today. If this is a bad time…"

"It sort of is." She immediately regretted it. "I mean, no. I was in the middle of something, but I'm being a total, total ass. I mean, I wake you up just to blabber and then you come all this way . . . Come in, come in." Nicole protested but at the same time followed Callie into the living room, stepping around a minefield of toys along the way. "Can I get you something? A lemonade or iced tea or some coffee?"

"A Coke, if you have it. Not Diet. Hate the taste."

"I remember. One Coke it is." Retreating into the kitchen, she kept up a barrage of small talk, just to fill the air. "What are you up to? You probably told me last night, so I apologize. Are you still at KXAN? Do you want ice with that?" If Nicole had heard her or was talking back, she couldn't tell. Callie moved as quickly as possible, taking the last can of Coke from the wet bar and filling a water glass with ice. To make her own drink look a little more like water, she added ice cubes and a straw then brought the can and both glasses into the living room. "You wanted ice with it, right?"

"Thanks." Nicole poured her Coke over the ice, all the while keeping focused on Callie. "What's wrong?"

"Wrong? Nothing's wrong. You know, there's all the stress of coming home and then my new job." Callie averted her eyes. "Did I happen to say anything about my job – like the stories I'm working on?"

"No, not much." Callie was relieved. "You were mostly going on about your dad and your pain-in-the-ass boss." Nicole's face brightened. "Oh, speaking of jobs, I'm a segment producer now. Evening news. I know I told you that last night, but…"

"Hey, congratulations." Callie smiled and sipped and wondered how far she would have gone at the station in those same three years had she not said what she'd said, live on air. Her very first time on air, a trial run, to see if the famous man's daughter could make the transition from assistant editor to on-air talent.

It had been a standard puff piece on Barton Pharmaceuticals, a local company that was expanding right here in Austin. The company spokesperson mentioned to Callie, just in passing, that the stock was worth twenty times what it used to be. And Callie, also just in passing, trying to put a personal spin on the story, mentioned that their father had given her and her brother stock in Barton Pharmaceuticals a few years ago for Christmas, old-fashioned stock certificates hidden in a big box of tissue paper. It had seemed like a peculiar Christmas present at the time, but in hindsight… In hindsight, what a gift! And from that innocuous anecdote, the trouble began. One thing led to another, led to Callie's testimony in a closed-door session with federal prosecutors, led to Lawrence "Buddy" McFee's disgrace and resignation.

"You're not looking too good." The words had come blurting out. Nicole instinctively covered her mouth. "Sorry. Sorry. But you really don't." And this from a woman who was always twenty pounds overweight and used to mimic Callie's hair and clothes and everything else about her.

Callie ran a hand through her curls. Maybe tonight she would wash her hair. "You caught me at one of those moments." She tried not to glance at her water glass. "I haven't been sleeping well."

"You're taking Ambien, you said? My grandmother takes Ambien."

"This piece I'm working on... Kind of stressful."

"I get it." Nicole looked away. "Hey, maybe we should do a raincheck."

They agreed that a raincheck might work best. Callie promised to call her when things weren't quite so stressed. Perhaps a nice brunch at Tommy on the Lake. Nicole had heard of the place and said she looked forward to relaxing and catching up. Callie promised to call. Soon. Maybe next weekend. It would be fun.

Callie waved good-bye from the front porch, water glass in hand, then retreated back inside and got as far as the living room before collapsing onto the sofa. After digging an ounce or two of Fruit Loops from between the cushions, she fell soundly asleep.

When she woke up, Yolanda was standing over her and what sounded like a pair of juvenile car alarms were screeching through the house. Larry and Brad had returned after a long day of school, ready to reclaim their territory. "What is this?" Yolanda held up the water glass and glared over the rim. Callie thought she was about to be reprimanded for not using a coaster. "Bradley almost drank this. My son almost drank this."

Her sister-in-law's sanctimonious tone brought out Callie's belligerence. "Did he drink it or not?"

"He could have. He was sniffing it." Yolanda lowered her voice but not her energy. "What the hell are you doing, drinking in the daytime. With a straw, no less? Aren't you supposed to be at work?"

"I'm working from home."

Yolanda grunted. "This is work for you, really? Sleeping on the couch and drinking?"

"Mom!" came a voice. "Larry's playing with Aunt Callie's computer."

"Am not. I'm just looking at it."

"Whatever you two are doing, stop it. Stop it now." Yolanda handed Callie the glass then marched toward the kitchen.

It took Callie longer than it should have to piece together the situation. If Yolanda got this upset when one of her boys sniffed a glass of watered-down wine, what would her reaction be… "No, no, no," she moaned then tried to get up. A pounding sensation surged through her head and on her first step, she realized that one of her legs, the one tucked underneath, was asleep. She hobbled through the throbbing and the stinging. But she was too late.

Yolanda had already shooed the boys away from the laptop. "My Sugar?" she asked but it wasn't really a question. "Welcome to My Sugar," she read. "Let's take the first step in finding you a sugar daddy." Yolanda scanned the photos and text then looked up from the screen, eyes wide. "Is this your new career goal? Finding a sugar daddy? Good lord, Callie. Good lord!"

"I want sugar," Larry bellowed. "Mom, can I have a cookie?"

"We're not supposed to have sugar," Brad reprimanded him. They were fraternal twins, not at all alike, even at the tender age of five.

"But the computer says…"

"Boys, go up to your room," Yolanda said in a voice that

no sane person would argue with. "Now." And the boys scurried off.

Callie grabbed the laptop away from Yolanda. "Did he press 'join?' Oh, my God, your son pressed 'join'. Why? Why did he press 'join?'"

"Because it says sugar. 'Do you want some sugar?'. He wanted sugar."

"You mean they can read?"

"They can read 'sugar,' yes. It's on everything I won't buy them at the store."

"I wasn't serious, for God's sake. I just need to get information. For a story."

"A story about hookers and sugar daddies?" Yolanda scowled. "Does the story also involve daytime drinking and sleeping on the couch?"

"I can't believe your stupid son pressed the button."

"My sons are not stupid."

"Sorry." Callie tried to back it up. "Yolie, I'm sorry. I didn't mean… Look, you can ask State about the website. He knows."

"You've been discussing sugar daddies with my husband? Your own brother? Callie, I need you out of my house. Now. Today. Seriously. I don't care where the heck you go."

CHAPTER 14

CALLIE HATED IT when people stood in her cubicle while she reviewed their work. She felt uncomfortable and put on the spot, which was probably how they felt, although they could avoid it all by going away and coming back later, damn it. She kept her eyes on her screen, plowing through to the end of the second installment before looking up. Jennie Larson was still there, trying not to pace, looking even more uncomfortable. "So, what happened to that single father – what's his name?" Callie scrolled back to the top of the article. "Todd Brenneman."

"What do you mean, what happened to him?"

Callie did a word search in the article, just to be sure. "You have several very emotional paragraphs about him trying to get his daughter into a non-religious charter school. Very good, by the way. But we never hear from him again."

"His daughter didn't get in," Jennie said. "I thought I made that clear. Page two."

"You did, except we still need a follow-up. Did she adjust

any better to the public school? Is Brenneman happy or sad or angry? Is he going to try again?"

"I thought about that, but it doesn't really have anything to do with the direction of the article. It felt like a diversion."

Callie swiveled and looked up, ready to dispense her pearls of wisdom. "Every time you tell a personal story, the readers care, or they should. It's how we're wired. Is this man good or bad? Do I want his daughter in the charter school, or do I want her to stick it out in public? Is it his fault or the system's fault? And the way you phrase whatever happened to him influences everything. It's your viewpoint speaking without you having to state it directly, which was what you did in the last two paragraphs, state it directly, which was too much. Too much editorializing."

Jennie seemed to understand. "You're saying I should cut the editorializing and replace it with a follow-up on Todd Brenneman that does the same editorializing."

"Evokes the same emotion, yes."

"Isn't that being manipulative?" Jennie asked. "I mean, making this guy evoke my point of view?"

"All good writing is manipulative." Why were these things so clear for her and so foggy for others? All through her child-hood, she had seen firsthand the great persuasion of language, always couched in a joke or an anecdote. "If you feel a certain way after reading a story, it's because that's what the writer wants. Even if you think this is some unique, subtle insight that you alone are getting, the writer has been there before you. It's not an accident."

It took Jennie a moment to process this. "Thanks. I'll

rework it." She smiled and made eye contact, then her mouth went down at the edges. "Is everything okay?"

"With me? Yes, of course. Why do you ask?" *Why did everyone ask?*

Jennie looked away. "No reason. It's just that you seem a little, I don't know, frazzled this morning. Sorry."

"You mean this?" Callie's hand went up to her unruly mop. "I was planning to wash it last night, but the evening got away from me." She knew that wasn't exactly what Jennie meant, but it gave both of them an easy out.

"I know how that happens." Jennie spoke evenly, without judgment. Good for her.

"I'm fine, Jennie, really."

"Callie?" It was Billy, one of the interns, arriving at the mouth of her cubicle. He glanced at Jennie then lowered his voice. "There's a detective here to see you."

She had been expecting this. State had called her three times last night and twice this morning. She could tell them right now that the detective was her brother. That's all she needed to say. State himself could have explained that much to Billy when he walked in but had evidently chosen not to. "Oh, yes, the homicide cop. I was wondering when he'd come looking for me." Billy's face grew ashen and Jennie's eyes dilated to the size of the buttons on her Ferragamo jacket. "If you guys will give us a few minutes alone…"

Both muttered in the affirmative and rushed away. It had been a cruel little trick, easy to correct, and not really her fault. Her brother had started it. "Detective," she said as State strode into view. "Is this about last night?"

"Why aren't you answering my calls?" State said, his gaze shifting to the neighboring cubicles.

"Are you here to explain why your wife kicked me out of the house?"

"Jesus." He held out his hands and lowered his voice. "Do you know how that sounds?"

"I know exactly."

"Can we discuss this somewhere private, okay? Please?"

Oliver's office was the only part of the *Free Press* with four walls and a door. He was inside, on his computer, so they couldn't ask him to leave. The best alternative was a stairwell connecting the building's two floors. "Are you okay?" State asked as he closed the door. His voice echoed in the empty space. "I thought you might have gone home."

"You mean to the ranch? Oh, no. That's the last place. I'd sooner sleep under a bridge."

"I think Dad would like having you home."

"You're living in a fantasy. I spent the night at Briana's."

"Is that a friend?"

"Briana, your homicide victim."

State winced. "Ms. Crawley. I didn't make the connection."

"I didn't have a lot of options. Sherry Ann's couch is just as comfortable as yours."

"So, you just called and asked to move in? That was nice of her."

"Very nice," Callie said. "Although I did hint that your wife kicked me out due to my investigation of your investigation – which is true, basically."

"You get it from him, you know that? Your talent for spinning."

Callie ignored this. "Briana's mother is using the other bedroom, but the living room has a pull-out couch, not as private as yours, but it'll do for a few nights."

"I'm sorry about Yolanda," he said. "I tried to explain about you and the sugar site."

"You can't find out anything unless you join."

"I understand. It was a dumb move on your part, but I understand."

"I didn't even join. Your son joined."

"Yes, he owned that move; he wanted sugar. I had a tougher time trying to explain the daytime drinking through a straw."

"It was a bad day, okay? Yolie doesn't have bad days?"

State shuddered. "She's pissed about that, too. I know, I know. It slipped out."

"It did. Can we change the subject?"

"No, we can't. Are you all right? You look like shit."

"Jesus. I will wash my hair! And get more sleep. And not use straws when I drink." She could feel his eyes boring into her. "Joking. No daytime drinking, I promise. Now can we change the subject?"

"Fine."

"Anything new on the Crawley case?"

State massaged the bridge of his nose, a habit he'd picked up from their father. "Is this what you call changing the subject? What is it? You want a murder to play with? This morning a kid drowned in a backyard pool, except it was a chilly day and there are pre-mortem bruises and we're looking at the step-mom. Any interest?"

"Is Dad involved in that one?"

"No, but the kid's still dead. So, it must be the fact that Dad's involved that makes her worthy of your attention."

"That's not true."

"It sure looks true."

Her brother had a point. "Okay. Look, if the woman killed her step-kid, you'll catch her. No problem. But if our own father is shielding a killer... And his alibi? By the way, Dad told me. A Skype call. A freaking Skype call."

State paused and wagged his head. "Why the hell is he telling you anything? The man must be going senile."

She could tell he didn't mean it, that he still didn't have a clue. Why couldn't her brother pay attention and take some of the burden off her?

"Cal." He saved the name Cal, using it only when he was desperate for her to listen. "Why are you pitting yourself against Dad? If you print anything about Blackburn and you're wrong, you'll get sued and run out of town. And Dad will hate you. If you're right, Dad will see this as another betrayal. And he'll hate you." State raised a hand. "I know, not your fault. But that's the way he'll see it. That's how everyone will see it. So, why? Tell me why?"

Everything he'd just said was true, and yet... "Because there's a dead girl."

"And you don't trust me to figure this out. On my own. That's what you're saying."

"I'm not saying that."

"Cal, I'm a good detective." State stared straight ahead into a wall. "Maybe not the best. Maybe it took some of Dad's juice to get me on homicide. I wasn't savvy enough to follow him into politics, and I don't have your brains. But I don't need you peering over my shoulder, second-guessing me. Getting to restaurants before me. Knowing more than you should."

"I'm sorry. I… I just…" She edged him over and settled in beside him on the top step. "I had never seen a body laid out in a morgue. It was worse than I thought. She was so young, and it was so heartbreaking. And her folks…"

"I know, I know." He said it as a sigh. "My first homicide was a boy, three years old, suffocated with a pillow. Looked totally asleep, surrounded by his toys. His grandmother gave me a photo of him. I used to carry it around."

"Oh, my God. The Crawleys did the same. I have Briana's picture taped to my laptop."

"It's not uncommon. They want us to remember, like we need any help." State wriggled sideways on the step. It reminded Callie of the two of them in the back of the Cadillac, with him squirming to get more room on the leather seat.

"Anything about the MySugar website?"

State refused to meet her gaze. "I am not your police source."

Callie didn't reply, just remained seated, nudging him gently with her elbow. She kept doing it until they both started chuckling. "I'm not going to stop," she teased. Just like the old days. 'Mommy says you can't hit me back 'cause I'm a girl.'"

State could have ended it by standing up, but he didn't. Instead, he licked his finger and stuck it in her ear.

"Augh," Callie screeched, jumping to her feet and swatting it away. "That is so gross."

"Wet Willie!" he announced. "Remember?"

"God. That is no way to win an argument."

"It worked when you were eight."

She wiped at her ear. "I'm going to teach it to your sons. It'll serve you right."

"Dad already taught them. The boys rushed off and taught everyone in class. Pandemonium. They nearly got expelled."

"Did Dad fix it? Sounds like the kind of thing he could fix with a two-minute call."

"He actually showed up in person, at his most charming self."

"Of course." Callie kept one hand over the moistened ear. "So, tell me about MySugar. I'm a member now. Maybe I'll have some insight."

"Not much to tell." He reached over and gently lowered her hand. "These websites encourage their hook-ups to exchange emails and phone numbers, to start communicating privately. It's smart policy, especially when they start talking pay for play. We have a list of the men who contacted Ms. Crawley on the website. Also their pics. But a lot of guys, especially the married variety, use fake pics. And some of their email addresses are burners."

"Burners?"

"Like prepaid burner phones. Addresses you can create with fake information, in case your wife is nosing around your emails. They leave no trace. We contacted all the non-burners on her list. To a man, they denied ever setting up a date with her."

"What about checking the men's emails?"

"Not without a court order."

"What about Briana's laptop?"

"We retrieved her deleted history, including the back-and-forths with her sugar daddy."

"You know who the daddy is?"

"We know what was in his emails. He called himself Dr. Feelgood. He never mentioned his other life and we have no way of tracing him. A burner address."

"What about Briana's phone? They must have called each other."

"We don't have her phone, remember? Verizon has a record of her calls but we have no access."

"This is a murder case. You can't get a court order?"

"The first thing a judge will ask is probable cause. True, we have a hunch that her death is connected to her sugar status, but there's no probable cause."

"What about the guy who emptied her bank account? Dylan Dane. He withdrew it in person, so the bank must have footage."

"Gee whiz, why didn't I think of that?"

"No need to get snotty."

"I'm just saying I do my job. We lifted the footage from Horizon Bank. This Dylan Dane knows his security cameras. And while there are rules about not wearing a hat in a bank, this is Texas. Getting a Texan to remove his hat, even in a bank, can be like…" He paused, trying to think of an analogy. "You know. Something hard."

"I know." She gave it some thought. "Like getting a French baker to go gluten-free."

"What?" State crinkled his nose. "What the hell? Where did that come from?"

"You know, French baguettes. Brioche. They all have gluten. I was trying to come up with some national trait that people won't give up even if you try to force them. Like Texas hats."

"Jeez Louise. Ain't you the fancy one."

"Never mind. Sorry."

"Gluten-free and French bakers. Ooh-la-la." He pursed his lips and waved his fingers, making his sister shake her head and roll her eyes. "Anyway, between Dylan's hat and his mustache, the security footage isn't helpful. He's a large fellow, we got that. But the teller can't remember the transaction. And the image is black-and-white, so weren't not even sure about race."

"Can I see it? Send it to my phone." She was reaching for her phone and didn't see her brother wetting his finger again. The second Wet Willie was even more annoying than the first. "Augh, augh. State. Come on."

"What are you going to do with a bank photo? Print it in your rag? Try to track down the guy yourself?" He handed her a handkerchief from his jacket pocket. She took it, thoroughly wiped her ear and handed it back.

"So, you're not even going to let me see it?" Callie's disappointment was tempered by the fact that she'd never expected him to share as much as he already had.

"Nope. I think that's the limit of my cooperation with the fourth estate. Remember? Dad used to call the press the fourth estate."

"No, he called it the goddamn fourth estate. And now I'm a card-carrying member. Gotta love it."

Almost in unison they pushed themselves up from the stairwell steps. Before Callie could open the door, State placed a hand on her shoulder. "Does Dad have anything to worry about with you?"

"Worry about?"

"Don't repeat."

"Repeat?"

"Come on. That's a stalling tactic."

"Dad doesn't have to worry," she assured him. "I just don't want him getting into trouble."

"Buddy McFee can take care of himself. He's been doing it all his life."

"But now it's different." She hadn't meant to say this.

"What do you mean, it's different?"

"I mean… I mean he's been bending the law for years. Someday the odds are going to catch up with him. He should retire."

State erupted into a laugh, a genuine laugh, one that rattled down the stairwell. "He can never retire. You know that."

Callie pulled open the door and they stepped back into the world. "Yeah, I know."

CHAPTER 15

BRIANA'S SUITCASES WERE piled in the living room, ready for tomorrow's flight, along with three boxes that Sherry Ann promised to have shipped. Every time Callie looked at the pile, she couldn't help thinking about the smallness of a life, the scant physical evidence someone leaves behind. All of Briana – her past, her plans, her studies, her dreams, the little pieces of artwork she'd taken the trouble to have framed, even the shoes and the Hermes handbags she had probably lusted over and debated with herself about buying – were all reduced to the size of a coffin, a few pieces of luggage and three boxes waiting to be picked up by the UPS man.

Helen and Sherry Ann had gone out for a farewell dinner. Callie didn't mind not being invited. She didn't have the same history with them and had never even met the girl who now preoccupied her every waking hour. Plus there was the sad fact that Callie had probably come to represent Briana's death. She had first met Helen at the morgue, viewing Briana's body, and every meeting thereafter, every conversation, had been focused on the unsolved case.

She was in the process of making her own dinner, a Lean Cuisine, when she happened to notice the Kindle in a red cover, half-wrapped in a T-shirt near the top of one of the boxes, the one Helen had left open just in case they ran across some forgotten item at the last minute.

Seeing the e-reader made her suddenly curious. What kind of things did Briana read? Traditional chick lit? Artsy millennial fiction? Sci-fi with political overtones? That was Callie's favorite, but she doubted Briana would be into that. It occurred to her that, for all of her delving into Briana's death, she knew almost nothing about her life. Would they have hated each other? Would they have been friends?

Callie ignored the ding from the kitchen. Reaching into the box, she unwrapped the Kindle from the T-shirt. For a second, it felt like a violation of privacy, but of course it wasn't, no more than looking on someone's shelf and discovering their taste in books. There was still a fair amount of juice in the Paperwhite, the same model that Callie herself used. An ad flicked on the screen as soon as she opened the cover, for a romance novel about a duke and a peasant farmgirl. Ugh. But then Callie often got this kind of Kindle ad. Swiping right got her into Briana's library.

A second ding reminded her that the Chicken with Pasta in Ranchero Sauce was cooling in the microwave. She retrieved it then set herself up on a stool at the counter with a glass of white wine and a paper towel for a napkin, realizing as she sat that this was perhaps the most pathetic dinner ever in history. She should take a photo and put it on Instagram, just to commemorate it.

Propping up the e-reader, she proceeded to scroll through

Briana's books. There were the familiar best sellers, summer reading as her mother used to call it – legal thrillers and dark mysteries featuring damaged female leads. Peppered throughout were non-fiction titles like "U.S. Diplomacy, a History" and "The Wise Men." She checked this last book's description and found it about a group of U.S. policy makers who had tried to contain the U.S.S.R. during the Cold War – obviously related to some of Briana's course work. Another title, near the top of her list, was "The Architect's Legacy, A Memoir." It stood out as an unusual purchase, an anomaly nestled among the predictable. Why would a prelaw student majoring in International Relations buy an architect's memoir? It wasn't a textbook. Or a best seller.

Callie clicked on the title, accessing the book's title page. It was from the University of Texas Press, published three years ago, and the author's name, Dr. Samuel Paget, strongly suggested a faculty member. When she pressed forward to the author's page, she found a grainy, black and white image of a middle-aged black man with a shaved head and a sad smile.

Callie put down her fork and wiped her mouth. Did Briana have some great love of architecture that no one had mentioned? On a whim, she fetched a pair of scissors from the kitchen, found the box labeled "Books, Etc." and slit through the packing tape. Inside were a dozen or so books, mainly textbooks, a few fashion magazines, a framed photo of Briana's parents in the stands of a basketball game, and other memorabilia, the reminders of a young life. Callie checked the covers.

In the very bottom of the box was a surprise. It was indeed another book on architecture, but the same one that was on the Kindle. "The Architect's Legacy, A Memoir" by Dr. Samuel

Paget. Having both an e-copy and a hardcover of such an obscure book seemed odd. But then Callie recalled a friend who had self-published a novel. Callie had bought an e-copy of the book, to show support. And then a month later, for Christmas, the friend gave her a hardcover copy, nicely autographed. She had never gotten beyond page ten in either copy.

Callie flipped to the title page and was rewarded with something she was fairly sure her brother, the great homicide detective, hadn't seen. "To Bri," read the inscription in a small neat hand, "A student of all that life has to offer. Sam Paget."

She sat cross-legged on the floor in front of the box, staring at the mentor-like, quasi-intimate inscription, trying to figure out what exactly to do. Should she turn this over to State, or just follow up on her own? After all, she was the one who'd found it. The book would have been sent on to Phoenix and eventually, probably thrown out, if she hadn't done a little snooping.

Callie slipped the book in with her own things, then re-packed and re-taped the box.

The saving grace of a depressing meal is that it doesn't involve much clean-up. Her plate and silverware went in the dishwasher, her paper towel in the trash and the Lean Cuisine box and its plastic container in with the recyclables. Her empty wine glass she was saving, just in case. Then she considered the rest of her evening. Should she call State? She would have to think about this.

Her usual distraction on a lonely evening was an hour or two of Netflix on her laptop. But ever since her nephew enrolled her in MySugar, Callie had taken to checking her profile, tweaking it here and there. Just last night, she'd switched out her photo to a sexier one, making sure her face was still obscured. She hadn't received many responses with the original photo, which was something of a blow to her self-esteem. Was it not provocative enough? Was she just not sugar material? Did her profile make her sound too dumb or too smart or not fun enough? Her guess was not fun enough. That had always been a problem. Even her sugar avatar was turning out to be a downer.

Of the few responders, the only one to show real enthusiasm, went by the screen name "Iwill4you", a cleverish handle. He'd seemed charmed by her profile and listed himself as 32 and a successful entrepreneur. The man in the photo could have been 32, or a few years older. She had sent him a tepid response and was now logging on to see what, if anything, was new.

The first thing Callie noted was that her banner ads had changed, not just on the MySugar site, but everywhere. She'd had no idea that Frederick's of Hollywood still existed. But Frederick's and several other lingerie companies were now paying Google good money to tempt her into buying the skimpiest, most over-the-top outfits she'd ever seen. Great!

Just how long would these ads follow her around? Would they pop up on her Facebook page, too? And what other marketing surprises were awaiting her? A twofer condom sale at Trojan.com? A half-page ad for edible underwear?

Callie toggled through to Heather111's home page. There were two new contacts. One called himself Glenn and was posing in front of a Bentley, which probably wasn't his. The other called himself ClarkKent14 but didn't look at all like Clark Kent, at least from his soft-focus, off-center profile pic.

Clark described his body type as athletic and stated in his headline, "I have a glass slipper. Let's make it fit." She crafted a "sounds intriguing; let's meet" kind of reply to both and sent them off before she had a chance to change her mind. What exactly was she looking for, anyway? To satisfy some cheap curiosity? To make some soulful connection to Briana's life? Or was it just a harmless fantasy game, a diversion from one more Netflix original movie?

Iwill4you had also left a message. Callie retrieved the last of the white wine from the fridge and made a mental note to (a) apologize for stealing half a bottle of wine and (b) buy two bottles of the same wine. That way she could save one for herself. Then she returned to the message. Iwill4you hadn't been put off at all by her lukewarm response and suggested that they switch from conversing on the site to using personal emails. "Then we can arrange a romantic meet-and-eat at the high-end restaurant of your choosing." She loved the phrasing – so cute but awkward.

Callie didn't want to give out her email but also didn't want to end the conversation. Her response was a hybrid; flirty but not too eager, chatty but not too revealing. She'd never done anything like this before, she told him, and needed to take things slowly. Then she signed off without giving him her email.

She had just disposed of the empty bottle and washed out her glass when her two roommates walked in. Helen made a point of ignoring the suitcases and boxes. Had Callie remembered to return the red-covered Kindle to its T-shirt nest in the open box? Yes. Good. All three settled in around the coffee table and shared the usual, end-of-the-day talk. How was dinner? How was your evening?

"I'm glad to be heading home." Helen emitted a deep sigh

and finally acknowledged the suitcases. "I thought I could stay here, be strong for her, but . . ."

"You are strong," Callie protested. "And maybe you can do more good in Phoenix. That's where Briana's real friends are. With social media and everything, you can still have an effect." She placed a hand on the older woman's arm, her voice turning heartfelt. "And don't forget I'll be here."

Helen's eyes turned from the suitcases to Callie. Gently but firmly, she removed the hand from her arm, got up and crossed to the tote she'd dropped by the door. "I assume this is the new issue. It's got today's date." She pulled out a newspaper. Callie recognized the distinctive size and the red logo. She and Oliver had labored for hours on the cover photo, adding saturated color and a quirky headline, trying to make the charter school debut article look as exciting as possible. Helen dropped the paper on the coffee table. "I found it in a rack by the restaurant. I thought you were going to write something. At least something."

"I know," Callie said. "I'm sorry."

She had pushed Oliver to start the ball rolling, perhaps a small piece on the metro page, detailing what they knew about Briana's death. *The Free Press is investigating. More to come.* But the publisher hadn't wanted to roll the ball without knowing there would be enough momentum. "The worst thing is to pique people's interest and then have nothing new the following week." It was an easy decision for Oliver. He didn't have to face Briana's mother.

"We'll start it next week. I promise."

Helen's frustration was palpable. "I'm sorry, but you're no better than the others."

"Helen!" Callie managed to maintain her composure. "It's not that simple. If we say that a man was arrested and released then we need to answer more questions, like who he is. And if we give his name... We would be opening ourselves to a lawsuit."

"Who is this man? You haven't even told us."

"What would you do if I told you? What would Frank do?" Callie waited ten seconds for the answer, which was an answer right there. "It's to protect you. To protect my publisher and my source. The man involved is very powerful."

"He was trying to bury my daughter."

"Jesus!" Sherry Ann's hand flew to her mouth. They hadn't forgotten she was there, just that there were things she didn't know. "Is this for real? Someone was caught like that and he wasn't arrested?"

Callie did her best to explain. That included revealing to them the essentials of Keagan Blackburn's alibi – not his name or position – but the fact that at the time of death set by the medical examiner, this non-suspect had been on a video call with respected businessmen all over the world.

"You mean like Skype?" Helen asked, her voice rising.

"Yes. And please don't tell my brother I told you."

"That's it? He was on a Skype call? Those things can be faked, can't they?"

"I don't see how." Callie was trying to imagine Blackburn carrying on a conversation, at the same time raping and choking the life out of a young woman. "Mrs. Crawley. Helen. I need more answers before I start telling her story."

Helen shook her head. "Isn't the point of telling her story to get those answers?"

"That's the whole point of journalism, isn't it?" Sherry Ann had decided to join the debate, speaking more timidly than usual. "I'm sorry. Look, all I know is from Journalism 101. Literally. I took Journalism 101. But didn't guys like Woodward and Bernstein start reporting before they knew all the answers? And they were up against the president."

"You're right," Callie had to admit. "Both right. There are things I can put out there that won't get us sued. The next issue, I promise you. I promise."

CHAPTER 16

CALLIE WAS ALREADY up and dressed when she heard the muted morning rustlings from the bedrooms. She had put away her sound machine and her pills – always the first thing to do when sleeping in someone's living room – and was in the process of transforming her bed into a couch. By the time Helen's bedroom door opened, Callie had made coffee, checked her email and was a third of the way through the *New York Times* online crossword.

"Good morning." Helen's tone was soft but distant. "I'm sorry about what I said. I know you're doing your best. It's more than anyone else has done."

Callie was grateful. She doubted that she herself would be so understanding. "No. You're right. This story needs to get out there, even if we don't have the answers."

Both women half-apologized once again and might have continued. They were stopped by the emergence of Sherry Ann from the other bedroom, drawing a brush through her hair and checking her phone. Was Helen ready? It was almost time. Sherry Ann would be driving her to the airport. "We'll be stopping for breakfast on the way. If you want to come with us, Callie…"

"No, no," she replied and felt like a coward for refusing. "We can say our good-byes here."

"At least you get a bedroom now." Helen's soft smile dimmed as she eyed the boxes by the door. "I think I've got everything."

"Don't worry," said Sherry Ann. "If I find anything else, I'll send it on."

"The police still have her laptop," Helen reminded them. "If you could ask them to get it to us in Phoenix."

"I'll tell my brother," Callie promised. "But you'll be talking to him. You should call him. He won't mind. And he'll call you with updates. I'm sure you'll be calling each other. It's a very active investigation, I promise."

"Thank you for everything." Helen reached out and framed Callie's face in her hands. "I think you and Bri would have been very close."

Five minutes later, Callie watched from the kitchen window as Sherry Ann's BMW pulled out of the parking lot and made a left onto Rio Grande. As soon as the car disappeared, she left the window and found her phone.

"Hey, State."

"Hey." He sounded less than happy to hear from her. "Before you ask, no I don't have anything more I can give you."

"Well, I have something to give you. Is that all right?" She didn't mean to sound pissy, but her brother could bring that out in her. "You should check out a professor. Dr. Samuel Paget."

"One of her professors?"

"I don't think so. Different department." She went on to explain about the Kindle and the inscription in the book.

There was no immediate response on the other end. Then… "So? I have an autographed Stephen King."

"Really? Did he also write, 'To State, a student of all that life has to offer'? Because that really would make it a horror novel."

There was a pause on the other end. "You're right. That is suggestive."

"Plus he used her nickname, Bri. To me, it smacks of mentoring, the bad kind, when you have to keep it a secret. And he's a doctor, like our anonymous Dr. Feelgood. I think he's the sugar daddy."

"A sugar daddy professor?" State sounded skeptical. "Any philandering professor worth his salt wouldn't need a website. He'd just do it the old-fashioned way."

"That would open him up only to the students in his class. And it's not as safe. A regular student might want a relationship. A girl on MySugar would know the situation going in. You know what I would do if I were you?"

"Can't wait to hear."

"I'd show Paget's photo to the wait staff at Anthony's. They might be able to ID him."

A third pause, the shortest one yet. "Do you have the book he signed for her?"

"I do. Somehow Helen forgot to pack it. You need it?"

"It might be helpful if I want to get a straight answer out of him."

"Tell you what. I'll give you the book. In exchange, you let me sit in on the interview."

"What do you mean, sit in?"

"I want to be there. I won't ask questions. It can be

off-the-record. Ten to one, Emily will have better things to do. You can tell him I'm your partner."

"You mean like impersonating an officer?"

"Okay. Not that. Sorry. Look, you have to give me something," she pleaded. "I'm the one who gave you this."

"Callie…" She hated it when he spoke slow and calmly, as if addressing a child. "I'll do my best to keep you in the loop, okay?"

"No," she insisted. "Look, I didn't have to tell you. You had the same chance to find the book as I did."

"Okay, okay. I'll think about it." The audio went out for a fraction of a second. "Hold on," State said. "I gotta take this." Then it went out again.

Eventually there was a click, followed by ambient sound on the other end. "Hello? State?"

"Callie?" His voice was shaking. "I gotta go."

"What's up? What's wrong?"

"Nothing's wrong. I mean, not nothing. I'll call you later."

"Does this have something to do with the case?"

"Not everything's about you."

"Well, the case isn't about me."

She could hear him moving, closing a door as he walked. "There's been a fire at the ranch."

"What do you mean, ranch? Our ranch?"

"The fire department just called. Dad and Gil are being rushed to St. David's."

"Oh, my God. Are they okay? When were you going to tell me?"

"Again, not about you." She could hear the beep of a remote as State unlocked his car. "He said it's not life-threatening, but that's what they say for anything less than critical. It's what we're trained to say."

Callie scanned the counter for her own car keys. "I'll be there as soon as I can."

CHAPTER 17

NORTHBOUND TRAFFIC WASN'T usually bad at this hour. But today, of all days, a three-vehicle accident was blocking all the lanes. Three years ago, as Callie tried to cope with Buddy's resignation, her psychiatrist had suggested mindful meditation. She'd given it a shot, two classes a week for over a month, but it wasn't for her. Now, as car after car inched its way around the twisted metal and the police presence and the ambulance, she tried again, focusing on her breath, pushing away all outside thoughts. But being in the moment wasn't going to be possible. Well over an hour later, worried and frustrated to the point of almost screaming, she found a parking spot on the fourth level of the hospital's parking structure and followed the signs to the elevator.

She expected someone to be here, waiting in the medical center lobby. When her father had his heart attack on the fourth fairway at the Austin Country Club, the mayor had been here waiting for her, along with the best heart surgeon in the state who'd been flown in from Dallas to perform the double-bypass. Today there was just an ill-tempered woman at the reception desk who barely listened. Callie had to spell out her name twice before receiving a printed guest pass. "The burn unit is on the third floor."

At the elevator bank, Callie pressed "up" and didn't let go until the doors slid open. "Callie? Oh, my goodness. Callie." It was Sarah from the ranch, alone in the elevator, wearing a white wristband and looking exhausted. "I'm so sorry, little girl. I'm so sorry." There were two trails of dried tears leading from her eyes to her chin.

Callie's heart froze. "Oh, no."

"It's all my fault. I could have saved him. I ran right by the study. He's always there in the morning. I didn't think."

"Are you saying he's dead? He can't be dead."

"Oh, my goodness." Sarah stepped out and the doors closed behind her. "I thought you knew."

"Dead?" She was having a hard time understanding. "They said it wasn't life-threatening. That's what they said."

"Not life…" Sarah shook her head. "No, honey, he died in the fire. Mr. Gil went back in to try to save him. When the fire was almost out, I saw one of the firemen carrying him out to the lawn. He said they found him in a corner. All dogs are afraid of fire. It's the way they're made."

"Dogs?"

"That's my experience. The whole notion of running through a fire to get out the other side… That wasn't something poor Angus could even think about."

"Poor Angus," Callie repeated without inflection.

"If I'd thought a sec, I would have called for him or gone in myself. He's almost always on his bed in there. I wasn't thinking. There was so much smoke. I'm sorry, little girl. I know how much you loved him."

Callie was overwhelmed. Under any other circumstances, the death of her beloved Angus, the puppy Buddy had brought home right after Anita's diagnosis, the happy, beautiful setter who had first bonded with her mother on slow walks around the ranch then with Callie and finally with her lonely and disgraced father, would have been devastating. She could just envision the sweet old dog being roused from a morning nap by the smoke and the flames, cowering in the corner of the wood-lined room, whining and barking until the acrid smoke filled his lungs. But mixed in with this horrific vision was a sense of relief. Her father was alive, must still be alive. It was almost as if, quite illogically, perfectly illogically, Angus had given her one final gift, taking the news of a dead loved one on himself. Someone close to her had died, and Angus had some-how stepped up and assumed that role. It made no sense at all, but in the chaos of her swirling emotions, she still felt grateful.

"How is Dad?"

"Your daddy's okay. Doctor says he got kind of confused, from the smoke and everything. They put him on some kind of breathing mask. That's what a nurse told me."

"You were there at the house?" Callie was still trying to piece it together.

"They had a dinner last night for some bigwigs. One of them kindly recalled my fried shrimp and chicken and your daddy brought me in. Things went late, so I came back this morning to clean."

"And you're okay?"

Sarah displayed a small, toothy smile and snapped off

the white wristband. "Takes more than a little fire to put me down."

Callie left Sarah in the waiting area – the cook's son was on his way to pick her up – then took an elevator to the third floor. According to someone at the nurse's desk, Lawrence McFee wasn't in the burn unit after all, had never been in the burn unit, but was occupying a private room on the same floor.

When Callie walked in, she found her father wide awake and the nurse at his bedside fast asleep. His eyes were darting around. His breath was fast and labored. When his gaze fell on Callie's face, it took him a few moments. "Hey, sweetie pie," Buddy said, the words muffled by the respirator mask. The sound was just enough to wake the nurse. His anxious breathing began to slow. "Did you get off from school? Where's your mother?"

"Mother… Mother's coming later."

"Is this your daughter, Mr. McFee?" The name tag on her blue blouse identified her as Lindsey, RPN. Nurse Lindsey could barely suppress a yawn.

"Yes, I'm his daughter. Can you call the doctor, please?"

"I'm sure he'll be back shortly. If y'all want to talk privately, I'll go. I got other things to do."

"Just get the doctor." Callie added another "please" as an afterthought and watched the nurse amble out the door.

She took a seat in the nurse's still-warm chair. Her father reached out and she met him halfway, her hand settling into the warm, enveloping embrace of his. How long it had been since she'd held his hand? Perhaps as a child, crossing the street. Could it have been that long ago? She had no memory of hand-holding after his heart attack. He'd been too preoccupied with showing her and the world how strong he was and how this wasn't such a deal. Now she reveled in the quiet, intimate moment. She squeezed and he squeezed back. When he mumbled something soft and affectionate, she couldn't quite make out the word. A few seconds later, he turned his head, looked her in the eyes and said it again. "Anita?"

For a moment, Callie was tempted to remove her hand. "Yes, Lawrence. I'm here. How are you feeling?"

"Better now that you're here." He reached with his other hand and made a weak attempt to take off the mask. She stopped him. "They told me you weren't coming."

"Who told you?"

"I don't know. The doctor. Oppenheimer." Some strength was returning to his voice. "That fool, Oppenheimer. He said you weren't coming."

"I guess he was wrong."

Buddy chuckled and it turned into a cough. "Where are the kids?" he finally managed to mutter. "In school? You shouldn't take them out of school. It'll just worry them."

"The kids are fine. You should get some rest." Callie lifted his head and straightened his pillow. When he settled back down, she once again took his hand. Gradually, his breathing grew slower and deeper. Only then did she let go and get up from the chair. A tall, lean man in a white lab coat stood in the doorway. She vaguely recalled his face. "Dr. Oppenheimer?"

"Callie." He motioned with his head and she crossed to him, away from her sleeping father. "I gave him something for the pain. He's a little disoriented. That's why he might be acting this way."

"It's okay," Callie assured him. "I know. Uncle Gil told me."

"Told you what exactly?"

"He confirmed what I already saw. He says no one else knows. No other doctors or specialists. Is that true?"

Roger Oppenheimer checked the hallway, both directions. He would continue to check. "I've consulted specialists about this, without mentioning Buddy's name. I visit the ranch once a week for monitoring. Callie, I owe your father."

"Everyone owes him." Spoken with a note of resignation. "Is that good or bad? I don't know. We've heard it all our lives – how lucky we are to be Buddy McFee's children."

"I can't speak to that," said Oppenheimer. "I imagine it could be difficult." His calm, understanding manner just irritated her more. "The nurse said you wanted to see me."

"What's his condition? Is he going to be all right?"

"I'll take him off the respirator this afternoon and we'll monitor him through the night. He didn't take in a lot of smoke. I wrote on his chart that the event aggravated his asthma."

"I thought he was done with that years ago."

The ex-surgeon general glanced around. "Your father was pretty incoherent. The paramedics put it in their notes. The asthma was my way of covering."

"I understand."

"Someone's going to have to tell him about the dog. That won't be easy." Callie had a feeling that job would become hers. "I can get a nurse to stay with him for a few days after he's released, if you'd like."

"I don't know. We'll see. Speaking of nurses…" She pulled the sleeve of Oppenheimer's lab coat, moving him further into the room. "The nurse he has now," she said. "Lindsey. Is she the best? I don't mean to disparage anyone, but . . ."

"No, she's not," he replied bluntly. "The best nurses are attentive and curious and have a knowledge of general medicine almost as good as a doctor's. Is that what you want?"

Callie thought. "I guess that's not what I want."

"You can decide what you think best. Lindsey shows up on time, makes no excuses and is perfectly competent." Oppenheimer checked his clipboard. "Have you dropped by to see Gil?"

"Not yet."

"He's conscious now. I know he's anxious to talk to you."

"Thanks." She glanced back at her sleeping, snoring father. "I'll go see him now."

The burn unit was on the same floor but in a newer wing, around the corner and through two sets of double doors. A woman doctor, Asian but with a British accent, escorted Callie past a row of therapy rooms and around another corner. "Mr. Morales is stabilized. He has a hydromorphone drip but he refuses to use it. He wants to talk to you first."

"Me? Why me?"

"That's what he said. His sister's coming in from Houston. She should be here this evening – to see him and discuss treatment options."

"Whatever he needs," Callie said. "You hear about these new burn treatments. My father wants him to have the best."

"We are the best," the doctor informed her. Then a little more sympathetically: "I'm new to Texas. But the names McFee and Morales seem to carry weight. We even had a call from the governor." In the old days, the governor would have shown up in person, Callie thought. "Mr. Morales is in a semi-private because they're bigger in this ward, but he won't have a roommate. That's been made clear."

Gil lay face up, both arms, from below the biceps to the hands, wrapped in bandages and propped up on pillows. One leg was also bandaged, with a gauze bootie on the foot. His face was shiny and bright, as if he'd suffered a bad sunburn. Gone was his short-cropped beard, replaced by a slightly less shiny section of skin. Like her father, Gil was hooked up to a vital signs monitor, but the respirator stood unused beside the bed. In the crook of his left arm was an IV drip with nothing going through it.

Gil's eyes, brown marbles peering out from the red, focused on Callie. He said nothing as she took a visitor's chair and moved it closer in. "Thank you." Her words were heartfelt. "For trying to save Angus."

"Your daddy loved him." Speaking didn't seem to add to his pain, at least not much. The brown marbles flitted over to the doctor. "Can you give us some privacy?"

"Certainly. A few minutes, no more." She finished checking the monitor then retreated, turning as she reached the door. "Ms. McFee? Let someone know as soon as you leave. We really need to start his drip."

Callie promised, then waited until the door was closed. "Uncle Gil, what happened?" Gil motioned with his head, very slightly, toward a tumbler of water on the bedside table. Callie lifted it to his mouth and positioned the straw.

He took a deep draw followed by a deep breath. "What took you so long? Your brother's been here and gone."

"An accident on the 183."

"You should've taken the 35. I wanted to be alert for you, but you're not making this easy. You didn't use GPS?"

"It kept saying 183. Uncle Gil, I'm sorry."

He took another sip and eased back on his pillow. "Dinner last night. Felix Gibson came over. A few of his staff."

Callie knew Felix Gibson the way she knew most of her father's cohorts. On Buddy's resignation, he had taken over as attorney general. Felix was up for election now on his own and, barring any catastrophe, had a lock on a full term.

"Dinner did not go well. Your daddy was…" He searched for the right words. "…in a mood. Memory problems make him angry. And stubborn and antagonistic. Man had a mind like a steel trap. Now it's a steel sieve." Gil grinned at his own joke and winced.

"You think they got suspicious?"

"Hard to say. I tried to blame it on the whisky, but Felix is cagey. And his staff – scary bunch of shitheads, not like the old good old boys. I wound up picking a fight with them, as a distraction. A long evening where everyone pretends to be drunker than they are."

"What does this have to do with the fire?"

"Maybe nothing. I don't know. It started in his study, the inner sanctum. That's the room with the most damage, making me naturally suspicious." Gil returned to the straw and took another long draw. "This morning I wrote up the notes from last night. I shot them off to your daddy. Couple minutes later he came storming to the back of the house. Said I must've been drunk. The meeting didn't happen that way, he said. Said I'm an idiot. I'm jeopardizing the reputation he's built for over thirty years. I swear, Callie, if I didn't love the man so…"

"Was he... in a mood?" She wondered if this was going to be the euphemism they used from now on.

Gil tried to relax his face. "It's not like a light switch, you know, on or off. Sometimes he's aware of his lapses. Sometimes he makes up new memories, just as real as anything. Sometimes he's in the past. It's not distinct. You can't always tell."

"And this meeting with Felix Gibson. What was it about?"

"Really, honey? You're asking me that?"

"You're the one who mentioned it."

"It was about something that happened years ago. That's all I can say."

"Something you covered up years ago?"

"Not covered up. Helped people see reason."

"And you think Felix or one of his men came back and set the fire? Why? To destroy any records?"

Gil lowered his voice from a rasp to a half-rasp. "Lawrence always kept his original notes, on his yellow pads, to cover his ass. He kept them locked in a file cabinet. A wooden file cabinet, unfortunately. I saw when I went in to get Angus. All destroyed."

"Did anyone know about his notes? Did Felix know?"

"Who knows what anyone knows? Or suspects? Is it just coincidental? The morning after Lawrence goes off the rails, his records go up in smoke?" Gil squirmed and let out a soft groan. "I swear, my arms itch like the dickens. God damn."

"We need to get you on that drip."

"Yeah, we do," he finally agreed. "There's a remote by my left hand. You can hit the button up to three times at once. Why don't we try one?"

Callie found the small, square remote. It consisted of an

LED clock and a single button. She pressed the button once, as instructed. "It may take a minute or two." She returned to her chair on the other side and waited, wanting to take her cue from Gil. Whenever he was ready.

"Sometimes he realizes his condition and doesn't want to believe it."

"Is that what happened this morning?"

Gil nodded. Just knowing the drug was on its way made him breathe easier. "Buddy was half making sense, half not. Paranoid, like I was the one messing with his head. It took time to calm him down. Made him take a little shut-eye on my sofa. An alarm went off and I smelled smoke. We took the quickest way out, through my doors then around to the front."

The drip was starting to have its effect. Gil told her about getting to the front lawn where Sarah was waiting. Buddy had tried to go back inside to find Angus and had gotten close enough to inhale a few lungsful of smoke before stumbling out. That's when Gil ran in. He barely made it out, without the dog, collapsing on the lawn just as the firetrucks pulled up the drive.

"It could have been an electrical fire," Callie suggested. "It's an old house. Maybe Angus chewed on a wire or tipped something over." Gil grunted, unconvinced. "What else could it be?"

The question hung in the air like a cloud. "You're probably right. The fire department will figure out the cause." Gil tilted his head toward the remote control. "One more." He watched, almost hungrily, as she pushed the button. "Thanks."

"I can do another."

"Let's not go crazy." He smiled then his mouth turned serious. "Calista. You should come home."

"Home? You mean the ranch? To live?" She took in a gulp of air. "No. Why, for God's sake?"

"I won't be out of this place for a while. When the house gets a structural okay, you can take him home. It's an old stone building. I doubt most of it was affected."

"I am not moving... For one thing, Dad would never go for it."

"What are you talking about? He'd love having you home. He's mentioned it."

"What about State and Yolanda? He can live with them."

"They only have the office as a guest room. And your dad needs supervision. Last week he went wandering down Hacienda Road in the dark. Had no idea where he was."

"You never told me."

"I found him on a tree swing in the Thornbecks' front yard. Can you imagine Yolanda and the boys dealing with that? And him in a strange environment?"

Callie had to concede the point. "You're right, he'll be better at home. Sarah can move back in. And there's this nurse dealing with Dad – Lindsey something. Look, even if I wanted to take care of him, I have a job."

"It's not just taking care. You don't see it, but he's more manageable when you're around. Sarah can come full time, while you're at work, and if we have to let her in our secret, we will. As for a nurse, I think not."

"What about my life?"

"Since when do you have a life?"

It would have been more hurtful if it hadn't been true. "That's my new resolution, to get a life."

"Calista, this is your father. It'll be good for you, too. Just until I come home."

"Just until?" Callie could sense the invisible wedge. At first it would be temporary, then once the wedge was in the crack... "What happened between Dad and me is not the whole... I can't be my own person around him. No one can. No disrespect to you or to Mom. But this is not the long-term solution you want."

"Who said long-term? Just until I scab up nice and regain the use of my limbs. It could be longer if they have to do skin grafts. C'mon." He did his best to look pitiful and reasonable, a man with both arms and hands bandaged, with a bandaged leg and second degree burns across his face, a man who had gone back into a burning house to try to rescue her dog.

When she didn't respond, the sweetness in his brown marbles hardened. "It's payback time, Callie. You owe him this."

CHAPTER 18

With her jaw clenched and her hands gripping the wheel, Callie turned left from the road onto the drive. As always, the canopy of oaks framed the view, but the full view was blocked by a fire department pumper, its hose snaked along the gravel. She assumed that other response vehicles had been on the scene and that this was the last.

Okay, not too bad, she thought as she drew closer. Most of the damage was on the ground floor. The windows of her father's study had been blown out, the frames burned away and the smoky openings in the stone facade circled in black. The front hall windows were in the same condition and the charred remains of the front door lay splintered in the door-way, several pieces of it lying in a shallow pool of water. The room on the other side of the front hall, the day room, had fared better. The windows were gone, yes, but the soot around them wasn't as thick and there was no smoke, at least none that she could see.

To one side of the drive were State's car and a large SUV, red and white with "Fire Marshal" printed on the side. She had expected a few news vans. Even a small fire at Lawrence "Buddy" McFee's home would be news. But Gil must have said something to the first responders. There wasn't a reporter in sight – except her, she reminded herself.

Her brother stood by the open rear hatch, a uniformed fire official by his side, both of them bending over something in the rear section. They straightened up just as Callie got out of her truck.

"Callie." State rushed over to meet her. "Where have you been?"

"To see Dad and Gil of course. And then…" For the second time today she'd been caught in traffic, this time on the 35. "Sorry. Is Angus still here? He's not in the back of the truck, is he? I'm not sure I want to see." She backed away and balled her fists. "Does that make me bad, not wanting to say good-bye to the poor old boy? I should say good-bye."

"No, no, no." He opened his arms and she fell into them. "It doesn't make you anything. Angus was a good boy."

"He was." The tears were welling, but she didn't have time for this indulgence. Later maybe, alone, over a few glasses of wine. She pulled out of his embrace. "Tell me he's not in the truck."

"Someone from the vet's office took him away. They'll want to know how to… You don't have to decide now. This isn't the time."

"How to dispose of his remains? Is that what you were going to say?"

"They need to know about burial or cremation."

"Cremation of a burned dog? Oh, my God, I can't even think about that."

"I had the same reaction," State said and stepped back toward the SUV. "The chief and I were going over stuff. Want to join us?"

"Sure." It would be a welcome distraction. Okay, not welcome, but a distraction.

The fire marshal, a middle-aged, folksy man with an overhanging stomach, introduced himself and offered his condolences. In the open rear of the chief's SUV were a computer tablet, some half-filled-out forms and State's trusty notepad and pen. Off to one side Callie noticed a longneck bottle of Lone Star, open and half-empty. State took a swig and offered her the rest. "There's more in the pool house fridge if you want your own."

She was surprised. "You're not on duty?"

"I am. But they make exceptions when it's your house on fire. Or they should." Having a beer on duty was probably as close as State would get to showing stress.

Callie took the longneck and finished it off.

The fire marshal cleared his throat. "My men checked the smoke detectors. They were the old type – not hardwired. The three that should've worked had rundown batteries and were useless. The one in the dining room finally went off." He shrugged. "The good news is the damage was limited. Water damage as much as fire. We'll get the structural engineer in as soon as we can. The bad news is we don't have a clear cause, so the arson boys – excuse me, arson officers – will need time before anyone can resume residency."

"Arson?" Callie asked.

"That's their title," said the chief. "Until we have a clear cause, everything is arson. Most household fires start in kitchens or bedrooms. Up north in chimneys. A fire like this, in a home office where no one's a smoker… I'm thinking electrical." He went on to outline the current situation, the rooms affected, the estimated intensity, the personnel involved and their estimated time of departure. He entered something on his tablet. "We'll keep the pumper here for another hour, in case of a flare-up. I know you hired a private security firm. That's your right. But the study itself is off-limits. To everyone, including you two."

"Security firm?" Callie asked.

"On Gil's specific, insistent instructions." State regarded the empty beer bottle. "Want another?"

"No, I'm fine. Can we go inside?"

The fire marshal gave his permission, once more warning them about the study. They gave him custody of the empty bottle and walked through the doorway puddle into the entry hall. The first thing Callie saw were the blackened remains of the parquet floor their mother had found in a classic Beaux Art hotel in Paris that was undergoing renovation. After several onslaughts of Texas charm, she'd persuaded the owner to sell her the old floor, then had it shipped over and installed piece by piece in the grand entry hall. For years after, she made the children take off their shoes before coming inside. Now it was just square pieces of charcoal. An armed guard in a private security uniform sat in a folding chair just outside the study door, examining his phone.

"Uncle Gil hired security?"

State nodded. "Seems like overkill. The department's putting a patrol car at the front posts, 24/7, but Gil insisted on his own."

"You don't argue with a burned man."

"I guess not. After Dad resigned, Gil installed an electronic system. But they stopped using it. I guess it would go off accidentally." Callie could just imagine her father roaming the house at night in his bathrobe, tripping alarms and getting belligerent when the police showed up. "Now, of course, no system is gonna work, not until they get some doors and windows."

The guard – thirtyish, overweight, seemingly devoid of energy – glanced up then returned to his phone. Across the doorway were stretched two rows of yellow police tape. Beyond the tape, it wasn't much more than a shell. The room where so many crucial meetings had taken place now looked small, square and cold. Callie tried to recall where everything had been – Buddy's burlwood desk, his desktop computer, now a cube of twisted metal; the brown leather chairs; the Japanese folding screen; the tartan dog bed where Angus had spent so many sleepy hours. She tried not to think about that.

The side of the room that seemed most damaged was the side with the oak bookshelves on top and the row of file cabinets underneath. In some spots, all that was left were lines of discoloration on the wall, dark gray on a darker background, like rectangles in a tic-tac-toe game, with burned rubble below. Gone was her father's library – leather-bound volumes, collections of Texas history, forty-year-old best-sellers, the books she'd looked at all her life but had never opened. Gone were…

"What do you think?" State was beside her at the tape, staring in. "Dad had this ancient PC, a decade old at least, that he never turned off. Maybe…"

"Maybe. The marshal also mentioned accident or arson?" She phrased it as a question.

"Well, Dad and Gil were in Gil's part of the house. Angus was here, but I don't see how he could have done it. Sarah was in the kitchen."

Callie focused on the tic-tac-toe wall. "Could anyone else have come in? Angus wasn't the best guard dog."

"What?" State pulled his neck in, giving himself a momentary double-chin. "Who would want to burn down Buddy McFee's house?"

"Well, doesn't it strike you as a little suspicious that the fire destroyed his files and melted his computer? Did he back up his stuff on the cloud?"

State pondered the question. "That doesn't sound like a Dad thing, trusting his files to some mysterious super-computer. What are you saying?"

"I'm just putting it out there."

State made another double-chin. "Hold on. You're saying someone sneaked in and torched his records? Why? Because of what was in them?"

Callie shrugged. "Dad kept a lot of secrets."

"That's right. He kept them. For decades. Never broke a promise or betrayed a confidence. Why do this now, after all these years?"

Callie could have answered. Instead, she turned to face the burned-out entry hall. "Gil is under the impression this place is inhabitable."

"Maybe some parts, once they finish the inspection and get rid of the smell. That could be days or weeks."

"That may work for Gil. He's not coming home anytime soon. Meanwhile, Dad's going to be released."

"Oh." State took a moment. "Well, he can't stay with us. Yolanda's not ready to deal with any more family." He made a guilty face. "No offense. What about Dad's friends? They've all got big houses."

"Staying with friends is always weird," Callie said and left it at that.

"What about the gatehouse?"

"The gatehouse?" She hadn't thought of this possibility. Various gardeners and handymen had lived there. She knew it to be a roomy two-bedroom but she'd never been inside. "Is it livable?"

"Livable? It's nicer than my house. Every time Mom got something new she gave them the old furniture, remember? You're honestly saying you've lived here your whole life and never been in the gatehouse?"

"It was someone else's home. When were you in there?"

"In high school. I used to pay George to let me use it for dates. Remember Maggie Weaver? I think she was in your class."

Callie recoiled. "Maggie Weaver? Really? Ew!"

"What do you mean 'ew'? You admired the hell out of her."

"Exactly."

State ignored the provocation. "Anyway, it's got water, electricity, cable. The place probably needs a good cleaning, but until the main house is ready…"

It wasn't the worst idea. "Maybe."

State didn't push her. "Did you happen to bring the book? Paget's autographed book?"

"Um, yeah. It's in my truck."

"Good. Can I have it?" When she didn't answer immediately… "You want this case solved?"

"Remember what we agreed? That you would let me sit in on the interview?"

"That's not what I agreed. I agreed to keep you in the loop."

Callie shook her head. "That can mean so many things. Do you want the book or not?"

"Do you want to be in the loop or not?"

"Depends what the word loop means."

A pair of footsteps echoed in the hall. It was the fire marshal. "I'm afraid we've got some press," he announced then led the way back out the gaping, black hole.

The three of them stared at the news van, parked half on the gravel and half on the lawn. The two doors swung open and the side panels slid, disgorging a small team from KXAN – a cameraman, a tall blond guy in a fresh haircut and a nice suit, and Nicole Whitman. A fourth person, a technician, stayed in the back of the van. Callie felt a mixture of irritation and pride. At least it was her ex-station that was the first to show.

When the camera pointed their way, State adjusted his tie and his expression – professional, concerned, yet welcoming of any legitimate inquiry. Nicole surveyed the scene, her eyes lighting up when she saw Callie. Callie knew what was going through her friend's mind. This was going to be a twofer – a fire at the Buddy McFee ranch plus the public revelation of Callie McFee's return to Austin. It was a piece of news that would have seemed intrusive and opportunistic on its own, but one that would dovetail perfectly with the fire at her childhood home.

Nicole whispered something to the man with the fresh haircut as she handed him an earpiece. He nodded then inserted the earpiece. A microphone appeared in his hand, as if by magic. "Callie," he called, still from a respectable distance. "Can we have a word with you, please?" He and the cameraman began their approach.

Callie's instinct was to turn and make a quick, dignified retreat. But she knew how that would look on camera, avoiding a news team from the same station where she'd once worked. So, she adjusted her own expression – professional, concerned, yet welcoming of any legitimate inquiry – and prepared herself for whatever hell was about to come her way.

CHAPTER 19

By four o'clock, she was in Oliver's office, door closed, unwrapping a Chick-fil-A grilled sandwich she'd picked up at a drive-thru. "Sorry," she said. "With all that's going on, I didn't get a chance." Then she buried her face in the wrapper.

"I understand." He twitched his nose uncomfortably. Callie saw it out of the corner of her eye and wondered if he might be a vegetarian.

On her drive in, she had put Oliver on speaker and filled him in on her day, from the autographed book to the fire, to her interview with the neatly coifed reporter. Oliver expressed his condolences and concerns at all the right spots. That's the kind of person he was.

"So, the fire department thinks it was arson?" he said, twitching his nose again.

"They're investigating," Callie mumbled between bites. Why had she even brought it up?

"Who would want to burn down your house?"

"You're right. I'm sure it was an accident," she said,

hoping to close the subject. "Meanwhile… Meanwhile, we have an article to write. Right?"

"Right." Oliver pushed his forearms off his knees and turned back to his desk, rapping the desktop in a little drum roll. "We've got ourselves a new series," he announced with a flourish. "One in which we can't mention Keagan Blackburn's name. 'A Death in Westlake'. Working title."

"It's good." Callie nodded and wiped her mouth. "As far as layout goes, obviously we start with the murder – who Briana Crawley was and why people should care."

"Do we mention the sugar aspect?"

She'd given this some thought. "Not in the first install-ment. It would take away public sympathy. Also, I promised her mother I would do it only if absolutely necessary."

"If any other paper investigates, they're going to find out. Don't you want to control the narrative?"

"Not in the first installment," she insisted. "I promised."

"Okay, we'll do it your way," he agreed. "So, first article. What have we got?"

Callie cleared her throat. "A powerful, unnamed man, Mister X – we can think of a better name – was discov-ered by a state trooper trying to bury the body of a raped and murdered girl. Someone in law enforcement made the arrest disappear, so we can't reveal Mr. X's identity, for fear of being sued. But X suddenly has an alibi. And…" She raised an index finger. "And the only person who can corroborate our story, Trooper Josiah Jackson, was given an unscheduled leave the very next day to an undisclosed location."

"Wow." Oliver scrunched up his mouth, accentuating his stubble. "Laying it right out there."

"It's all true. And we're not libeling anyone."

Oliver's mouth stayed scrunched. "Readers will want to know more. Who is X? Who is covering for X? Who is our source?"

"They'll be dying to know. But we can't say. And it's not like we're teasing them, not intentionally." She could feel his hesitancy and resented it. Why did she have to be the macho one? "I thought you were on board."

"I was. I mean, I am." Oliver steepled his fingers. "A lot of our information comes from your brother, our reliable source."

"Not all. Some we unearthed ourselves."

"Enough came from him. Is there going to be trouble?"

"We never mention State's name. It'll be fine."

Oliver's steeple collapsed into a prayer. "Callie, come on. He's the detective working the case. His sister's name is on the byline. How does that look? He can get into real trouble."

"State can handle himself. He can deny it."

"Then he'd be lying." Oliver shook his head. "I don't want to be the one responsible for your family getting screwed up again."

Callie didn't need reminding. Every time she'd played the sister card with State, coaxing and teasing him for more information, promising to keep things off the record, this had been in the back of her mind. "Okay. What if we take my name off the byline? Would that work?"

He thought it over. "Your name's still on the masthead."

"No, it's not."

"What do you mean?"

She smiled. "You never added my name to the masthead. I was vain enough to check."

"Damn." Oliver smacked his desk. "I told Chuck to add it, I really did. I'm so sorry."

"No reason to be."

"And I meant to officially welcome you, too. In my *Notes From the Editor*."

"All perfectly fine."

"I got sidetracked by the charter school series. I'm so sorry."

"No, it's perfect. Just keep my name out of the paper and we're fine."

He thought for a second. "Yeah, but people know you're working here."

"Not many. And if my name's not in print, no one will make the connection." She reached out to touch his arm, a gesture she'd seen her father use. "Oliver, we need this. It'll get the whole town talking. And maybe bring Blackburn to justice."

"There are safer ways. More ethical ways."

"How?" she asked and removed her hand.

"Well…" Oliver avoided making eye contact. "We tone it down. Make it one article instead of a series. We don't use our source and only print things we know independently. And if State's information led to other information, we can't use that either. Ethically."

"Are you kidding me?" Callie asked. "What's left? Are we just going to let someone get away with murder?"

"Hey. We're reporters, not the police. You said yourself that State's a good cop. Let him do his job. If he tells you stuff on the record, then we'll use it."

"Or…" And here she also avoided eye contact. "Or we

take my name off the byline and the masthead, and we get a big story. Pulitzer Prize big."

In his pause, she could sense him starting to come around. "I don't know. You'd be willing to take your name off? Really?"

"If it gets her story out there." She stepped up to his desk and extended her hand, hoping it wasn't still greasy from the Chick-fil-A. "Do we have a deal?"

"Deal, I guess," he said, and they shook.

"But if it goes all the way and you get a Pulitzer, my name goes back on."

"Deal."

CHAPTER 20

SHOULD THE SLIGHTLY plumper pillow go on top or underneath the slightly firmer pillow? That's the question she focuses on now, adjusting her head side to side and up and down, testing it.

Okay. Try it the other way, she thinks, sitting halfway up and reaching behind her head to switch pillows. That's better. Softer one on top, tucked under at the sides. Why can't she ever remember? How many years has she been sleeping and she can't remember? Why is it so difficult? The whole thing has become more an art than a science, depending on how much she tucks the top pillow or which direction the pillowcase is facing, which sounds silly, but it's not, because the open end of a pillow case plumps up differently from the closed end.

Bed firmness plays a role, too. It's all about neck support and how the face rests in the pillow. She needs to make herself comfortable for the hour after hour when she's lying still awake. If she settles onto her back until the Ambien kicks in, then switches to her stomach, facing right, toward the sound machine, there won't be quite as much discomfort to keep her restless and annoyed. For stomach sleep, after the Ambien, she goes into a swastika position

— *right arm up, bent at the elbow (not touching the pillowcase edge), left arm bent and down, right knee up, left leg down and slightly bent. None of the limbs can touch the body; the tactile sensation makes her too aware. Of everything. Okay, now for the covers. They're bunching around her feet, so she awkwardly tries to kick them into place. Then she gets out of bed to adjust them. Then the pillows are off again.*

There are some nights like this when she feels like she's reinventing sleep, analyzing every aspect, her mind obsessed with each detail. She thinks of the Princess and the Pea and tries to figure out how many figurative peas are under her mattress and pillows and limbs and brain. Should she get up and take another Ambien? How about a Xanax, which she takes for the anxiety caused by the Ambien not working, which is pretty much every night? And how many of each does she have in the pill bottles? Long ago she learned not to count her pills at night. No matter how many are left or how many refills are listed on the bottle, she only gets more nervous and more alert when she counts.

She knows there aren't that many. Her last appointment with Dr. Faber was three months ago when she stopped going to the sessions where they sat in matching chairs and always seemed to talk about the same things. She can't very well call his office and ask for a new prescription, not without a trip to Dallas and a world of apology, begging more than apologizing, having to face his lectures and the stern disapproval in his voice. Maybe Dr. Oppenheimer could cut her a break. He's dedicated to the McFees. He must have prescribed untold amounts of drugs to her mother in her last days and to her father in trying to deal with that. What's the use of connections and owed favors if you never use them? She realizes that in her drugged state she's thinking like Buddy, a man who counts up favors the way she counts pills. At the moment, as she switches from the swastika to a side position, left hand under her head, the thought doesn't upset her at all.

The side position will be comfortable for a while, twenty minutes or so, before her arm gets numb and she has to change. She's nostalgic for the old days when she could fall asleep instantly, when she would have to struggle to stay awake until her mother came in for the goodnight kiss. Even years later, sleep was easy, coming home from school and letting Angus jump on the bed and snuggle, totally unbothered when he would scratch at the covers, get up then make his little circles before settling back down. Oh, yes, Angus. Poor Angus. So terrified, terrified and helpless, barking and clawing, making desperate little circles as the smoke and fire stalked him down in his own little corner of the study.

*

Callie fought off her medicated grogginess with a long, hot shower, stopping only when the building's industrial-size water heater finally began running lukewarm.

Sherry Ann had already gone off to class, leaving Callie to deal with a growling stomach. She promised herself a grocery expedition as soon as humanly possible then almost miraculously discovered a leftover slice of pepperoni pizza suffering from frostbite in the freezer.

Sitting at the counter over the microwaved slice, a mug of coffee and her laptop, she did her best to bat away the cobwebs. It was surprising how wide-awake a person could be in the middle of the night and yet so foggy the next morning. She went to plug in her machine and found the outlet occupied by a phone charger, probably Helen's. Chargers always seemed to be the easiest things to leave behind.

An email from Oliver, sent at 8:12 a.m., stated that he had received her share of the article and would spend the rest of the morning collating it with his. It wasn't the blockbuster Callie had hoped for, but it portrayed Briana in a sympathetic light and featured the unidentified man with the shovel. Oliver asked if she wanted to do another pass or if she trusted him enough to send it off with just his edits. A combination of trust and exhaustion made the choice easy.

As she gnawed at the chewy edge, she reviewed her schedule. First would be a visit to St. David's to see Gil and her father. Buddy was originally supposed to be released today but Dr. Oppenheimer had arranged an extra day for observation – and for her to figure out what to do with him. Next would be the vet. She had already spoken to a very sympathetic technician who had agreed that cremation would be the best choice and informed her that Angus' remains would be ready any time after two. Squeezed in somewhere would be a trip to the grocery store and possibly a nap.

It was nearly eleven when she rinsed her breakfast dishes then went to answer the doorbell.

"Emily." She hadn't seen her brother's partner in well over two years. Emily Pasquale looked pretty much the same, same cynical half-smile, same bored demeanor. A bit more sallow in hue and definitely pregnant.

"Callie. Your brother mentioned you were staying here. Sorry for not buzzing from the lobby, but people enjoy opening doors for me."

"Come on in. Congratulations. How are you?" Neither

woman was much of a hugger and they both leaned in with a mid-distance air kiss.

"I could have been a burglar for all they knew."

She definitely looked further along than three months. "Are there many pregnant burglars?" Callie asked.

"Actually, there are. I think it's the hormones."

Callie smiled. This was the Emily she remembered. "So… how's the first trimester?"

"Entering its fifth month." She waddled through the door. "The vomiting's been replaced by back aches, leg aches, every possible ache. But thanks for asking."

"Oh. My brother said it was your first…"

"My fault. I told him it was my first trimester a couple months ago and that's what stuck."

Callie motioned to the sofa. "Do you want to sit down? Can I get you something?"

"If I sit down, I may never get up. I came to drop something off. Is Helen Crawley here? I need her to sign for this." Emily bent at the knees and lowered a Trader Joe's shopping bag to the floor.

"Helen went back to Phoenix. Don't you and State communicate?"

"Not so much. I've been dealing with the vacant lot where the vic was found. We brought in metal detectors, dogs, a search team from the police academy."

"All of that? Why?"

"The lot is one of our few leads, which isn't good for the property owner. He's trying to sell the lot, and our presence isn't helping. I guess murder brings all kind of annoyances." Despite her plan to the contrary, Emily eased herself into a flowery upholstered chair, probably a castoff from Sherry Ann's childhood home.

"What is it?" Callie pointed to the Trader Joe's bag.

"Briana's laptop. The techies found nothing helpful, but they transferred the data to our system just to be safe."

"Nothing at all? Are you sure?"

The detective pursed her lips. "State said you were second-guessing us. There's no coverup, Callie, just a murder we're trying to solve." She eyed the bag. "Now I'm going to have deal with the departmental mail system and verification paperwork."

"I have a charger cord that Briana's mother left behind. Maybe you can put it in with Briana's laptop."

"Sure," Emily said with the hint of a whimper. "Or you can do it yourself. Send them off together. Oh, what a good idea. Callie, please? It'll save a grumpy pregnant woman the hassle."

"Send it to her parents? I can do that?"

"You just sign for it. I trust you'll mail it in a timely manner."

"I'll do it today. But do you trust me not to snoop? I am a reporter."

"Go ahead and try. A. There's nothing on it. And, more important, B. you don't have her passcode. Come on, Callie. Do me a favor."

"Okay," she agreed. "I can have it sent from our office. Should I insure it? Or send it return receipt requested?"

"Probably not a bad idea. Either one or both." Emily grunted as she leaned over and pulled a large, sealed, cushioned envelope out of the Trader Joe's bag. The bag also contained a pen and Callie used it to sign on the red line marked Verified

Delivery. "Thanks," Emily said. "Now I can go home and take a nap. Don't tell your brother."

"No problem. So, how is everything else?" She was straining to remember Emily's husband? Rob or Ron? "Is everyone excited about the baby?"

"I wouldn't say excited. It hasn't been the easiest pregnancy. Ross's mother says the first birth is the hardest, which is true for me since I never intend to have a second."

"What about my brother? Has he been understanding?"

Emily made a face. "He won't let me interview suspects. We tried it. He says I get too emotional. That's why he sent me here instead, running stupid errands."

"Instead? Instead of…" It took Callie two seconds to piece it together. "You mean now? State is interviewing a suspect now? In the Westlake case? He's doing it now?"

Emily hemmed. "I didn't say that. We're working several cases."

"You are such a bad liar."

"I am not a bad liar. I'm just exhausted at the moment."

"So, it is the Westlake case."

"Augh." It came out as a combination growl and moan. "The guy's not really a suspect, Callie, more a person of interest. State went to talk to him."

"And by 'him' you mean Professor Samuel Paget. Damn. I'm the one who gave State his name." She made a fist. If there'd been a nearby wall, she might have punched it. "So, I'm right. Paget is his suspect. So much for keeping me in the loop. State promised to keep me in the loop."

"Callie, please. You're giving me a headache to go with my backache."

CHAPTER 21

BATTLE HALL WAS a Classical Revival building, designed by classic American architect. It seemed like a fitting home for the university's Center for American Architecture and Design.

Callie had always been good at piecing things together. From Emily, she knew that the professor had not been brought into the station. State was going to him. Before leaving the apartment, Callie visited the U.T. website and found that her old password still worked. With just a few clicks, she'd determined that Paget had office hours today. Right now, in fact.

As she rounded a corner into a marble-lined hallway, Callie noted a young male student, seated outside a faculty door, an art portfolio balanced on his lap, his left leg bouncing nervously. The office was 107, Dr. Paget's, and the student looked up as she approached the door. "There's a police officer in there. I don't know why. They kicked me out."

"Thanks," said Callie and twisted the knob. It wasn't locked.

"Excuse me. Can you ask them how long they'll be? I have a class."

"You should go to your class," Callie said right before pushing open the door. "This may be a while."

Sam Paget was behind his desk, a little slumped over, in a brown jacket that probably always looked wrinkled. "Student hours are by appointment," he snapped.

"Sorry, Professor."

State was seated across the desk. In just two words, he recognized the voice. "Oh, my God."

Callie was the only one prepared for this moment. She had rehearsed a dozen variations and had settled on the truth. She just had to say it with authority. "I'm not a student, Dr. Paget. I'm a reporter."

"A reporter?" He was sitting up straight. "No, no. I can't have a reporter here." Then he instantly changed his mind. "Wait, don't go yet. What do you want?"

"Oh, my God," State repeated.

"Sir, I think you had a relationship with Briana Crawley, a sugar daddy kind of arrangement, and that it ended not long before her murder."

Paget bristled. "You can't prove that. I'll sue. Who do you work for?"

Callie pointed to the familiar hardback lying prominently on the middle of his desk. "I'm the one who gave the police your autographed book."

State was on his feet, facing her. "I'm going to have to ask you to leave."

"Is this true?" Paget asked the detective. "You know this woman? She gave you the book?"

State paused. "She did. But she has no right to intrude." He stepped toward his sister and lowered his voice. "Did

Emily tell you I was here? I swear, she needs to go on maternity leave." He turned. "Mr. Paget, this woman is leaving."

"Fine," said Callie. "I'll just write what I have."

"What you have? No." Paget sounded desperate. He turned to State. "I want her to stay. I don't want her printing this, not without hearing my side. Can you make her not print anything at all?"

"I wish I could. But you can ask her to keep whatever you're going to say off the record."

"Would you do that?" Paget asked Callie, his eyes pleading. "Keep this off the record?"

State's tone turned reassuring. "Sir, I'm sure she doesn't want to ruin your life. How about it, Miss? If Dr. Paget's statement has nothing to do with her death, will you agree to keep his name out of it?"

"Um…" This conversation had obviously been going on for some time. "If it has nothing to do with it? Okay. Off the record. If I have to mention Dr. Paget, if it's unavoidable, I'll use a pseudonym – if he has nothing to do with her death." Already, she was feeling disappointed.

"There it is," State declared. "Her word in front of a witness. Now you can tell her what you told me." He pulled another chair out from against a wall and offered his sister a seat. Callie was reminded of the dozens of times she'd sat in a claustrophobic office just like this one, discussing grades and careers and life.

"Okay." The smooth-headed, slightly paunchy man swiveled his chair, facing them both. "One of my male students told me about this website. A lot of college girls use it, he said. Not that I was looking for…" He took a deep breath. "Look, my marriage wasn't in the best place, and I had some money from the sale of a property my aunt left me." With every sentence, he seemed to get smaller and more vulnerable. "I found Bri on the site. She wasn't a student in my department, so I thought, 'Why not?'. We would never meet outside the arrangement. And she seemed to need some guidance, being away from home. Bri was very special. You can laugh, but it wasn't just about sex."

Callie hadn't pulled out her phone or a notebook. She didn't want to spook him. "What was her screen name?"

"Holly G," State said. "We got it from her computer."

Paget nodded. "Like Holly Golightly from the movie. That's how she thought of herself, untainted, doing it for fun."

State checked his notes. "And you're Doctor Feelgood, I presume."

Paget emitted a closed-mouth moan. "It was a joke. I wanted a girl with a sense of humor."

"When did the relationship begin?" Callie asked.

"In the fall, right before classes. She wasn't demanding. I paid her rent and spoiled her. We liked each other. We were good for each other but we didn't have illusions. At least I didn't. It couldn't go on forever."

When he paused and lost focus, Callie primed the conversation. "You called it off, didn't you? Was it guilt? Did you finally feel guilty?"

"Guilt?" A gurgle formed in his throat. "My wife almost found out. I was leaving the office to have dinner with Bri, and Gloria called me. We have the same Google calendar. She said, 'What's this reservation tonight at Anthony's Trattoria? I thought you had a meeting.' I told her I did have a meeting. Then she told me to check the calendar. I did, and there they were, both listed for seven o'clock, my made-up meeting and my dinner with Bri at Anthony's. I don't know how it happened. I had called for the reservation personally, not Open Table or anything like that. Talked to the reservation girl personally. But somehow it magically popped up on our calendar. How the hell it happened… It's this damned connectivity crap. Everything's connected. There should be a law. So, I told my wife it was a weird mistake. And then I stood Bri up, just to be safe. The next day I called it off."

"What was Ms. Crawley's reaction?" State's trusty notepad was once again open.

"She was upset, but she understood. Excuse me." Paget swiveled to face State directly. "Can you answer a question for me?"

"Depends on the question."

"You keep calling her Ms. Crawley. Is there a good reason for that?"

State lowered his notepad and thought. "It's an old cop thing, I guess. The way I was trained. It's supposed to be a sign of respect. Do you find it annoying?"

"I do," said Paget.

"Me, too," Callie chimed in. "I get trying to be respectful, but it sounds so formal."

"Like she's not a real person to you," Paget added.

"Okay, I get that," State said. "Bri. Briana. Okay, I'll give it a shot." He raised his notepad. "You say Briana was disappointed, but not angry."

"Sounds better to me," Callie said.

"Yeah, that's what I live for. Dr. Paget, how did you leave

things with… her? Any severance offer? Any agreeing to continue the rent?"

Paget nodded. "I gave her five thousand in cash, to ease the transition. It was nearly all I had left from the property sale. Like I said, it couldn't go on forever. Right after that, I got rid of the phone we used, got rid of the email address."

"Five thousand's a lot of money," Callie said.

"I cared for her. I wanted to make sure she was okay."

State made sure he had eye contact. "Was the money a bribe so she wouldn't tell your wife? Was she threatening to make trouble?"

Samuel Paget looked from one red-headed interviewer to the other. If he saw any resemblance, he didn't mention it. "That's why you're both here. You're thinking maybe I killed her. What a horrible thing to think."

State shrugged. "That's my job. Can you tell us where you were on the evening of April twelfth?"

"The night she was killed? I'm not sure I remember."

Callie pointed to the smart phone on his desk. "Your Google calendar?"

"Oh, yeah." Paget picked up his phone, pressed the screen a few times and squinted at the result. "April twelfth." He smiled. "I was part of a panel discussion at Goldsmith Hall. 'The Future of Municipal Architecture'. Afterwards we all had dinner with Dean Atchison. Dinner was at eight. I assume we finished up around ten. I drove home and probably watched a half-hour of something before bed. When was Bri killed?"

State didn't have to check his notes. "Between eight and nine p.m. Give or take."

"Then I have an alibi." He seemed relieved. "I told you it wasn't me."

State nodded. "If it all checks out, yes. Congratulations. Was your wife at home when you got there?"

"She was."

State made a note. "Was your wife alone? Had she been home all evening?"

The professor jerked his head up from his phone. "Jesus. You're not saying my wife needs an alibi, too? She had no idea about us. And she could never do… Please don't talk to her. Promise me you won't."

"There was rape involved," State reminded him. "So we're not looking at any women right now. I'll talk to the dean about that evening. You say there were several people at the dinner?"

"Probably six of us."

"Good. Then I won't have to mention your name, just as part of the group."

"Thank you." There was relief in his voice. "I appreciate it."

It seemed to Callie that the interview, as disappointing as it had turned out, was almost over. All of this work to find Briana's sugar daddy, and for what? Her brother flipped to the next page. "Does the name Dylan Dane sound familiar?"

"Dylan Dane? Never heard of him."

"Did Briana mention any boy from school? Any other boyfriends? Perhaps another sugar daddy she had? Some girls do that, have more than one." Paget didn't answer. "Any business opportunity or relationship she talked about? Dylan, like Bob Dylan. Dylan Dane."

"Sorry," he replied. "Bri used to talk about her roommate

and a couple of girlfriends, but we never discussed boys. We were in our own little world, a separate world. As for the other thing, it's possible that she had another arrangement in her life. I hope not. She wasn't the type. I…" His voice broke. "I hope not."

"Almost done," State said with a sympathetic half-smile. "I know this is difficult." Callie could see that, despite her preconceptions, her brother was actually good at his job. "What do you know about Briana's bank account? Did you ever deposit anything directly into her account?"

"No. Never. I'm not stupid. I paid her in cash, even for rent and presents. The only mistake I made was autographing the book. And that damned Google calendar." He smacked a hand flat on his desk. "A lot of men must get into that fix. It's a life lesson. Never share a calendar with your wife."

When State flipped shut his notepad and put away his pen, it signaled the official end of the interview. They spent another few minutes listening to the sad, defensive man reminisce about his dead mistress, the college girl that Callie had bonded with from the moment she'd seen her lying in a metal drawer.

State stood first and shook Samuel Paget's hand. In his early days on the force, he had told his sister that one of the policies of old school cops was never to shake the hand of someone you honestly think is a killer. "If you remember anything or think of anything, please contact me, no matter how inconsequential," said Detective McFee." And with that, he pulled his wallet from his jacket and gave Dr. Paget his card. "There's my cell phone and my departmental email. Remember, anything at all. Thank you for your time."

They were in the parking lot, halfway to their cars, when State felt far enough away to speak. He stopped, hands on his hips. "What the hell was that about?"

"I was keeping myself in the loop."

"You were compromising an interview."

"Was not."

"This is the last time I'm letting you pull this shit. My badge could be on the line."

"I did nothing wrong," she said, emphasizing each word. "I told him who I was and he gave his permission. You think he's a dead end, don't you?"

"I do. We need to check his alibi, but it seems verifiable. I'll also check her banking history to see if she deposited five thousand in cash like he said. I suspect he's telling the truth."

"So that's it?"

"He's not our Dylan Dane from the bank footage. Not big enough."

"So?" Callie didn't want to give it up. "Paget hired a hitman. People do that. Your mistress is threatening to tell your wife, so you pay someone to kill her. And the hitman is Dylan Dane, the one who emptied her bank account. That was his pay-off."

"So, Paget paid a hitman to rape his mistress."

State had a point, but… "The hitman did that on his own."

"Hitmen don't do that, even amateurs. They do it the easiest way, usually with a gun. And remember, half the money gets paid after, so you don't want piss off your client by raping his girl. Even guys who want their mistresses dead get particular about that." State pulled out his car keys. "He's not our guy."

Callie frowned. "Maybe it's the wife. What's her name? Gloria. And she paid the hitman extra to rape her."

"You're saying the wife knew all about the mistress – name, address, etc. – without the husband having a clue. And she felt strongly enough to hire a rapist hitman."

"I've read about things like that," Callie said weakly.

"In novels. Okay, we'll check the wife's bank account," he said with a distinct note of condescension.

"So, that's it?" She couldn't believe it. "Hardly seems fair."

"It doesn't work on 'fair'," State said. "From what Briana told her friends, this guy was her first and only daddy. That leaves us the usual angles – old boyfriends, neighbors, strange cars seen in the Westlake area, people with violent rape arrests. We're asking around about her movements that night. And we're still talking to Blackburn's law team, trying to pressure him to say… anything." State clicked his key and the beep from his car was followed almost instantly by a ding from his phone. "Excuse me." Callie gave him a little space while he checked it. "Damn," her brother said under his breath. "Damn it all."

"What's wrong?"

"Paget sent me a text. 'I want you to remember who she was.'" State handed the phone to his sister.

Below the text message was a photo. It was Briana, fully clothed, lying stomach down on a bed, her face propped up in her fists, smiling coquettishly, with just a hint of Audrey Hepburn about her. The leather and gold necklace, the birthday present, peeked out from between her forearms. "Congratulations. Now we both have a picture of Bri."

State took back his phone. "I hate it when they do that."

CHAPTER 22

ON CALLIE'S NEXT visit to St. David's, her father seemed himself again. But he was cranky and restless, anxious to get home, not accepting the fact that going back to the house was impossible. On the other side of the third floor, Gil was looking more alive but less coherent, falling in and out of consciousness. His sister Maria sat by the bed where she'd spent half the previous night. She was in charge of the hydromorphone drip and was more liberal in its use than Gil might have wanted.

Next was the Westridge Pet Hospital, where she had a comforting talk with the veterinarian in charge. He had been Angus's vet for most of the dog's life. "Do you plan to bury his remains?" A small wooden box, smaller than Callie would have imagined, sat on the side table between his desk and her chair. "I would recommend it fairly soon. The longer you put it off… I'm sure Angus wouldn't want to be stuck in a drawer somewhere forever." Callie agreed. She promised that, as soon as things settled down, she and Buddy would have a little ceremony and bury the good old boy under the shade of his favorite willow.

Dinner came early, in her truck, parked twenty yards beyond the drive-thru window of a Chick-fil-A. By the time she walked into Sherry Ann's apartment, she was ready for a drink.

She was relieved to find the place empty and to find another half-bottle of white wine hidden in the vegetable crisper. She made a mental note to replace this bottle as well, bringing the total of three – and counting. She took a glass from the shelf, retrieved the cushioned envelope Emily had given her to mail, and settled into Sherry Ann's flowery uphol-stered chair.

She had to send off the laptop tomorrow, she reminded herself. It was a sobering prospect, letting go of her one remaining contact with Bri. If this little machine could talk . . . Without thinking too much, she tore through the seal and pulled it out. There was no note or documentation, just the MacBook Air and a power cord. Oh, and something attached to the back, rustling under her hand. Callie turned it over and was surprised to find a Post-it note. *Bc*1234*, written in light pencil. Really? She had to laugh. So much for police department security. Of course, the tech geeks had no reason to think that it would wind up in the hands of anyone but Briana's family.

Taking the MacBook to the kitchen island, she plugged it and powered it up. The passcode worked, bringing up a photo of a smiling white kitten on Briana's screen and a dozen or so icons, including a familiar-looking 'M" superimposed over a 'S". Callie double-clicked the icon and waited while the MySugar site loaded its classy-looking homepage. A log-in box materialized on the upper right and when she typed in

"B", the auto-fill feature suggested Briana's email address and eight dots for her password. Another double click and she was in. It was that easy. A selfie of a shy but sexy-looking Briana materialized above the name Holly G.

Callie retrieved her wine, took a gulp followed by a deep breath then checked the dead girl's message history. She tried to tamp down her expectations. State had already accessed this information. But her brother didn't know everything. For example, he hadn't bothered to look at Briana's Kindle or to check the autograph in Sam Paget's book.

There were a fair number of messages to Briana, twenty or more, including a flurry of contacts in the fall, when she'd first signed on. Some sugar daddies were replying to her inquiries. Others were reaching out on their own. All of them commented on her looks and fun-loving attitude. "Let's get to know each other," wrote a man calling himself LuxuryMate. "We'll have a swinging time. No strings." Each communication featured a thumbnail photo – men in their forties or fifties, some younger, some serious, some smiling, one in a karate pose. One of the September notes was from Dr. Feelgood, Dr. Paget's online name. The photo was not of him but of another black middle-aged man, this one a little younger and with hair.

Their correspondence had continued – playful and chatty, with talk about school and Briana's life goals – before Paget asked for her private email address. That was the last entry from Dr. Feelgood.

Scrolling down, she saw that the message history went semi-dormant, just a few incoming inquiries, no responses from Briana, until March 31. Callie did the math; just 12 days before her death. On that date Briana sent out five inquiries and received two responses. Only one of them went private, from YrValentine, a mid-thirties, mid-attractive white male who had given her a phone number, not an email. Could this man be involved? Not Briana's ex-daddy but her new one?

She took another sip, using the other hand to grab her phone and dial the number. Sure enough, a recorded voice came on almost immediately, informing her that it no longer in service. One more long sip and Callie had emptied the wine glass.

Her gaze returned to the MacBook screen and the two messages from YrValentine. The second, the one with the phone number, was longer than the first. He was married, he admitted, but was sure they could work out a great relationship. She should respond soon, and they would set up a "meet-and-eat at whatever high-end restaurant you prefer."

She read this sentence again. She read it once more. A meet-and-eat at a high-end restaurant. Callie stopped breathing. This had to be the same daddy who'd contacted her. It had to be. Iwill4you. The odds of two men on the same sugar site using exactly the same phrases…

Retrieving her laptop from the bedroom, she accessed the MySugar site with her own password and clicked through to Iwill4you's thumbnail. She studied the face, comparing it to YrValentine's. They were similar but not the same by any means. The one thing the man didn't change, perhaps didn't think to change, was his language, something that Callie was particularly attuned to.

A chill went straight through her. Here was a sugar daddy who'd gone private with Briana not long before her death, who'd then changed his name and profile and was now approaching Callie. Could this be a normal thing? Did men regularly change their names and pics and descriptions? She herself had changed her profile and photo. But no, this felt different.

Her first impulse was to call someone, to get their opinion and support. What about State? She smiled. Oh, she would love to rub his nose in this little morsel. He'd been so dismissive when she – actually one of his sons – had joined a sugaring website. His wife had thrown her out of the house. But now, because of that, she had a brand-new lead. No, Callie decided. The last time she came across a clue she'd done the right thing, only to have State try to freeze her out.

What about Oliver? Well, Oliver was her partner and her boss, the man who was putting his paper on the line in order to bring this to light. But he, too, had been problematic. She thought back to their interview with Crystal. They might have gotten Blackburn's name out of her and into their article if Oliver had been such a nervous Nelly. What if the same thing happened again? Would Oliver still want to play by the rules when playing just outside them might help put the bastard in jail?

Callie sat with her empty glass, thinking over her options. Neither was perfect. But going it alone seemed even worse. And then a sharp ding interrupted her musings. It was one of the laptops. Hers. At the top right corner of her MySugar page appeared an alert, a personal message from Iwill4you. The icon, a glowing, pulsing red heart, was intended to be romantic, but that's not how she reacted.

She clicked through and read. "Hey, Heather. Got your

message. You didn't include your cell, but I get it. A girl can't be too careful. Here's my cell, just as a show of faith. I'm quite excited to meet you. Let's do dinner. BTW, my name really is Will, which makes my handle a pretty lame joke. Is your name really Heather?"

Callie had no intention of calling him and letting him see her number, so she stuck with the website. "Hey, Will. Yes, I'm really Heather. I would love to get to know you. Dinner sounds terrific. How about somewhere near campus? That makes it convenient for me."

They went back and forth a few more times, settling on Mikimoto, a fusion restaurant just a few blocks away. Will suggested making a reservation for tomorrow at seven and Callie, or rather Heather, accepted. She saw no reason in postponing it, which would only give her more time to change her mind. This was something she had to do.

It was just dinner in a public place, she told herself. Her brother wouldn't be there to take over. And Oliver wouldn't be there to protect her virtue or insist on full disclosure.

As soon as they signed off, Callie went into the bathroom and started the process of washing and air drying her thick, rather problematic hair. She had learned how to deal with it from her mother, and the procedure always brought back a flood of memories.

CHAPTER 23

THE NEXT DAY, from the moment she woke up, it hung over her like a cloud – the upcoming date, interview, meet-and-eat, whatever. A busy morning and an equally busy afternoon helped keep her distracted.

It began with a call from Briana's mother in Phoenix. This week's *Free Press* was online and Callie had texted her a link to "A Death in Westlake". Helen thanked her for portraying her daughter in such a sympathetic light and for not mentioning the sugar aspect. But there was no mention of a series, Helen pointed out. Was there going to be another article? Callie told her the truth. There probably would be, yes. It all depended on what new information they could dig up. It might come very soon, Callie thought but didn't say.

After that came the packing up and the labored thank-you note to Sherry Ann, followed by a walk to the post office to mail off Briana's laptop, going to the extra trouble to send it insured, return receipt requested. On the way back, she dropped into Junior's Wines and Spirits to buy a bottle of Champagne and three bottles of a decent, mid-priced white.

She left the Champagne as a thank-you and two of the whites as reimbursements, putting the third in her backpack. The door locked automatically behind her and she lugged her backpack and two suitcases into the elevator and down to the lobby.

Sarah had overseen the preparations for the McFee gatehouse. She had a set of keys and knew the property. Two of her nieces had spent the previous day cleaning. Also enlisted was the ranch's handyman/gardener, to move Buddy's clothing and personal effects into the larger of the two bedrooms. Burned-out light bulbs were replaced. Small repairs were made – a loose door hinge, a broken shelf. The cable and wi-fi were up and running. Callie had learned from her mother that any problem could be solved if you had a sweet attitude, knew where to throw your money and tipped generously. Gil had told her where to find the household checkbook, in the center desk drawer in his office.

Callie turned off Hacienda Road and stopped to say hello to the uniformed officer manning the gateposts. Down at the end of drive, a lone motorcycle stood by the blackened doorway, evidence of the rent-a-cop still on the job. For a moment, she toyed with the idea of driving up, just to reexamine the damage, but there was already enough on her mind.

She pulled up to the small driveway fronting a faux French Provincial chateau but on a tiny scale, like something built for Epcot Center. It was a strange feeling to be home again and yet walk into a house she'd never been in before. Generations of gardeners had spent their working lives in this gatehouse, laboring for the McFee dynasty, and yet she knew almost nothing about them.

One of Sarah's famous enchilada casseroles was waiting in the oven, making the strange house smell like home. She treated herself to a healthy slice, then wrapped the rest in tin foil and found a spot for it in the freshly stocked fridge, complete, she noted, with two bottles of chilled white wine. Those, plus the one in her backpack, made three. Thank you, Sarah!

As she unpacked in the bedroom, a decent-sized ensuite with new towels and sheets and her old blue comforter from childhood, Callie second-guessed her living situation for the umpteenth time. From a practical point of view, it made sense. She needed a place. This would be familiar ground for her father until the ranch was once again inhabitable. And it would keep him away from prying eyes. On the other side of the pro-con ledger was just one item, her great discomfort in the two of them living under the same green copper mansard roof. It would be temporary, she promised herself. The majority of her belongings still sat in a storage unit in Dallas, where they would stay, awaiting a saner, more permanent solution.

Throughout the day, she'd been on and off the phone with Oliver. The article was already garnering attention and she could sense his excitement. Despite his low-key persona, despite his role as the publisher of a weekly handout, Oliver loved being in the middle of the action. "My phone is ringing nonstop. I'm so embarrassed your name's not on this."

"When the time comes, we'll have a long discussion with the Pulitzer committee."

He laughed. "I know you're joking, but…"

"No, I'm not."

Oliver's very first call had come from the Police

Community Liaison, denying any such arrest and demanding to know the name of their source. The second and third inquiries were from the mayor's office, and the district attorney's. The Austin Justice Coalition had also called, trying to judge the racial implications. Social media soon joined in, with links to the article appearing on Twitter and Facebook. Some took the feminist approach, wondering how the police could justify protecting the identity of a man like this. "There are also a few dozen theories about who the suspect could be. Every local celebrity from the governor to Lance Armstrong. One theory says it was Keagan Blackburn.

"You think it's a lucky guess?"

"Yes," Oliver said, "although my heart skipped a beat, I have to tell you. The rationale was that he lives in the vicinity and that his wife walked out, turning him into this serial rapist-killer."

"Serial? It was just one."

"You know the internet. All in all, pretty manageable. We didn't blow up nationally, but it's good local attention."

Callie had thought about bringing Oliver up to speed on tonight's plan and decided against it. He would only try to talk her out of it. Or try to come along.

It took her over an hour to get ready. The gardener – Lou, she thought his name was – had brought over the dressing table from her old bedroom, the one she'd inherited from her mother. Anita McFee would sit there, staring into this same mirror, applying her party face, while Sarah, in her gray and white uniform, brought up a dressing drink, a small gin martini with an olive. It had been a tradition for women of a certain station to sip a little concoction while preparing for the evening. Callie smiled at the memory then went down to the kitchen, poured herself a glass of white wine, her own dressing drink, and returned to her mirror.

Will, if that was his name, would be expecting real date attire. He basically knew what she looked like, a redhead named Heather with her face half in the shadows. Callie pulled back her hair and wrapped it in a ponytail. Now, how should this Heather dress? What kind of make-up? Should Callie use her own taste or go a little cheaper and more obvious? More eyeshadow maybe? It was like going undercover, complete with a disguise and a backstory. Her plan was to leave early, giving herself plenty of time, which meant, of course, that there was no traffic and she arrived there early.

Mikimoto was on the low end of high end, with white tablecloths and reasonable enough prices. Definitely a date place. It was relatively empty on a week night but not uncomfortably so. She gave Will's name – Will Peterson – to the hostess and was given a choice of being seated or waiting at the bar. She chose a corner table with subtle lighting, hoping that it might conceal that she was half a decade over her stated age of twenty-one.

She had just ordered a glass of pinot grigio when a tall, well-built, rather handsome man in a blue blazer stepped up to the table. "Heather?" he asked. "Heather111?"

"Will? Oh, hello. How are you?" Reflexively, she stood. Just as reflexively, she shook both his hands and gave him an impulsive kiss on the cheek. "Oh, I'm so sorry." She had to laugh. "Starting off on the wrong foot, aren't I?"

"Not at all." His smile was bright and slightly crooked. "Exactly the right foot, as far as I'm concerned. Good to meet you."

"I don't usually kiss strangers." He was a pleasant surprise. There was nothing creepy looking about him and his posted age of 32 seemed about right. The blazer was stylish but not expensive looking, and his face was square-jawed and thin-lipped, with just the hint of a dimple in his chin. His hair was dark brown and thick, combed back and curling over his ears. "That's not your photo," she said. "On the website."

"It's not," he admitted. "I'm married, so I didn't want to post… Is that going to be a problem?"

"No. It's just… Most people, when they fake their pics, go for someone more attractive."

"Well, thanks. I guess." His smile was wide and open, his manner a little awkward but charming. "I guess I didn't want to over-promise."

"No, I'm happy you didn't over-promise. It's lovely."

Will chuckled. "You know what's kind of weird? A first date where the man gets all the compliments." He leaned in, enough to be suggestive but not overly. "You're gorgeous. And I love your hair." Callie was so glad she'd finally washed it.

Her pinot arrived, along with the menus and a recitation of tonight's specials. Will ordered a bourbon and branch on the rocks. This was State's drink of choice and, for a moment, Callie was reminded that this wasn't a real date, but part of her investigation.

"Have you ever done this before? I mean, the sugar daddy thing?" Callie covered her mouth, pretending to regret the question. "Oh, I'm sorry. Was that a rude thing to ask?"

"Not at all." Will said. "We shouldn't have secrets, at least not about this." He paused, looking a bit embarrassed. "Twice before. Once last spring. It lasted nine months. She loved animals and wanted to be a vet tech. I helped her go to school and she wound up getting a job in Galveston. It was just what she needed and the two if us stay in touch. The other was just recently. I don't know why it ended, to be honest."

"What do you mean?"

"We saw each other twice. Then she just stopped responding. I tried calling, texting. She'd said she needed help with her rent, which was fine. I would have been happy to help." He spread his hands and shrugged. "Not every relationship works out, I guess."

Callie was a little startled. He was obviously referring to Briana. "She just disappeared on you? That must have been annoying."

"It was. I told myself I would never do this again. I tried an escort service for a while. They're discreet, but too impersonal." The corners of his mouth turned up, stretching out his little dimple. "And then I saw your profile."

Callie felt both relieved and disappointed. She didn't want this guy to be a cold-blooded killer. On the other hand, she'd been so proud to have tracked him down. Was it possible that he didn't even know about Briana's death? Callie thought back to her own situation. If she hadn't talked to State and met Briana's parents, she might not have heard about it either.

On the third hand, she knew from her father just how skillful a liar could be. The good ones stick as close as possible to the truth. Yes, he had started a sugar daddy relationship with a girl who had just disappeared from his life. All perfectly plausible and innocent.

"You're being very quiet," Will said. He reached across and took her hands in his long, strong fingers. "Maybe I shouldn't have mentioned it. I didn't do anything to make her ghost me like that, I swear."

For a second, Callie thought of telling him about Briana's death, just to gauge his reaction. But how could she bring up the subject? There was no conceivable way. "I believe you," she said, aware of just how lame and condescending that sounded.

The conversation quickly began to lag, probably more Callie's fault than Will's, as they stared down at their menus. The server returned with his bourbon and branch water and they talked over their selections, with Callie ordering the trout special and Will choosing the pork and peanut noodles. After the server left, they clinked glasses, tasted their drinks and tried again.

This time it went better. Will asked smart, personal questions and seemed genuinely interested in Callie's life and goals. Heather's, actually. In Heather's cover story, she had transferred from U.T. Dallas at the beginning of the semester to escape a bad relationship that had followed her out of high school and stayed way too long. Will knew a fair amount about Dallas and, thanks to her time at the *Morning News*, Callie was able to keep up the charade. Heather was just finishing up her junior year and hadn't made many friends here. The girls were too cliquish, and the boys... They were just too much like boys.

Will sympathized. He even apologized for the callow frat boy he himself used to be. "Somehow we got raised without manners or consideration, especially to women. I'd like to blame it on our spoiled upbringings, but that would just prove how spoiled I still am."

The rest of the evening flew by, despite Callie's disappointment in the trout special. Will was a tech investor, he said. Through an old roommate – Texas A&M – he'd gotten in on the ground floor of two big I.T. businesses. He made some mistakes along the way, but still came out well financially and now was involved in something new. Ever since college, he'd done nothing but work. The marriage had produced no children and his wife Tammy, feeling bored and ignored, developed her own interests. Will wasn't specific about what these interests were, but now that the business life was less demanding, he was developing interests of his own.

Callie had intended this to be more of an interview than a date, but it was nearest thing to an actual date that she'd had in a while. She could almost understand the attraction to the sugar lifestyle, if all of the daddies were guaranteed to be like this. Once every ten minutes or so, she had to remind herself that she was mirroring the behavior of a poor twenty-one-year-old who'd been raped and murdered less than two weeks ago.

They were still deep in discussion, mulling over the pros and cons of Heather's psychology major and whether or not it would make sense for her to go to grad school, when the check came and went and they found themselves stepping out into an unexpectedly breezy spring evening. She had to physically restrain Will from taking off his jacket and draping it over her shoulders.

"Okay," he said and rebuttoned his jacket. "At least let me walk you home. Which way?"

If Callie hadn't had those three glasses of pinot grigio, she might have thought before answering. "No, that's all right. I'll call an Uber."

Will looked puzzled. "I thought you lived nearby. That's why we picked Mikimoto."

"I know, I know," she improvised. "But I don't feel like walking."

"Then I'll drive you. I'm just up the block."

"No, that's okay," she insisted.

"You don't want me to know where you live?" he asked. "That's no way to start a relationship. I know how to be discreet, Heather. And if I'm going to be helping you with your rent and other such things…"

Up until around noon today, this wouldn't have been a problem. But her home was now the gatehouse of one of the nicer estates in the toniest section of Austin. How could she possibly explain this? "Okay, you can walk me. I'm on 22nd, this side of Pearl." It was Sherry Ann's address.

"That's just a few blocks." Will chuckled. "I didn't take you for such a diva."

"Oh, I'm full of surprises."

On the entire walk, as she kept up her end of the small talk, Callie tried to remember. Had she left the keys on the kitchen counter as instructed or had she forgotten? She often forgot things like this. It would be wonderful if she had forgotten, if Sherry Ann's keys were still in her purse, but she couldn't remember.

When they stopped in front of the glass doors of the building, Will took a moment, gazing up at the limestone façade and the shiny balconies. "No wonder you need help with your rent."

"Oh, it's not terrible. I have a roommate," Callie said and began rummaging through her purse.

"I disagree. I think a roommate is terrible. It means I probably won't get invited up."

"Not tonight." She kept rummaging. She'd found her own car keys, but the search for Sherry Ann's was not going well. "Well, thank you so much. It's been a great evening."

"First of many, I hope."

"Me, too." She started to flip her ponytail back over her shoulder then in mid-flip decided it was too much. "I'm not sure where we go from here."

"Next time," Will said. "We'll get to know each other better and talk over the arrangement – including getting you a private apartment."

Before she could reply, Will pulled her in. The kiss was warm and soft and unexpected in a way that made her inhale and taste the peanut noodles mixed with bourbon. She didn't pull away but wrapped her arms softly around his waist. She could feel his whole body responding to hers and felt herself responding in the same way. Two long, deep breaths. Exchanging the same sweet, spicy air. Will pulled away on his own, just a moment before it would have become too much. A lovely, romantic kiss and not a prelude to anything more.

"Wow," he said, echoing just what she felt. Under any other circumstances, she told herself, then floated back down to reality.

"I think this is where we say good night," she said. Will nodded but didn't move. He was waiting, she realized, for her to take out her key and open the door. "Good night, Will."

He seemed slightly insulted. "I'm not going to push my way in."

"I know that, but . . ." She actually didn't have an end to

that sentence. Instead, she returned to her purse and rummaged. Maybe she could say she'd lost them. Then what? He would insist on waiting while she buzzed her roommate. Would Sherry Ann be in? If she was, would Callie be able to phrase things to make it seem like she still lived there. "Hi, I forgot my key." No. "Hey, Sherry Ann, can you buzz me in?" Better. But could they get through the exchange without Sherry Ann saying Callie's real name? Unlikely. And if Sherry Ann wasn't home…

A movement beyond the glass doors caught her eye. Someone was just getting off the elevator. Thank God.

Callie pulled out her own key ring, rattled it and tried to smile. "Ugh, I swear they could have bit me." She stalled for time by gazing deep into Will's eyes, then aimed her gatehouse key toward the keyhole just as the door opened.

It was a boy from Sherry Ann's floor – short, slim, a little dorky – someone Callie had had a nodding acquaintance with during her few days here. He was dressed for a run, his white earbuds in place. "Hey," she said, trying to make herself heard. "Good to see you."

"Hey," he said back and held open the door.

Callie stood on the threshold while Will stood at a respectful distance and didn't repeat his request to come up. Then she gave him one last peck on the cheek and walked in as if she owned the place.

For the next few minutes, she hid out in an empty, unmoving elevator, trying to gauge how soon it would be safe for her to leave.

CHAPTER 24

SARAH WAS IN the gatehouse kitchen, making lunch, when Callie and State brought their father home from the hospital. Gil had suggested Sarah be there, a familiar presence, to help ease him into the unfamiliar surroundings. Buddy was having a lucid day, which did not always correspond to a good day, as Callie had learned. His first demand was to go up to the big house to inspect the damage.

The three McFees walked through the leaf-dappled sunlight, arm in arm in arm, with Buddy in the middle. At the doorway, the children stepped aside, letting him go in first. The study was still protected by yellow tape and the security guard, a middle-aged woman this time, kept a careful eye on them.

Buddy leaned over the tape and glanced around the room. "Could've been worse," he said in a calm, matter of fact way.

Callie watched her brother watching their father and wondered. Yes, today was a lucid day. But State had observed enough of Buddy's behavior. Did he really not know? Or did he just refuse to admit it. If State never acknowledged it, then maybe it wasn't happening and his father would remain the invincible Buddy McFee.

State stayed for lunch, Sarah's smothered chicken with rice, and got Buddy settled in his new bedroom before leaving. Callie toyed with the idea of phoning Oliver and telling him of her date last night, but she wasn't sure what she would say. She had followed a false lead with the first of Briana's daddies. And Will be just as innocent.

There would be one more date, she told herself, during which she would use her journalistic skills to discover whatever she could. For example, was his name really Will Peterson or was that just his way of shielding his marriage? The internet had turned up dozens of Wills, Williams and Bills, plus endless numbers of "B" and "W" Petersons. Another question: Did he have any connection to Keagan Blackburn? Or did he live near the vacant lot where Briana's body was found? This was all information that was worth a second date with an attractive, charmingly awkward man.

She was still culling through her Google list of Petersons, trying not to glance down at Briana's graduation photo clinging stubbornly to the bottom corner of her laptop, when a ping alerted her to a MySugar message. It was Will, saying how much he'd loved last night. He thought they'd made a "thrilling connection" and, at the risk of repeating himself, said he would love to work out the details of an arrangement. What did she think?

Callie agreed. How about tonight?

Will replied that tonight was out. This was date night with his wife Maggie, an idea foisted on them by an optimistic marriage counselor. How about tomorrow? They settled on who counts up favors the way she counts pills. At the moment, as she switches from the swastika to a side position, left hand under her head, the thought doesn't upset her at all.

The side position will be comfortable for a while, twenty minutes or so, before her arm gets numb and she has to change. She's nostalgic for the old days when she could fall asleep instantly, when she would have to struggle to stay awake until her mother came in for the goodnight kiss. Even years later, sleep was easy, coming home from school and letting Angus jump on the bed and snuggle, totally unbothered when he would scratch at the covers, get up then make his little circles before settling back down. Oh, yes, Angus. Poor Angus. So terrified, terrified and helpless, barking and clawing, making desperate little circles as the smoke and fire stalked him down in his own little corner of the study.

*

Callie fought off her medicated grogginess with a long, hot shower, stopping only when the building's industrial-size water heater finally began running lukewarm.

Sherry Ann had already gone off to class, leaving Callie to deal with a growling stomach. She promised herself a grocery expedition as soon as humanly possible then almost miraculously discovered a leftover slice of pepperoni pizza suffering from frostbite in the freezer.

Sitting at the counter over the microwaved slice, a mug of coffee and her laptop, she did her best to bat away the cobwebs. It was surprising how wide-awake a person could be in the middle of the night and yet so foggy the next morning. She went to plug in her machine and found the outlet occupied by

n the University District, even

allie left him in Sarah's care
t stop was Sherry Ann's
r for Callie to borrow
counter just yester-
e explained that
uilding's front
vestigation
rry Ann.
, like
d dan-
up the nerve
pful 19-year-old
flip-phone. He asked
she said she didn't honestly
eight gigabytes of talk and text.
meone, will this number show up?"

t your name won't, and it's almost impossible
e number back to you." Henry eyed her curiously.
doing something on Craigslist? Or is this some kind of
boyfriend thing?" Callie smiled but didn't answer.

She was still in the parking lot of the strip mall when
she tested it with a call to Will. "Hello?" His voice sounded
tentative and a little annoyed, as if he were expecting her to
be a telemarketer.

"Hey, Will? It's Heather."

His voice brightened. "Heather! What a surprise! So,
you're finally giving me your number. I'm honored."

— right arm up, bent at the elbow (not touching the pillowcase edge), left arm bent and down, right knee up, left leg down and slightly bent. None of the limbs can touch the body; the tactile sensation makes her too aware. Of everything. Okay, now for the covers. They're bunching around her feet, so she awkwardly tries to kick them into place. Then she gets out of bed to adjust them.

Then the pillows are off again.

There are some nights like this when she feels like she's reinventing sleep, analyzing every aspect, her mind obsessed with each detail. She thinks of the Princess and the Pea and tries to figure out how many figurative peas are under her mattress and pillows and limbs and brain. Should she get up and take another Ambien? How about a Xanax, which she takes for the anxiety caused by the Ambien not working, which is pretty much every night? And how many of each does she have in the pill bottles? Long ago she learned not to count her pills at night. No matter how many left or how many refills are listed on the bottle, she only

nervous and more alert when she counts.

She knows there aren't that many. Her la...

Dr. Faber was three months ago when
sessions where they sat in matchin...
talk about the same things: S...
ask for a new prescripti...
world of apology. ...
his lectures o...
Oppenh...
H...

"As you should be."

They chatted for a few minutes and reconfirmed their dinner tomorrow at Dante's. Will was not looking forward to his date night with Maggie and wished that he could spend the evening with Callie instead. Callie told him that he should keep an open mind and give it another chance.

*

The next morning, Callie got in early to go over the metro layout with Bob, the paper's graphic designer, then went straight into a staff meeting. Oliver wasn't fond of staff meetings and liked to keep them short. It was one of the few things he and Callie agreed on these days. Minutes after the meeting ended, Sarah texted her, asking her to come home. Nothing urgent, but please come home. Because of the fire and her father's condition, everyone at work was cutting her slack and not asking too many questions.

Sarah was just putting on her hat when Callie pushed open the front door. "Just in time," Sarah said, even though they both knew she would have waited. "I need to do some shopping for dinner and I didn't want to leave Mr. Buddy by himself."

"Is he okay?"

Sarah cocked her head and stared over her half glasses.

"We'll talk about this later."

"Oh, Sarah, please. I can explain."

Sarah rechecked her reflection in the mirror then crossed behind Callie and out the door. "He's in the kitchen."

Callie took a long moment, which somehow reminded her to plug both of her phones into the charger on the entryway table. When she walked into the kitchen, she found her father in the process of pushing the retro, Formica-topped table over toward the bay window. "What's wrong with this place?" he grunted as he pushed. "Why does your mother always have to change things? The door used to be over there. What was wrong with the door?"

"It's a different house, Daddy." Callie pulled him gently away. "Mom's redecorating the main house, remember? This is the gatehouse." She was probably doing it all wrong, making up a story to explain whatever confusion his mind was going through at that moment, a story that would cause the least upheaval and that he would quickly forget. If some doctor knew of a better way of dealing with it, she'd be glad to listen.

"Oh, yeah," he said, obviously embarrassed. "Why the hell didn't Sarah say that? Redecorating. I forgot."

"You have more important things to think about."

"I thought for sure…" Buddy looked around. "Some of this furniture I remember from the other house."

"It was in the other house."

"Darlin', darlin'". He grabbed her by the shoulder and shook his head. "Why do I get so confused? My mind was never fuzzy like this. It's not right."

"Why don't you sit down and read the paper? I'll get you the paper, okay?"

Buddy let himself be led to a plush couch in the living room. His breathing slowed. "You want some tea, darlin'?" he asked as he settled into the cushions. "English breakfast tea with a little cream?"

Callie smiled. "I'll get you some tea."

"Just a little cream, no sugar," he called out as she left the room. "You're my favorite, you know."

"I know."

She made the tea just as ordered and delivered it in one of her mother's china cups. A copy of the *American-Statesman* was in the magazine rack. It was yesterday's, but in his current state it didn't matter. "Just relax and read the paper," she said then kissed him on the forehead and went out to get some air.

The day had turned into a prelude to summer, with the humidity shooting into the uncomfortable range. It was second nature for her now to start walking up to the main house whenever she stepped outside. This time, as she walked, she saw the fire marshal's red and white SUV parked by the charred remains of the door. The marshal emerged from the house just as Callie came within hailing distance. "Ms. McFee. How y'all doing? Your daddy got everything he needs?"

"He's fine, thank you." Callie reminded herself to keep an eye open, just in case the marshal decided to stop on his way out and pay a visit to the great man. "Is there something I can help you with?"

"No, no." He was holding a clipboard and now rested it on his sizable stomach. "The arson squad finished their report. Just thought I'd check it before filing."

"Their report?" Callie tensed. "Was it arson?"

"Undetermined," the chief drawled, rebalancing the clipboard as he searched for the right paragraph. "Not electrical," he summarized. "No accelerant detected. The hot spot was between the desk and the file cabinets, in the vicinity of the wastebasket." He flipped a page. "This doesn't rule out arson. But if it was, it was very good, a professional job."

"How could it be accidental?" She reached out for the clipboard, but he ignored the silent request. "It was in an empty room that hadn't been used in maybe fifteen minutes. If the fire wasn't electrical…"

"That's why it says 'undetermined'. Their job is to look at the physical evidence, not grab at one conclusion or the other." He removed the clipboard from its perch and flipped the page back. "You'll be glad to know we're releasing the site. The officer's coming off your front gate, so it won't look like you're living in a crime scene. Gil and your daddy can get their insurance people in here and whatnot. I know they got a small army wanting to start repairs."

"That's good," she said, forcing a smile. "Thank you."

"You're most welcome. It was good seeing you, Ms. McFee." He checked his watch and began waddling toward his SUV. "Got go meet with the attorney general right now. Can't be late."

For a second, she thought he meant her father. "Oh. Felix Gibson."

He laughed. "I guess I'm dealing with two of them, huh? How do you say that? Attorneys general? Mr. Gibson is very interested in this case, no doubt 'cause it involves an old friend. He wants to review everything before the report goes out."

She watched the marshal drive off then walked through the blackened doorframe. The remains of the French parquet floor, the one her mother loved so much, would soon be torn out. Callie's choice for its replacement would probably be a dark mahogany. It would match the rest of the house much better than Anita McFee's choice, but it wouldn't be the same.

The guard, in a folding chair by the winding staircase,

didn't notice her until she was halfway through the entry hall. "Excuse me?" he said, looking up from his phone. The name on his tag announced J. Durban while the patch on his sleeve said Eagle Security. The man himself – thirtyish, overweight, seemingly devoid of energy – was armed with a black handgun in a side holster, half-hidden by his paunch. Callie wondered how long he'd had this job and if he'd actually ever used the gun nestled under his layer of fat.

Callie introduced herself, adding that she was Buddy McFee's daughter and was living with him in the gatehouse. "The guy who owns this place, right?" said J. Durban. She found his clueless response oddly liberating.

"Right," she said. "And you are . . ."

He pointed to his nametag. "Jeremy."

"Well, Jeremy, the fire department has released the house, so I'm just going to take a look around."

"Does that mean I can leave? Job over?"

"No. First of all, you can't walk off because some woman comes up and says so. That's not exactly security."

"Sorry," Jeremy stammered. "This is my first assignment."

"No problem. But you wait till your boss tells you. Your company's being paid by Gil Morales. Gil's in the hospital, but I'll ask him next time I have the chance. My guess is he'll want it guarded until he can get a security system installed. Until then, your orders are to keep everyone out." Then, in direct defiance of what she'd just said, Callie walked from the front hall back into the rest of the house. Jeremy didn't try to stop her.

The odor of wet charcoal permeated the lower story. Would it go away, or would it always be there, the faintest of scents lingering under every other scent? It was disconcerting to be in a place so familiar, the only real home she'd ever known, and yet have it be so different. Even in her darkest days, when she and her father had lost contact and she was in a claustrophobic one-bedroom in Dallas, the ranch had been there, comforting and full of memories, six generations full. And yet, like all material things, it was impermanent, something that would be sold some day, or fall into ruin. Or burn to the ground. This had been an incomprehensible possibility, right up to the day it almost happened.

After making a slow circuit of the main floor, she emerged back in the hall and waved good-bye to Jeremy. He was back on his phone and didn't see her leave.

The unmoving, muggy air enveloped her as soon as she stepped outside. At the end of the corridor of live oaks, by the gatehouse, stood a black limousine, the kind her father had once used, its black-suited driver lounging against the passenger side door. Next to the limousine was the fire marshal's red and white SUV. What was it the chief had told her right before driving away? That he was going off to meet the attorney general? Not Buddy, of course, but the current one, Felix Gibson - although he did make some joke about dealing with both attorneys general, she recalled.

Oh, shit!

Callie began to run. Her pace slowed to a brisk walk only when the driver looked up and saw her. "Hi," she shouted from a distance. She'd never realized how hard it was to appear nonchalant when you're shouting and race-walking. "Hi," she said again, combining it with an open-mouthed smile. "I'm Buddy McFee's daughter. Sorry I'm late. Where are they, the living room? Mr. Gibson told me to come…"

The driver raised a hand, his face expressionless. With his other hand, he took a police-style communicator from his belt and spoke a few soft sentences into it. Callie recognized the breed, a driver/bodyguard, the same macho, intimidating type that had attended her father for so many years. He lowered the communicator and deigned to speak. "It's a private meeting. You'll have to wait out here."

"I'll do no such thing. This is my house."

"I wouldn't know about that. I have my orders."

"I don't care about your orders. You can't keep me out of my own house."

The driver took a few steps, placing himself firmly between Callie and the front stoop. "It's a private meeting, Miss. The fire chief and the attorney general and Mr. McFee." His mouth turned up into a slight, totally fake smile. "You'll just have to talk to me."

"Sounds lovely, but I don't know you. I do know Felix Gibson, however."

"Ma'am…" He had progressed from Miss to Ma'am, not a good sign. "I'm going to have to ask you to step back from the door."

Callie had a decision to make – to push things, make a scene and further arouse whatever suspicions Felix Gibson may already have; or to let it go and deal with the aftermath. She decided to let it go.

She was still pacing the driveway when the front door opened and the fire marshal walked out, clipboard tucked under his arm. "Ms. McFee, good luck with the repairs. And don't forget new smoke detectors, ones with fresh batteries this time."

"Is the meeting over?" Callie asked.

"All over. Have a good one," he said and headed for his red and white SUV.

"Calista, long time. How are ya'?" Felix Gibson stood in the middle of the living room, motioning her to come inside. Felix was State's godfather and had been a ranch regular, always ready to laugh at Buddy's jokes, to whisper in his ear and be part of whatever backroom deals were in the works. Gil had never been a Felix fan. Callie thought it was because the men were too much alike. Both were political animals. The difference was that Gil proved to actually have loyalty, which had probably been his downfall. Felix had gone on to be lieutenant governor and was now attorney general, a much more powerful position. Gil could have left the McFee employ at any time, even after the scandal. He'd had offers. But he stayed by Buddy's side.

Felix was about the same size and build as Gil, but clean shaven and of Scottish descent. "Tim, my boy, let the girl in. Don't tell me you've been keeping her out here."

"Sir?"

"Me and Calista are old friends. Come in, come in."

Callie didn't gloat, just stepped over the threshold and looked around. Three half-empty glasses of lemonade sat on leather coasters on the coffee table. "Where's Dad?"

"Little boy's room." Felix waited until Tim the driver had left and closed the door. "The marshal told me he was doing his sign-off. Thought I might as well drop by. Your daddy seems none the worse for wear."

"The whole experience was very hard on him," Callie said, hoping to explain away whatever Buddy might have said or done.

"I can see," Felix said. "He likes talking about the past, things I barely remember. I guess we all do when we hit a certain stage in life."

"Like I said, it hit him hard." Callie put on her good hostess face. "It was so sweet of you to come."

"Nonsense. We've been through a lot, me and your daddy. You know, I was up at the house the night before the fire, in that very same room."

"That's what Uncle Gil says."

"I'll bet we brokered more deals there than in the State Capital. Boy, if those walls could talk…"

"Well, they're not going to talk any more, are they?"

If Felix understood her innuendo, he didn't let on. "Ah, it'll look as good as new. Just you wait. Do you mind if I go up and take a look? Marshal Regan showed me pictures, but…" His smile broadened. "Do you mind?"

Why does he want to see it? she asked herself. *To see if Buddy's files were all in cinders and ash?* "Of course I don't mind."

"What doesn't she mind?" It was Buddy, just exiting the powder room and zipping up his fly.

"Us going up and taking a look at the house."

"In the midst of the redecoration? I wouldn't mind that myself, though I gotta warn you. It may not be looking its best."

"Redecoration," Felix cackled. "I love it."

"No, Dad. You stay here and rest." She had no idea how Buddy would react to it in his current state of mind. "I'll take Mr. Gibson up."

"No, I want to see the redecorating."

"But you promised you would wait."

"I did?"

It took a little persuading, but Buddy gave in and Callie got her way. She and Felix walked up the shady drive and did the tour by themselves.

That evening on the phone – her real phone, not the burner – Callie informed Gil of what had happened. He seemed low-key but attentive, undoubtedly still in pain.

"You did the right thing. I'm proud of you. Having Lawrence go up to the house could have been a disaster. Do you think Felix suspects?"

Callie had spent hours thinking about this. "Dad was in a mood, so he has to suspect something. Whether or not he attributes it to old age or the shock of the fire or exhaustion, I'm not sure."

"Did Felix go into the study?"

"He did," she confirmed. "He pretended not to stare at the wall where the file cabinets used to be, but he definitely did."

"Well, that's understandable. I would have stared, too."

"Is Dad in danger?" It made her nervous to even ask.

Gil's tone was reassuring. "No, not at all. Felix is a sly, vindictive son-of-a-bitch, but if he set that fire, he's probably feeling pretty safe for now. I think we're okay with him."

"That's good to hear." The new topic of safety and danger had just reminded her. "Oh, the fire marshal is through with the house, so there's no more officer at the front. The guy from Eagle Security wants to know if you'll still be needing them."

"Good God, yes." His voice erupted into a painful cough. "Yes," he finally managed to add. "I'll give Eagle a call. We should add a perimeter walk to his schedule, too. Thanks for telling me."

"I thought you said we were okay."

"Oh, honey, there are many different kinds of okay. You know that as well as I do."

CHAPTER 25

"My brother says this is just another form of prostitution." She didn't know why she mentioned this. But she had consumed most of the bottle of Chardonnay with only a shrimp Caesar salad to absorb it and felt, in her foggy, happy state, that such an admission might seem authentic.

The evening was warm and moist with barely a rustle of air. A full moon illuminated their way as Callie and Will walked hand in hand, a little boat of calm passing through the waves of rowdy college kids. "You told your brother about us?"

"Not us in particular," Callie said quickly. "But we discussed the general topic. He's a good sounding board."

"And he disapproves?" She didn't need to answer. "I never thought of it as that," Will said. "My first sugar baby – God, there has to be a better term – it started as a sexual transaction, I guess. First time for both of us. We were just feeling our way. Then we got to know each other and, I think, care for each other. Not in any permanent way. Just two people sharing what they had. The money wasn't much, from my point of view, and I got to be a part of her life. Listen to her hopes and dreams. Watch her eyes light up when I gave her something." His chuckle was soft and sad. "Makes me sound pretty pitiful, doesn't it?"

"No, not at all." She shook her head and felt the ponytail wave between her shoulders. It was part of her Heather persona but she actually liked it. Maybe she would keep it. "We all need certain things at certain times. In a way, I guess that is transactional."

"And is this something you need now?" Will asked. "Or something you want?"

It wasn't what Callie wanted at all. But she felt herself envying the mythical Heather who might have embarked on a little adventure of being spoiled and having an older, wiser, very attractive mentor. As for her investigation, it really wasn't one, she had to admit, more like an excuse to have a couple of great dates and discuss some alternate universe where he would put money into her account every month and spoil her rotten. And the sex. Who knew what the sex would be like?

Will, she remembered, might still be a killer. But what would drive him to kill someone he barely knew? Did they have a fight? Had Briana threatened to tell his wife? Briana had never threatened to tell Sam Paget's wife. And how would she even contact the wife? Callie had gone on two dates with Will, just like Briana, and she had no idea if Will Peterson was even his real name. Asking to see a driver's license is not something she usually did on a date.

When she didn't answer the question, Will rephrased it as a statement. "I would love to take care of you, Heather. But we're both going to need more than great dinners. I know you're hesitant. That's obvious."

They had just arrived at Sherry Ann's building. This time she found her set of keys without a problem. "You're right. I should jump at this. It's everything I imagined it would be. You're a terrific guy."

"Uh-oh." Will combed a hand back through his hair. "Not sounding good."

"Give me a night to think it over."

"I can get you the money tomorrow. Then we can go about renting that new apartment."

Callie was surprised. "So soon?"

"I want to prove I'm serious. I already checked with the rental agent in this building."

"You did?"

"It was one quick phone call. There's a great one-bedroom on the top floor. Monthly rental. Fully furnished. You can move in tomorrow."

"Tomorrow?" She had to laugh. "What if it doesn't work out?"

"Then I'm out a few grand, and you have an apartment for a month. But I'm betting it works out. I'm betting on us." He waited for an answer and when it didn't come, he turned serious. "It's an arrangement, Heather. If you don't want an arrangement, you shouldn't have signed up."

"No, it's not that."

"Then why wait? Just text me your bank info and the money will be in your account – first, last and security. Then we can celebrate." He reached over and pulled her in close. "I could really use some celebrating, if you know what I mean."

"You've been very patient," she said in a flirty voice that she didn't realize she had. "We'll talk tomorrow."

"I take it your roommate is in tonight?" he whispered in her ear. Callie nodded. "Damn, that girl needs to get out more."

They parted with a kiss, not as long or as passionate as their first, but definitely in the same ball park. Callie knew it would be their last. Between the alcohol and Will's reluctance to talk about his life, she had managed to extract nothing new. So, unless she was serious about becoming a sugar baby...

This time she didn't get into the elevator. She found a corner of the chrome and leather lobby and punched in her brother's number before she could change her mind. "State, don't yell at me." She tried not to slur her words.

A TV was playing in the background. "Callie? Okay, but I reserve the right to yell at you later. What have you done?"

"I have someone for you to interview. You're much better at it than I am."

"Thank you. It's my job. Now what am I going to yell at you about?"

"I'm dating Briana's second sugar daddy. Hold on, it's not as bad as it sounds. Well, maybe it is."

"Mother of God." She could hear the TV fade as State walked into another room. "Tell me."

Callie started to pace the open, airy lobby and tell the story from the beginning, how she had gotten into Briana's laptop and recognized the wording from one of her sugar daddy contacts. "It was the same guy who contacted me, but with a different handle and photo."

"And you know he dated Briana?"

"No," she admitted. "Their communication went private. But the timing's right. And he told me he had two dates with a girl and then she disappeared. Just like Briana disappeared."

"Callie!" He sounded just like their father. "What the hell are you doing dating a suspect?"

"He's not a suspect. Well, I guess it could go either way."

"Did you put out?"

"What? Jeez." She was incensed. "You don't get to ask me that question. No."

"Good. Well, he's definitely worth talking to. Do you have his contact information?"

"Probably not his real information. He has this wife he needs to keep things from."

"Well, you need to stay in touch. Make plans to see him tomorrow."

"We more or less have plans," Callie said. "He wants to rent an apartment for me. Well, technically, I'll be renting it. He wants to put the money into my account. We haven't settled on how much, but he seems pretty rich."

"Putting…" State paused. "Callie, how is he putting money into your account?"

"Well, he asked me for my bank info, so…" It was her turn to pause. "Oh, shit!"

"He asked for your account information."

Callie felt she had to sit down. "Shit. Is that all he needs?"

"Well, he also needs your bank passcode."

"What are you, nuts? I'm not sending him my passcode."

"Maybe not. But you're not a naïve twenty-one-year-old desperate for a sugar daddy."

"Like Briana," Callie said, her voice flat.

"Exactly like Briana," State confirmed. "I'm betting your guy's a scam artist. All this daddy stuff is just his way of stealing from young women."

"No," Callie said but meant yes. She was both incensed and disappointed. Will, she suddenly knew, had never really been interested in her. That was the part that hurt. "I can't believe it. He is so not the type."

"He sounds exactly the type. My guess is he'll get you to text him your routing number and the passcode, and you'll never hear from Mr. Sugar Daddy again. Remember Dylan Dane?"

Callie had nearly forgotten. "You think he's Dylan Dane? Do you have the surveillance photo from the bank?"

"It's on my phone," said State. "Hold on. I'll send it to you."

"If you'd given me the pic days ago when I asked you to, I wouldn't be in this mess." Her claim didn't make sense, but she didn't care.

"Here it is," he said. Two seconds later and her phone dinged with the text.

Callie enlarged it as much as she could. It was what she'd expected: a high-angle shot over the teller's window, black and white, grainy, showing a large man with a wide-brimmed trucker cap that shielded his eyes. The mustache was a distraction, as State had said. But there was something about his bearing – a tilt of the shoulders, the long angle at the nape of his neck. And then the hair, just visible enough, dark and curling over his ears.

"It's him," she said, absolutely sure of it. "That bastard."

"What's the matter? Your pride hurt? You thought you had this sugar baby soul connection? Is he cute? I bet you he's cute."

"Shut up."

"A cute guy buys you dinner, pays some attention. That's all it takes."

"Shut up. I have what's left of Mom's money in that account. Almost thirty thousand. Goddamn bastard."

"Okay, Cal, fun's over. I'm sorry I teased you. Honestly." State's tone helped her to focus. "This guy of yours. Do you have anyway of ID-ing him?"

"His name has to be fake. I'll bet you he's not even married."

"Ooh, the bastard."

"All I have is his cell number."

"That's not going to help. Any pictures?"

"No. I doubt he would've let me take any if I'd tried."

"How did he pay for dinner?" State asked.

"He paid cash."

"Well, we can't lose track of him. Can you get him to meet you again?"

"We're supposed to rent that apartment tomorrow."

"Well, that's not going to happen." Callie could make out some noise in the background. "It's Callie," he shouted. "Jeez, Yolanda, I'll be back in a minute." State reverted to his normal voice. "Sorry about that. She hates it when I interrupt her shows. Look, call this dirtbag in the morning. Or text him if you think you'll be too nervous. Say you need to meet again."

"He'll keep pushing for my account info."

"Well, if worse comes to worst, give it to him."

"What? Did you just say...? I'm not giving him thirty thousand."

"Hey, he won't get away with it. He can transfer the money somewhere else, but If he wants it in cash, then he has to show up in person, like he did at Briana's branch. We'll alert your bank. They'll keep track of it."

Callie got up again and continued pacing. The lobby was empty, illuminated as much by the moonlight as by the artfully placed table lamps. "You think he killed her, don't you?"

"It's looking good, yes. The guy has a sugar daddy scam. He took Briana's money. Those are our facts. I'm figuring she tracked him down. There could be dozens of other victims out there. He'd be facing serious jail time unless he got rid of her. The rape also makes sense in this context." Callie didn't answer, not that he'd asked her a question. "Are you all right?"

"Yeah, I'm fine." Her voice was shaking. "I suppose I should be happy or relieved or something."

"But you're nervous," State said. "That's because you just had a date with her killer and he's still out there. Where are you now?"

"I'm in the lobby of Briana's building. It's a long story."

"Well, get back home. Have you had a few drinks?"

"No more than usual." Well, a few more than usual.

"Do you want me to pick you up?"

"No, I'm fine. Really."

"Don't call him tonight, okay? You don't want to spook him. Text him in the morning. Ask for a meeting. If he's skittish, then apologize and send him your bank info. Don't worry. You won't lose it. Are you sure you're okay to drive?"

"I'm fine," she repeated. "Thanks, State. You're a good brother."

"No problem. Drive safe."

Callie had found a parking spot directly across from the apartment building and once she got out of the University district, traffic was light. Sarah was still at the gatehouse, like a babysitter waiting for parents who'd stayed at party too long. "He had a good dinner, watched a little TV and went to bed," Sarah said. "I checked on him just a minute ago. Sound asleep and snoring up a storm."

Callie thanked her profusely. She wanted to say that Sarah could come in late tomorrow but stopped herself. She had no idea what tomorrow's schedule would be like.

They said their goodbyes and Sarah drove off, leaving Callie to plop herself into the roomy armchair by the window, Buddy's chair, open her laptop on the side table and play a few games. An hour or so of spider solitaire would help calm her down. After that would be her pill regimen and bedtime and the sleep that wouldn't come. Not tonight. When a car pulled up a minute or later, she didn't think twice. Sarah must have forgotten something.

Callie was still in the armchair when the front door swung open.

CHAPTER 26

THE MAN WHO called himself Will Peterson loomed in the open doorway. "What do you want from me?" His arms were straight down his sides, his fists balled.

"What do I want from you?" Callie repeated before she could even process the moment. Her brain raced to fit the pieces together. "You saw me in the lobby, on my phone." How ridiculously stupid of her, to be talking to State in full view of the street. "You saw that I was upset and you were curious. Maybe concerned. That's understandable. Sweet of you. I guess you were in your car when you passed by and saw me. Otherwise, you wouldn't have been able to follow me."

As she talked, a plausible story was forming. She, Heather, had been on the phone to a sick friend who was living here. Heather was worried enough to go visit her friend right away. If Will didn't believe her, they could always tiptoe up the stairs and peek in on Buddy, her sick friend, now asleep. An uncle perhaps, not a friend. Yes, that would be better.

"You're Callie McFee," Will said.

"Um, excuse me?" How on earth could he have known?

She was stunned. She was also grateful that she hadn't blurted out her first story.

He held up his phone and wagged it. "I Googled this location. Buddy McFee. It's a famous house. Like something from *Gone with the Wind*."

"Yes, but that doesn't mean…"

"A lot of articles came up. Your picture came up."

"Okay, okay. I'm not a twenty-one-year-old student." Callie got up slowly from the armchair and pushed aside her laptop. "Sorry. And I don't live in an apartment. I live here." She didn't start out being afraid, but now she was. She just couldn't let it show.

"You're a TV reporter. That's what they said."

"That's an old article. But yes, I'm a reporter." Another story was forming. "I'm doing a newspaper article on the sugar baby scene in Austin," she explained. "My editor asked me to go undercover, to see firsthand how sugaring worked. He thought it would be a good angle."

"Good angle? What does that mean? You were just playing with me? Were you recording what I said?"

"No, I promise you I wasn't. No recording. No photos."

"Were you going to take my money?"

Take your money? You bastard. You were trying to take mine. She tried to keep her thoughts out of her expression. "No. It was just the two dates. And I'm changing your name in the article. I was going to tell you tonight, but I had a little too much wine."

Will shook his head. "I knew something was up."

"Look, I can reimburse you for the dinners. My paper can. The *Austin Free Press*."

For the first time since walking in, Will unclenched his fists. The lines between his brows relaxed, and Callie noted how, with the slightest change, the same face that had seemed romantic and masculine could seem threatening and cold.

"I can't believe I invested all this time and energy. I mean, you seemed so perfect."

"You seem perfect, too. And I know you're disappointed. I'm sorry."

"You can't use my picture, or anything else that identifies me."

"Agreed." Her goal now was to keep herself safe. "Will, it's kind of late and I've had a few." She made a guilty face. "Can we please meet tomorrow? I can buy you lunch and you can tell me about the experience from a daddy's perspective, for the article. Again, no names or pictures or recordings."

Will hesitated. He rubbed his chin. "I'm not sure that's something I want to do."

"Why not?"

"It's a waste of time. You wasted enough of my time."

"It's lunch. You have to have lunch. I'll meet you anywhere you like." She softened her voice. "Your wife will never be able to identify you, I promise. We had two great dinners. I think people would want to hear your point of view."

"No. I have to think this over." His hand went from his chin toward his jacket, as if reaching for his car keys.

"Okay, think it over. I'll call you in the morning." But she knew it wouldn't happen. Tomorrow's lunch would never take place.

Callie looked out one of the tall front windows. A gray, stylish sedan was parked right behind her truck. Maybe… As he walked out of the house, maybe she could turn on the front lights, a polite gesture, then take a photo of his license plate as he drove off. That would do it. Now where had she left her phone? Probably on the side table, beside her laptop.

Will was standing by the side table, staring down at her laptop. "I'm sorry, Will, for misleading you, I am. If we had met under regular circumstances, just two people…"

"What are you doing with her photo?" His voice was soft but intense.

Callie knew immediately and her blood ran cold. It was that photo, stubbornly clinging to the lower right corner of her machine. Bri's inspiration.

"It's Briana Crawley," she said. Up until this moment, Callie hadn't known for sure. But his reaction told her everything. She took a deep breath. "The girl you raped and murdered."

Will turned to face her, his body clenching again. "Who are you?"

"Like I said, a reporter. I'm investigating her murder."

"Are you with the police? How did you find me?"

"I'm not sure that's important."

He repeated himself, shouting the words. "HOW DID YOU FIND ME?"

"I didn't find you," she reminded him. "You found me."

"HOW?" he bellowed.

She stumbled back, as if pushed. "I went on the website, putting myself in Bri's situation. The phrases you used for her were the same ones you used for me. 'Meet-and-eat.' 'High-end restaurant of my choosing'."

"Phrases, huh?" He winced. "I guess I was sloppy."

"And then there's the security footage of Dylan Dane

at her bank. I recognized your hair. Your neck. Your way of standing."

"You know about the bank?"

"I do." She didn't know which would be better, to tell him that her brother the cop also knew, or to let him think that she'd been acting alone. "The police are…"

"Callie!"

It was Buddy's voice, coming from the top of the stairs. He sounded half asleep but fully annoyed. "What the hell's the racket? What's wrong?"

"Go back in your room and lock it," she shouted. "Call 9-1-1. Home invasion." And then a sharp pain shot through the left-rear part of her skull.

CHAPTER 27

CALLIE WOKE UP slowly. At first, she thought she'd been unconscious for a split-second, just long enough to fall to the floor, her face tilted sideways. A strangely mangled object, black, was in her direct line of vision and it took her several seconds to recognize it, her laptop, nearly broken at the hinges, the monitor twisted open. Something wet was streaming down her face and the back of her head. She assumed it was her own blood and decided against using her tongue to confirm this.

Will, his shoulders and back looking huge in his blue blazer, was in a corner by the TV, busy with something. Callie wasn't conscious enough to be afraid, just in pain and calmly fascinated. When Will finally stood and moved aside, she could see her father sprawled on the floor in his white, half-open bathrobe. His eyes were closed and there was a gash across his head, too, running from just above one eye up to his hairline. She focused and tried to see if he was moving. His hands were tied, she saw next, tightly bound across his stomach with the sash from the bathrobe. His feet were bound with something else. She instinctively knew this was good.

Why was it good? Oh, yes. It meant he was alive. People don't tie you up when you're dead. She kept staring until everything faded once more to black.

The next time she opened her eyes, Buddy was still there, still in the same position, still unmoving. She thought she could see his chest rise and fall, but she wasn't sure.

"I know you're awake." Callie didn't respond. "If you don't say something, I'm going to come over there and kick you in the ribs."

"I'm awake," she managed to mumble.

"Good. I just don't want you to think you're fooling me."

When she finally got up the strength to fight the pain and turn her head, she saw the man who called himself Will in the armchair, casually examining his phone. "Hello, sunshine," he said. "Be with you in a sec. Just working out my plan."

"Plan for what? Escaping?" Callie didn't feel like being antagonistic right now, but she had to stay on the offensive. It was a Buddy strategy. Always play strong. "You're not very good at escaping. I managed to track you down. Bri managed to track you down."

Will shrugged. "That was bound to happen, I guess, dealing with university girls. You hang around the same part of town and one of them's bound to see you on a street corner or in a bar with another babe. Lesson learned. Time for a move, anyway."

"You're moving? To do what? Steal money from more girls?"

"Makes a pretty good living," he said without the least hint of shame.

"Until you get caught. Is that what happened? Bri saw you on the street?"

"Total fluke. I was heading to a new meet-and-eat. Sweet little Asian girl. Very eager. Dinner at Mikimoto. I like that place 'cause their security cameras are shit. Anyway, just got out of my car, a block or two from the restaurant. Briana happened to be right there. Started shouting at me, taking pics of my license plate. Then she took pics of me. It was just luck on her part, bad luck, taking a shortcut from somewhere to somewhere. One of those alleys behind the stores where you sometimes find parking spots between the Dumpsters."

"And that's why you killed her?" Callie was incensed. "You could have just taken her phone and driven off."

He smirked. "How many numbers are on a license plate? Seven? Even a college girl can memorize seven numbers."

Callie turned her head, then painfully pushed herself to a half-seated position. She couldn't look at him. How could this be the same man? Will must have sensed her disgust.

"C'mon, Heather – Callie," he corrected himself. "I'm not a monster. I tried to talk sense. I told her the bank withdrawal was a mistake. I'd been preoccupied with business and didn't even notice. One of my assistants must have got into the wrong account and pressed the wrong key. I could fix it tomorrow morning, I said. You know me, I can be persuasive."

"But she didn't believe you."

"She'd figured it was a scam, so I had to change gears. Okay. I told her, yes, I'd stolen her damned money, but I'd give it back if she didn't go to the police. I'd do it right then. I told her I had enough cash at my place, which I didn't. I wouldn't have given it back anyway." Will sighed, as if it had all been Briana's fault. "She was stupid enough to get in my car."

Callie could visualize a desperate college girl, desperate

and trusting, wanting to believe that this last promise might solve everything. She might never have to tell her parents or the police or anyone else. "How did you do it?"

"You know how. I choked the bitch to death."

He had meant it to shock, perhaps to scare. "And then what did you do?" Callie asked. "With her body? Did you have an accomplice? A friend? Where did you take her body?" Even now, she was trying to reconcile his confession with Keagan Blackburn's actions.

Will looked up from his phone and smiled. It was the same bright, crooked smile that used to fascinate her. "You ask very stupid questions. Enough questions."

"The police know," Callie blurted out. It was the only way she could think of to stay on the offensive. "When I was in the lobby, that's who I was talking to. They know all about you."

Will took the news seriously. Then he smiled. "What do they know? Some good-looking guy named Will? I assume you told them I was good-looking. As for actual witnesses, ones who can describe me to a sketch artist or pick me out of a line-up…" With that, he opened his arms in opposite directions, one toward Callie and one toward her father in the corner by the TV.

Buddy was just beginning to move, groaning and pulling weakly at the bathrobe sash binding up his wrists. Callie's heart went cold. "You can't kill him. That's Buddy McFee."

"I know," Will said, pointing to his phone. "Very impressive resume."

"All of Texas law enforcement will be after you."

"Well, they'll be after someone." He scrolled down his screen. "Your dad has a lot of powerful friends – and enemies.

I was just looking at some out-there website. It claims the fire at the house had to be some kind of revenge, maybe a murder attempt. One of Buddy McFee's foes from days gone by. Can you believe that? Well, it gave me an idea. One more visit from Buddy's enemies. Of course, there'll be a little collateral damage." He looked up from his screen and winked.

"It's not going to work," Callie said. "The police know about you. They'll know it was you." She was sitting up now, her back pressed against the side of a chair.

"How could it be me? I don't know who Callie McFee is. Even if they manage to find me, which they won't, so what? I had two sugar daddy dates with a girl from the University district who told me her name was Heather." His eyes darted around the living room. "You don't happen to have a gun I can borrow? Buddy McFee must have guns."

"Up at the main house," Callie said, "under lock and key." Up at the main house, she repeated to herself, where there's an armed security guard.

"Do you happen to know where the key is?"

Callie pretended to be frightened by the idea.

Will brightened at her reaction but then glanced from Callie to Buddy and back and changed his mind. "Nah, better keep it simple. Blunt instrument, something I can wipe the prints off."

Callie now focused her thoughts on the main house. Could she get through this door and outrun Will up to the house? If she shouted as she stumbled away, would the guard hear her from wherever he was right now? Asleep in a folding chair or roaming the grounds? Or could she get just as far as her car and then drive there, honking all the way? The keys were in the bowl by the door, where she always dropped them as soon as she walked in.

Will was up from the armchair, scanning the room for the perfect blunt instrument. He didn't seem to notice that Buddy's eyes were open – not hazy or dazed, but alert. *How long had he been awake and alert?* she wondered. Their eyes met, father's and daughter's. Callie looked to the bowl by the door and Buddy nodded, a slight, painful nod. Do something, he seemed to be saying. Do something. But the throbbing in her head made any movement seem an impossibility.

And then Buddy did something.

Will's search had brought him to the hearth. At some point, someone – probably Callie's mother – had made a design choice and installed a useless fireplace stand by the gas fireplace, complete with a poker and a shovel for the non-existent coals. Will saw the poker and grinned. He had just crossed the room to get it, passing by the TV, reaching down, when Buddy extended his legs and pushed himself, groaning loudly with the effort. He rolled just far enough to hit the back of Will's legs. The shock, Buddy's surprising groan and the impact sent Will tumbling.

Callie had seen it coming, had seen her father tense his body and move his arms and prepare himself for the roll. Three seconds later, with Will still on the floor, she had snatched the car keys and was out the door, heading for her truck in the driveway.

She fumbled with the fob and was rewarded with the clear, single beep from the driver's door. Ignoring the clumsy, heavy footfalls behind her, concentrating on the silver door handle, Callie reached out. A split-second later he was there, grabbing her by the arm and spinning her around. Callie fell back against the door and he loomed in front of her, pressing against her, as close as a lover.

In an instant, his hands were up and around her throat. When they tightened, the pain was intense. Callie grabbed at his wrists, but very quickly became light-headed, hungry for air. And then, for no reason, he let go. With the wind knocked out of her and her head still pounding, she slid to the ground, on her back, gasping.

Will stood over her now. Even if she could get up, he would be blocking any escape. "I have to say I'm disappointed in you," he purred. "Abandoning your dad? I wasn't quite prepared for that."

Callie tried to maintain eye contact, to carry on a conversation not built on screams or pleas, to not look like a victim. "You're after me," she rasped. "You're not after him."

"True," he admitted. "You're the bigger threat. I doubt he got much of a look at me. Still, abandoning your dad. That's cold."

Callie opened her mouth to shout for help, but between the trauma to her windpipe and the lack of air, nothing emerged but a moan.

He smiled at her effort then looked puzzled. "Is there someone nearby?" He glanced around in the semi-darkness, illuminated by a bright moon in a cloudless sky. There were no sounds to indicate neighbors. No dogs barking. No car engines. And no nearby lights, only a glow from the doorway of the burned-out entry hall at the end of the driveway of live oaks. "Is someone there?" he demanded.

"A guard," she choked out. "He circles the grounds."

Callie managed to crawl a foot or so away, wriggling on her back. "All the time."

"I don't know how much of that to believe."

"Believe it."

"True again," he allowed calmly. "I should believe it. And I should hurry, to be safe, although I would absolutely love to take my time."

Callie felt a surge of anger. "The way you took your time with Bri?"

"Yes, the way I took my time with Bri."

Will paused, as though savoring a memory. A deep sigh. And then he was on top of her, straddling her torso with his knees. He leaned back for better balance and then cracked her, open palmed, hard across the face. Callie exhaled in a whimper just as his hands once more went for her throat.

It was shocking how quickly she needed to breathe. Almost instantly. Her reflex, as before, was to clutch at the hands. It was only then that she realized she was holding a sharp object. Re-grasping the key, making sure she had a solid grip, Callie swung upward. She aimed the wild, arcing swing for the man's face and was surprised when it made contact. The hands around her throat loosened as Will let out a howl. A gash of blood opened up, streaming from his left cheek, from the outer edge of his eye almost to his chin. Drops of red fell on her face as he kept leaning in, pressing down on her windpipe. "Bitch!"

Callie still held the key, now slippery with his blood. She slashed up at his face again, but he leaned back out of reach and allowed himself a little chortle. "You think you're so smart." Blood began to drip from the fleshy rip across his cheek.

Callie aimed the long, red-tipped key at his hands now, but she didn't have the strength to do much damage. Releasing one hand from her throat, he used it to snatch the key ring and toss it. She saw it skid, useless, a few feet away, under the front of her silver Yukon.

"What the hell did you do to me?" he howled. He removed his other hand and sat back, resting his full weight on her upper legs. Will seemed tempted to touch his face, to try to assess the disfigurement, but afraid of what he might find.

Callie gulped in deep breaths and stared into his eyes. She was proud of the damage she'd done. Proud and horrified. The gash on his once-handsome face appeared to be widening, pulsing with his heartbeat. Blood was now dripping onto the gray silk skirt that she had agonized about wearing just a few hours ago. She was strangely glad that she hadn't worn her favorite white dress tonight.

Will's fingers trembled as he reached up to his neck and wiped away a little pool of blood that had gathered just above his in his collarbone. He flicked it onto her face. "You're going to pay for this."

With a grunt, he leaned forward to finish the job, coming to his feet for more weight and freeing her legs. His hands found their place again, covering the red marks he'd already forged on her throat.

Callie felt the familiar pain, the on her larynx, the instant cutting off of air. Her hands went wide, one hand trying to swat at him the other one flailing under the truck. For a moment, she thought about the key ring, but what good would it do her now?

She lay there, mesmerized under the force of his hands,

staring up at that face. The expression in his brown eyes was almost one of affection, almost sweet. Had he looked at Briana that way, with those wide, affectionate eyes, as he squeezed the life out of her?

Will bent at the elbows. His blood-dripping face was directly over hers, making her shut her eyes to try to avoid the sickening drops, his blood mixing with her own blood from the gash on her head. One bitter drop fell into her mouth. She wanted to gag it up but couldn't. His ear was right next to the wheel well when Callie happened to lay her flailing hand on the key fob.

The truck's panic alarm was excruciating, sudden and deafening. It startled them both, Will more than Callie. She felt his hands loosen around her throat as her instinct for flight kicked in one last time.

Later, as she relived this moment, in her memories and in her nightmares, Callie had no idea how she had gotten out from under her attacker. She couldn't recall how she might have gotten to her knees and then to her feet, or how she could have started to put the slightest amount of distance between them.

She did remember making her way down the gravel drive, weaving, half-conscious in the direction of the big house. She also had a memory of the rent-a-cop stepping out of the blackened doorway, hand over his eyes, staring curiously through the trees toward the source of the panic alarm.

In her hazy memory, it was Jeremy, the thirtyish, overweight guard still on his first assignment. He stared at the young woman he'd met once before as they'd discussed security measures. She stumbled toward him, her face streaked with blood, trying to speak or maybe to scream. At some point, the guard looked beyond her, his eyes widening. Callie stopped and fell to the gravel. Jeremy, just a few yards in front of her, was struggling, nervously trying to unclip the handgun from his holster. His hands were shaking as he used them both to pull up and aim his weapon. He may have shouted something.

The rest she didn't see, but she could imagine. The sight of a large man, his face slashed from eye to chin, lumbering toward them, coming closer and closer, not heeding whatever warning Jeremy might have been shouting to him.

Callie counted five shots in rapid succession, although there may have been more.

CHAPTER 28

THE NIGHT CRAWLED by in a confusing blur as her mind slid in and out of consciousness. She was vaguely aware of her brother sitting at her side, being uncharacteristically, almost frighteningly nice. Someone, a woman, had also been nice, holding her hand, first one hand then the other, doing her nails. No, not doing her nails, she decided. Gently scraping under her nails. People asked her questions – her brother, the woman. The same questions over and over. Did she answer them the same each time? She couldn't remember.

When she woke this time, her mind was clearing and sunlight was streaming through the hospital room window. *I'm not in so much pain*, she thought. *It's not so bad.* She could sense someone watching her. When she turned to see, there came an ache, radiating from the back of her neck to her shoulders, but nothing so terribly bad. "I'm on a lot of meds, aren't I?"

She was surprised to see Yolanda McFee in the visitor's chair, her expression warm and sympathetic. The first thing to go through Callie's mind was, *I must be worse off than I thought.* "How are you?" Yolanda asked. "You look better. My husband was yelling at you last night, but he didn't mean it."

"He was yelling? I thought…"

"He didn't mean it. He was worried for you and mad at himself. You did a very brave thing."

"Really? How bad off am I?"

"You mean because I paid you a compliment?" Yolanda's thin, hard face eased a little. "Not bad, I think. A concussion, of course. They had to shave a patch in order to stitch you up."

"My hair? They shaved my hair?" Callie reached up to touch the throbbing spot above and behind her left ear.

Yolanda stopped her before her fingers could assess the damage. "Don't worry. It's not too much."

"I can't believe they shaved my hair."

"You can arrange it so it doesn't look so bad. I was always jealous of your hair." Yolanda was quick to add, "I mean, I still am."

Callie lowered her hand. "And it will grow back."

"Of course. It will grow back and you're alive."

"Is he dead?"

Yolanda glanced toward the bathroom, as if looking for guidance. "Yes, he's dead," she said. "I don't think they're going to file any charges against the guard."

"Good. On both counts. Can I have some water?"

There was a plastic cup on the metal bed stand already half full. Yolanda secured the lid and adjusted the bendy straw. Callie had just finished two long sips when they heard a flush from the bathroom. State walked out, looking exhausted.

"Awake. Hey, how are you?" His sympathetic smile almost matched his wife's.

"Yolanda told me he's dead."

"Yeah, I heard from the bathroom."

"How's Dad?"

"Better off than you. His skull's thicker, I guess. The EMTs were concerned at first, but then they were concerned after the fire. He'll be fine."

"I should leave you two." Yolanda pushed herself out of the chair. "I need to go see Buddy then check with Gil's doctor about the surgery. See how that's going. At least you're all in the same hospital. Lucky me."

"How is Uncle Gil?" asked Callie.

Yolanda said, "He's having three skin grafts today. Wants to get them over with, against the surgeon's advice, of course. That's Gil."

"Is he going to be okay?"

"They say there'll be scarring and maybe some nerve damage. On the plus side..." Yolanda gave her sister-in-law a little peck on the cheek. "I'm glad you're okay." Then she headed out the door.

Callie waited several seconds before whispering, "Why is Yolie being like that?"

"She feels bad about kicking you out. She thinks if you'd been with us instead of living at the ranch... I'm not sure I get her logic, but don't look a gift horse."

"Hey, I'm grateful for anything." Callie settled her head into a pillow and closed her eyes. She could feel her brother's eyes boring into her.

"His real name is Gavin. Gavin Hollister, in case you want to know."

"Thanks," she said and kept her eyes closed.

"He has – had – a decent apartment in Hyde Park."

"Was he married?"

"No. Never been."

"That's good. He caused enough pain."

"Until a year ago, he worked for a security company, installing cameras and other equipment. After that, he had no employment record, so we assume the sugar daddy scam began around then."

"How many others?"

"If you mean, how many other murders; none that we know of. No unsolved homicides of young women in that demographic, not in the Austin area." State reached into his jacket and removed his trusty notepad. "If you're asking how many other scam victims, we're not sure. There have been five police reports from young women describing a man like Gavin. Others may have been robbed and not come forward. That's fairly common. Briana didn't come forward."

Callie opened her eyes. "Did you find any connection between Gavin and Mr. You-know-who?"

It was a subject that had provoked her brother several times before. "None," he said evenly. "I was actually hoping you might have some insight. Did Gavin say anything?"

She thought back to that nightmarish moment in the living room when Will, as she knew him then, had confessed to murder. "I asked him if he had any friends or accomplices. He said I should stop asking stupid questions."

"So, he didn't answer one way or the other." State turned to a blank page and made a note. "We'll need to do a cross-check of Gavin and Mr. You-know-who. Also another interview, if his lawyers are amenable."

"If his lawyers…? It's their choice?"

"It is. We have no arrest record."

"Thanks to our beloved father."

"Plus we have a confession from a dead killer, which covers all the bases. Okay, except for that base."

"Which is a big base. Like home plate."

"No, no," he scoffed. "More like second or third. Gavin is home plate."

Callie sighed. The pain was returning to her skull. "When am I getting out of here?"

State checked his watch. "Well, it's almost one p.m."

"One p.m.?" She was shocked.

"Yes, sleepy head. They'll probably keep you overnight for observation."

"Okay," she said, thinking through the ramifications. "Make sure they keep Dad overnight, too."

He chuckled. "Wow, the two of you <u>are</u> becoming joined at the hip, aren't you? That's sweet."

Callie reached out for his arm and lowered her voice again. "If I'm spending the night, I'm going to need my meds. They're in my medicine cabinet. Just bring the bottles. Ambien and Xanax."

State frowned. "When did you start taking those?"

"None of your business. Just bring them."

"Shouldn't we check with the hospital? In case of interactions?"

"No," she insisted. "They're going to want to talk to me

and examine me and supply their own pills. It could take a day. Just stick them in your pocket on your next visit."

"Well, I wasn't necessarily going to make a next visit."

"State, please. I've been taking them for a while. I have prescriptions."

"All right," he allowed. "You tracked down a murderer. You deserve a little contraband. Just don't die."

"I won't."

"I'll be in deep shit if you die."

It was only a few minutes after State left that Callie had another visitor. She was just dozing off when she heard a soft knock, followed a few seconds later by a more insistent knock. "No one home," she croaked, more to herself than the knocker.

When she opened her eyes, Oliver Chesney was staring down at her, studying her. "Are you okay? There are guards on the floor. They say no one but family."

"How did you get in?" It was only then that she noticed the light blue surgical scrubs and the mask hanging from his neck. She smiled. "Are you a law-breaker, Mr. Chesney?" she asked. "Have I turned you into a felon?"

"No, I did not waylay a doctor and knock him out. I tried the supply closets, but most of them are locked. I left the hospital and went to a uniform supply store, but they said I needed medical I.D. I wound up going to a costume shop. By the way, there are very few costume shops open this time of year. I had to drive all the way to…"

"You bought a doctor's costume?" Callie started to laugh but the pain stopped her. "You're impersonating a doctor?"

"Don't laugh at me. I needed to get in. Are you okay?"

"Yes, doctor, I'm fine." She wasn't really. Fine would have

involved a hairbrush, a mirror and just a little warning, for God's sake.

"You don't look fine." He leaned in to examine the purple welts across her throat. Self-consciously, she turned her head, accidentally exposing the left side of her skull, where Gavin Hollister had struck her twice with her laptop. Oliver seemed to be counting the stitches.

Callie turned back to face him. "Tell me it's not that bad."

"It's not that…" Oliver groaned and gave up. "Oh, hell, it looks terrible. Who did this?"

"I asked my brother to call you. At least I think I did."

"I had to find out from my newsfeed. They say you were attacked by an intruder at your family home. It couldn't have been Blackburn because – Well, no offense, but that would have been the headline: Keagan Blackburn killed by security guard. Subhead: He was attacking Buddy McFee's daughter."

Callie had forgotten how little she had kept Oliver informed. She felt bad. "It was Briana's sugar daddy. The second one, not the first. We went out on a couple of dates. Last night's date didn't go particularly well."

"Why on earth did he attack you?"

"Because he knew that I knew that he killed Briana."

"He killed…" Oliver shook his head, overwhelmed. "Wait. You dated Briana's killer?"

"Okay. Use that tone and you can make anything sound bad."

"And he's dead? You solved the whole case? And her killer is dead?"

Either this conversation was giving her a headache or

the painkillers were wearing off. Callie pointed to the plastic cup with the bendy straw. "Can I have some more water? With ice?"

Oliver got the ice from the mini-fridge and the water from the bathroom sink. When Callie was a little less thirsty and had settled in again, she told him everything, from the passcode on the back of Briana's laptop to the 'meet-and-eat' messages to the first and second dates and Gavin's request for her banking information. She began to describe last night's life and death fight on the driveway, but then decided to downplay it. Oliver was being very sweet, but enough was enough. He didn't need to get any more worked up.

Oliver listened, his scowl growing, until she finally finished. "Why didn't you tell me what you were up to? I thought we were a team."

"You're going to yell at me now? Really?" After all the talking, her voice was raspy, still a long way from recovery.

"I'm not yelling," he said, his voice raised to an almost-yell. "I'm just… surprised. I knew absolutely nothing."

She smiled, open-mouthed, hoping her breath didn't stink too much. "I'll try to do better next time."

"My newsfeed said 'unidentified man'. It didn't mention his name or his connection to Briana. The police obviously know all this. Why haven't they released it?"

"I've thought about that," Callie said. "I think someone's trying to protect me, at least for the moment. It's State or my dad or Gil or all three. I'm sure they don't want the family name associated with a sugar daddy killer."

"Or…" Oliver had another theory. "Or they want to protect your story. I mean, give the guys some credit."

"You think?" It was a much sweeter theory.

"It makes sense." Oliver took the empty plastic cup from her hands and put it on the side table. "You tracked the guy down. You put yourself in danger. You almost got killed. The idea of some other reporter running with this story while you're lying unconscious in the hospital … That must have occurred to someone, no?"

"Maybe it did." The throbbing in head was definitely getting worse. But she found she wasn't minding it as much.

CHAPTER 29

THEY WERE RELEASED the next day. Policy mandated that all discharged patients be wheeled out, but Buddy wasn't about to be photographed and videoed and interviewed while seated in a wheelchair. A negotiation ensued with the administrator and a compromise reached. Calista McFee would leave the hospital in a wheelchair. Lawrence "Buddy" McFee would walk behind, holding onto the handles just in case he needed support. Callie knew better than to argue, and the optics, of course, were perfect. The strong, caring father wheeling out his injured, estranged daughter. Buddy didn't have time to answer questions right now, he explained to the cameras. His family was more important.

By now, Gavin Hollister's name and photo had been released and the press had more questions than before. Had Callie been involved with her handsome attacker? What was Buddy's part in the story? Was there any connection between the attack at the McFee ranch and the fire? Callie's feelings about the public's right to know had suddenly become more nuanced, and she appreciated the patrol car that was once again stationed in front of the property.

The McFees spent the rest of the day by themselves, giving Sarah another day off. With Briana's killer dead, Callie had one of her better nights, waking up only twice and getting by on her usual dose of Ambien and only .5 milligrams of Xanax, plus two glasses of wine with dinner. It felt like an achievement, even though a month ago it would have felt excessive.

In the morning, Callie sat down at her dressing table and experimented. Luckily, she still had a crayon concealer, dating back to her last bout with acne in college. She applied this to her neck, under her foundation, and the result was passable. People would still be able to tell she'd been strangled, but might not be as distracted by it. The hair took more work. In the back of a dressing table drawer, she found a few of her mother's old bobby pins. For half an hour, she tried pinning her hair to drape over the shaved spot but only succeeded in accentuating it. At the end, she resorted to a baseball cap.

As soon as Sarah arrived, Callie left, driving into the office well after rush-hour. Oliver had set up a workspace for her in his office, on an old TV tray they'd found in a storage closet. With the door closed, they worked out the structure of "A Death in Westlake, Part Two."

It was an exciting process and Callie forgot to take her next dose of Extra Strength Tylenol until they stopped for a break and the soreness – head and neck, and her scraped knees from crawling on the gravel – came flooding back.

Callie would have the sole byline for part two, they decided, telling the story in first person and changing enough details to keep her father and brother out of the picture. According to part two, for example, she first met the Crawleys when they came to the *Free Press* looking for answers and not when she and State were catching up on old times at the morgue.

The focus would be on the MySugar site and Callie's undercover role as a sugar baby facing a charming, cold-blooded killer. They found a way not to identify Dr. Sam Paget, Briana's first daddy, but could not find a way to keep Briana's sideline out of the story. It was, in fact, at the very center and provided a cautionary tale for girls who could be victimized by men shielding themselves behind a slimy website and modern technology.

Story details, powerful phrases, rearranged time-lines and transitional paragraphs all flew back and forth as the beast took shape. At one point, Oliver looked up from his computer. "By the way, you should delete your profile from the site."

"Already done," Callie said. "So, if you want to hook up with Heather, you're out of luck."

"That's okay. I probably couldn't afford her."

"You most certainly couldn't."

He wagged his head in a 'we'll see' kind of gesture.

Callie readjusted her baseball cap. "I suppose we need to think about the guy in the field."

"What do you mean?"

"Well, the heart of the first installment was the suspect who was caught dragging her body through a field. You got calls from all over, demanding to know who he was. The police were denying it. What do we say?"

Oliver threw her a cagey look. "We can't say it was Gavin? Or at least imply it?"

Callie didn't even have to think about it. "No way. That

would mean the cops had caught him red-handed and let him go. There would be internal investigations."

"You're right, you're right. Dumb of me." Oliver leaned back in his swivel chair, lacing his fingers behind his head. "I got it. We promise the readers a part three."

Callie was intrigued. "Really? What does that accomplish?"

"It means we don't have to answer all the questions. They'll accept that."

"But then we'll need to write a part three."

"And we will. We just don't know when. Or what will be in it." Oliver raised and lowered a shoulder. "Look, the police case is still open. There's hope."

"That's true."

"Absolute worst scenario. Blackburn gets away with whatever he did. If someone comes after us about Mr. X in the field, we'll print a retraction saying there was no man. Our source was wrong."

"God, I would hate to do that."

*

The article went online the next morning and in the print edition the day after.

For two days, she made a point of not checking her newsfeed and not answering her phone, not even from Oliver and especially not from Nicole at KXAN who left four messages, pleading for an on-air interview. Callie knew it was out there, that she was a journalistic hero who'd risked her life. But she was happy to ride out the storm in their faux French mini-chateau, taking care of Buddy and dealing with Gil who was still in the burn unit. State did drop by one evening, on his own, for burgers that Buddy grilled on the Kalamazoo Hybrid. He mentioned that he had read the article all the way through, enjoyed it, and appreciated the fact that he was not mentioned once.

On the morning of the third day, Callie, with a second cup of coffee at her side, finally returned one of Helen Crawley's calls, eleven calls spread over the previous two days, each call angrier than the last. When Helen answered the phone, her tone was different. There was more hurt than anger now.

"Frank was devastated. You know how he heard? Some reporter showed up and stuck a camera in his face. 'This article says your daughter met her killer on a sex-for-hire website. Any comment?' Imagine opening your front door to that? It was the first Frank heard. He almost punched the guy. I pretended not to know either, which makes me such a liar, but I didn't know what else to do."

"Helen, I'm so sorry."

"He went right to her MySugar page and read everything. I finally had to take her computer and delete it all."

"Helen, I had to. I had to tell her story. Either I was going to control the narrative or it was going to be someone who didn't know anything and probably wouldn't care."

There was a pause at the other end. "You did write some nice things."

"And I think it did some good. MySugar put up a new homepage, warning girls about financial scams."

"Good," Helen snapped. "I hope they go broke."

"Me, too."

"I just wish you could have found a different way. You could have called him her boyfriend. You tracked down her boyfriend."

"Okay," Callie allowed. "And how did I do that?"

"I don't know," Helen said. "Maybe through a dating website. You found him on a dating website."

"Which one? Because whatever website I mention is going to be facing the worst P.R. They're going to check their membership files and find out that I'm lying. Then what?"

"I don't know," Helen said, her voice a little more modulated. "You're the writer. I just worry that everyone's going to blame the victim."

"I know." Callie had to be honest with her. "There will be blaming. People think, 'Sure, it's a tragedy. But it would never happen to my daughter because she'd never do that.'"

"It could be anyone's daughter."

"I know. But it's true for everything: crimes, accidents, diseases. They tell you Uncle Billy died of lung cancer and your first question – was he a smoker? A guy dies in a car accident. Was he speeding? Or not using a seat belt? A girl gets attacked in a bad part of town – you think, what was she doing there at 2 a.m.? People want to put as much distance as possible between themselves and someone else's tragedy. It's not really blame. It's…" She searched for the word. "Human nature."

Helen sighed. "You make it sound almost normal."

"It is normal. And it doesn't change who Briana was, not to you or anyone who knew her or cared about her."

"Okay." Helen seemed to be processing this new point of view. "I'll mention this to Frank, what you said. Maybe it will help. Oh." It sounded as if she'd just remembered something. "Have the police been to his home?" She was hesitant, almost apologetic. "Did they find anything there, anything that belonged to Bri? I don't know. It's so stupid. Just having him dead should be enough." It obviously wasn't enough, not for Frank or for Helen. "Can you ask your brother to look for the necklace? You know the one."

"The one you gave her for her birthday."

"If they find a necklace and don't know who it belonged to, I don't want them just…"

"Absolutely. I have a shot of it on my phone. I'll send it to State."

"Not that it changes anything, or that I would ever wear it, God knows, but it would be nice to have it back."

"Of course. I'll ask my brother. Anything else?"

"Um…"

Apparently, there was something else. Callie wasn't sure how much more supportive she could be, especially since Helen hadn't said a word about Callie nearly getting killed and solving their daughter's murder. "What is it?"

"Frank was curious. This man who murdered our girl, he wasn't the same man who was burying her body?"

Callie wished she could say yes. "No, he wasn't. We don't know what happened between the time of Bri's death and when the trooper found her."

"Well, then maybe, just maybe, this Gavin wasn't the real killer. Maybe her killer is still out there."

"Helen." She was starting to lose her patience. "Gavin Hollister did it. He confessed. He knew details. He had motive. And he was trying to murder my father and me because I found him. He almost succeeded. I have bruises on my throat and stitches in my head to prove it."

The woman on the other end of the line gasped. "Oh, Callie. I didn't think."

Almost instantly, Callie regretted her outburst. It had been selfish. This call wasn't about being thanked. Helen's anger was part of her grieving process, which Callie knew when she'd made this call. At some point, yes, she would like the Crawleys to thank her, but that shouldn't be now when Briana's story was just being told to the world. "That's all right. I shouldn't have brought it up."

"No, it's not all right. I'm so sorry." The woman sounded genuinely mortified. "If you hadn't been at the morgue that first day, I don't know what we would have done. You were the first person we met. You helped when no one else did, not the police or anyone. And you nearly got killed. Then finally it's over and I yell at you? What a horrible human being I am."

"You're not a horrible human being."

"Yes, I am. I'm so sorry."

For the next ten minutes, Callie tried to stay out of the way. She accepted Helen's heartfelt thanks and, when the subject returned to Bri, did her best to guide the conversation in this direction, turning their call into a small, audio memorial service, just the two of them, for this young woman she'd never met.

CHAPTER 30

CALLIE HAD PROMISED herself not to drink until cocktail hour. But as soon as the minute hand clicked to six o'clock, she was there, pulling out a bottle of pinot grigio that had been waiting for her in the lettuce crisper. She was just uncorking it when her father walked into the kitchen. "How can people live in a house with no wine cellar and no wet bar?" He'd been in the present and fairly clear-headed for a day and a half now and she was loving the stability of having him back.

Father and daughter settled into the armchairs in the living room. There was still a trace of blood on a corner of the Persian carpet that Sarah hadn't been able to get out. Callie had her wine and Buddy had his whisky-colored water. He actually seemed to enjoy it. "You know I don't blame you, honey, now that I've had three years to mull it over."

The subject took her by surprise. Was he really bringing it up? "I had no idea, Daddy. Honestly." They had never seriously discussed it. It had been yelled about and fought about but never calmly discussed.

"You <u>should</u> have had an idea. That was always my point."

He put down his drink and adjusted the cushion behind his back. "You were doing live TV, about a big-deal pharmaceutical company that you personally owned stock in. Did it not occur to you there might be a perceived conflict of interest?"

"No, it didn't," she shot back, raising her voice more than she intended. "It did not occur to me that my father might have given me a Christmas present that was in violation of SEC regulations. Didn't enter my mind."

Callie had never paid much attention to his work life. The things her father did were all vaguely important and illustrated just how crucial he was to the running of the state. She had heard about Barton Pharmaceuticals' new cancer drug. They had conducted clinical trials all over Texas, five years of rigorous tests and recordkeeping. But Barton's stock took a nosedive when the Texas attorney general's office began looking into allegations of faked records, allegations that had been made by a disgruntled ex-employee. Months later, the Texas attorney general, Lawrence "Buddy" McFee, dropped the investigation and the stock soared.

Buddy had no financial interest in Barton. That would have been illegal. But when Callie announced on TV that shares had been bought in her and her brother's name, it began an investigation into her father's actions. The Democrats accused him of everything from taking a bribe to insider trading.

The attorney general never addressed these accusations. The involvement of his only daughter made it too sensitive. But certain people within the Republican Party went into damage control. Her statement hadn't been accidental, the rumor-mongers said. She might pretend to be free of malicious intent, they said, but Calista McFee was a rabid Democrat, a muckraking reporter out to make a name. She hated everything her father stood for. She wanted him ruined. And her weapon – to many Texans this was truly the most egregious part – had been her dad's sweet little Christmas present. The rumors had their intended effect. Waters were muddied, public opinion was divided and Buddy managed to escape with a simple resignation.

"I never blamed you, Callie. I never said a word."

"But you never told them to stop. If you'd objected strongly enough or made a public statement on my behalf…"

"I never would have started it, you know that." There was real distress in his voice, mixed with regret. "It was someone in the governor's office. By the time I heard about it, it was too late. You'd been damaged. You couldn't be undamaged. That's not how political rumors work. So, what's the best result?" 'What's the best result?' It was a line she'd heard a hundred times, a key part of Buddy's negotiating language. "The best result, at least I thought at the time, was to let it ride out. I didn't defend you or blame you."

"I know. You got to be the injured father trying to keep his family together." The governor, her godfather, had used some similar phrase to explain away Buddy's silence in the matter. All the people she'd known growing up, the politicians she'd gazed down on through the staircase balusters, had stayed silent or closed ranks against her.

"We both made mistakes, darlin', mistakes that hurt."

"I am sorry," Callie said. She knew this wouldn't be the end of the discussion, but it was the end for now.

"Sorry, too." Buddy glanced down at his four fingers of

colored water and shrugged. "Damn it. I need a fake cigar to go with my fake whisky."

"And I need to warm up whatever Sarah left for us."

Sarah had left a batch of chili and cornbread, one of Buddy's favorite meals. They ate at the Formica-topped table by the bay window, a situation that led Buddy to mumble another question, "How can people live in a house with no dining room?"

Afterwards, Callie put the dishes in the sink and joined her father in the living room, him with his wooden cigar and his third colored-water, her with her third glass of wine. "Do you really like that?" she asked, pointing to the contents of the cut crystal glass.

"Keeps my mind clear, on the days when I have a mind. On the bad days, Gil pours me a snort of the real brown goods. Just a snort." He tilted his head slyly toward a bottle on the sideboard. Callie didn't recall seeing this bottle before. "You like it?" Buddy asked. On a bad day, make sure you pour me this one."

She walked over to the sideboard and checked the label. "Glenfiddich."

"Not just Glenfiddich. Fifty-year-old Glenfiddich. Best of the best."

Callie knew her father well enough. "All right. Who gave you the Glenfiddich and why? I know you're dying to tell me."

"You're not going to like it." Then before she could guess… "Keagan Blackburn. He messengered it over today while you were out."

"Jeez, Dad. Did you have to tell me?"

His grin was proud and impish. "People still appreciate my skills."

"And what were your skills in this case?" she asked. "Erasing his arrest record? Getting the state trooper to disappear?"

"State trooper and girlfriend." Buddy chuckled. "I almost messed up with the girlfriend. Clever of you to think of her."

"I learned from the master."

"There was no reason for the arrest, you know. That loser from the website killed her and almost killed us. Any doubt about that?"

"There's no doubt," she had to admit. "But Blackburn was involved."

"A misdemeanor. A two-year-old could make a misdemeanor go away."

"Doesn't it bother you, helping him get away with whatever he got away with?"

Buddy used a finger to stir the ice in his brown water. "Keagan's gotten away with a lot in his lifetime. You know, he cheated on all three of his wives, plus at least one fiancée he didn't marry. Not one of them found out."

"Quite the stud."

"Hey, you know I don't approve." He looked past his daughter into the distance. "Me, I sowed my oats early and married late. I was the luckiest bastard alive when I met Anita. I didn't want to outlive her. Didn't think I could. What Anita and I had was sacred."

Callie didn't know what to say. Her father had never talked about his grief.

Buddy shrugged. "If there's any karma in this world, I

think Keagan really loved this last wife of his. Ingrid or Elsa or Asta."

"Ingrid."

"Ingrid." He had a way of half-forgetting names, more a form of disrespect than anything. "This Ingrid, she paid him back in spades. You should've seen. You would've enjoyed it." Buddy eased back in the leather, ready to tell another one of his hundred stories. "This was some months back, before you came home. The two of them, Ingrid and her lover, ran off with the jewelry and everything else in her name. All she left him was this one-page note and an address in Buenos Aires to send her stuff. Keagan came over the night they ran off, pounding on my door. He was a God-awful mess."

"He came to see you?"

"The night she ran off. Pounding on the door, half-hysterical. Clothes all rumpled, babbling, sweating like a pig. At first, I thought he needed my services. But the man just wanted to talk, avail himself of a drink and a sympathetic ear."

"I didn't realize you were close."

"People generally come because they need me to grease the wheels or make things disappear. In this case… Guess he just needed someone to listen, to tell him it's not so bad. Hell, she's just some foreign sexpot who never made a real friend. Half of Austin knew about the polo player. Just check your pre-nup, I said. Go on with your life. People will gossip, but what the hell? Let 'em. You're goddamn Keagan Blackburn. What do you care? Take her stuff and burn it in a bonfire, why don't you? Good riddance."

Callie had to smile. "Did he appreciate your tender sympathies?"

Buddy grinned. "I think he did. Like I said, he came over

a blubbering mess, like her screwing around was his fault, like he was responsible . . ."

"Well, he was screwing around himself," Callie pointed out, "so in a way he was responsible."

"Hmm." The guttural sound was barely audible.

"Dad, what are you thinking? Dad?"

Buddy didn't seem to hear her. He was focusing his gaze downward, staring at the brown ice in his cut crystal glass.

"Dad?" she repeated, but her father didn't move a muscle. "Dad, are you okay?" Could it really happen this quickly? Could his mind have been taken away this quickly? One second here, the next second gone? Was it going to be like this from now on? Comfortable, heartfelt conversations cut short without any warning?

"Why, that sonofabitch," Buddy muttered under his breath. "That goddamn sonofabitch."

"Who are you talking about?" She reached across and touched his hand. "It's Callie, Dad. How are you feeling?"

"How am I feeling?" he asked himself, his mind still somewhere else. "Better now. I'm better now," he answered. "Thank you, sweetie. Much better. Sonofabitch."

"Good. Do you want to go to bed? Maybe lie down for a while?"

He laughed. "Hell, no. I want to go for a drive."

"A drive? Um, I'm not sure that's the best idea. You look tired."

"Tired? Who the hell's tired?" Buddy McFee shot to his feet. He wavered for a second then stretched out his arms and caught his balance. "I'll grab the Glenfiddich. You grab the car keys. The two of us are going for a drive."

CHAPTER 31

MOST OF HER life she had spent not questioning her father. Even now, as she pulled the silver Yukon out onto Hacienda Road, she didn't ask. Buddy seemed lucid and in control as, turn by turn, he barked out the directions. It wasn't even nine p.m., so she doubted they would be waking anyone up. It reminded Callie of when he used to pile the family into the Cadillac without explanation. It was always exciting, whether they were heading to a circus just come to town or to a political fundraiser.

This particular ride was short and they spent less than a minute idling by the roadside intercom for someone to answer. Then the wrought-iron gates swung inward and Callie drove onto the Blackburn estate and up to the house on the artificial hill.

Keagan Blackburn met them at the door and the unflappable Texas gentleman ushered them inside. He was wearing black jeans, a flannel shirt and a bemused but welcoming smile. Buddy brandished the Glenfiddich, swinging it overhead. He profusely thanked his host for the extravagant gift and suggested that the three of them open it to celebrate the ending of "the troubles". Callie mouthed a soft hello, apologized for the intrusion and left the rest to her father.

Half an hour later, she was sitting quietly, smiling mechanically and feeling exasperated, only half-listening as the men blathered back and forth. They were in the living room just beyond the entry hall, a well-proportioned room with classical moldings and a painting of an oil rig on a barren plain, gracing the fireplace mantle. Buddy had immediately scoped out the best seat for himself, a padded wing chair with a view out to the lush gardens, the stone wall and the field beyond it, the whole view illuminated by a halogen street lamp along a deserted country road. It was a pleasant enough view.

"Keagan," Buddy finally said, as if just realizing it, "Is this your chair? Did I come in here and steal your chair?"

"You're my guest." Blackburn waved a gracious hand. "It's an honor to have you there."

"Appreciate it." Buddy chuckled. "Let me just say, when you and the snot-nosed lawyer came to me, I thought you were hellbent on disaster. No way out, you stubborn bastard. But just look." It was at least the fourth time Buddy had expressed that sentiment, each time in a slight variation. Each time, Callie expected him to go further, in his patented way – to slyly reveal a new fact, to ask a pointed question, to insinuate or goad or guess, to somehow peel off a layer of the onion. Not tonight. And each time Buddy repeated himself, Blackburn smiled back, poured another toast with the 50-year-old whisky and expressed his gratitude for all that the fixer had done. It was becoming interminable.

"I hope your little girl has no hard feelings," their host

said. His speech was on the cusp of slurring. And that was when Callie noted that her father had not been downing his share of the Glenfiddich, merely holding his glass over the side of the chair, out of sight, bringing it up to his mouth occasionally, but barely imbibing.

"No hard feelings," she replied.

"You must understand, darlin', some things are private," Blackburn drawled between sips, leaning into Callie, like a tutor to a student. "That doesn't make them bad or illegal, just private. You want to know everything, whether it's private or not. I get it. That's part of your job."

"Part of the job." Callie was a little more alert now, a little more engaged.

"Part of the job," Buddy said then rocked forward in his wing chair, pushing himself up with a grunt. "Is it safe to leave you two alone? Keagan, buddy, I trust your powder room is still in the front hall?"

"It is," said Blackburn. "Make yourself at home."

Buddy headed in the right direction, drink in hand, swaying slightly. "I want you to keep Mr. Blackburn occupied while I'm gone, you hear me? The art of holding a man's attention is a woman's hallmark." And with that, he disappeared into the front hall.

"Is it safe for me to be alone with you?" Blackburn asked, showing off his bright smile.

"Maybe." Callie shifted on the couch. The last time they'd been alone had been at the brunch after he'd followed her in his Lamborghini. "Briana's parents still need answers," she said pointedly.

The brightness faded. "They have all the answers they

need. I didn't kill her, and the man who killed her is dead. I hope they can take some solace in that and go on with their lives."

"Hmm. I have this feeling you're getting away with something."

"What the hell would I be getting away with?" His question had some genuine bite in it. "Tell me. Did I rob a bank? Is there some local crime spree I'm unaware of? Because if there's no crime, then what the hell…" A cell phone jangled in the distance, interrupting his outburst. He swiveled his head toward the dining room and the kitchen beyond. "Office ringtone," he said. "I'm sorry, Ms. McFee, but I'm going to have to leave you for a few minutes."

"No problem."

Callie watched as he retreated toward the back of the house, replicating her father's slightly inebriated gait. She rearranged herself on the couch and thought over what he'd just said. What exactly did she think he'd gotten away with?

Within a minute, the light from the halogen street lamp drew her eye. *Was there something moving out there?* she wondered, *a breeze rustling through the branches or a car passing by?* She stood up to stretch her legs. Something was definitely moving, she deduced as she made her way to the window. It was not a car or a breeze. No, it was her father. The man she'd last seen ambling to the powder room was now ambling out under the illumination of a street lamp. Callie tuned her ear, identified the CEO's barely discernible voice behind one or more closed doors, then made her decision.

"Dad?" The pedestrian gate to the left of the wrought-iron gates was unlocked on the inside and had been propped open with a stone. Callie went through, made a left turn and raced to the end of the stone wall to one of the vacant lots flanking the Blackburn property. She had run most of the way and was now panting, the night air coursing through her tender throat. "Dad?" she called a little louder. He was already thirty yards into the field, bending down, passing his arms randomly through the spring grasses and bushes, like a day-dreaming child. "Are you alright? You should come back inside. Dad?"

He heard this last mention of his name, stood straight and turned. "What the hell are you doing here?"

"Looking for you. Are you alright? Do you know who I am? It's Callie, Dad."

"What the hell?" Buddy's eyes darted around, from his daughter to the road to the mansion and back. "I told you to keep him occupied. I distinctly told you. Could I have been any clearer? Hold his attention, damn it. Where is he now?"

"He had to take a call." She began to step carefully through the bushes, her path illuminated by the halogen. "When I saw you... I thought you might be wandering."

"Don't come to me. I'll come to you." He headed in her direction, no longer swaying, just trying to avoid the brambles and the gopher holes. "With any luck, we'll beat him back to the living room. If not, we'll say we went out to clear our heads. Too damn strong a whisky. The whisky's fault."

"Why are you here?"

"I wanted to see the world from his favorite chair. Then I let the curiosity get me. Stupid, stupid. Lit up like a stage. What could I do? You and me, we'll come in the daylight. It's his land, so we'll need some papers from your brother."

"I don't know what you're talking about."

"Doesn't matter." Buddy's left ankle turned on something. He caught his balance then tilted his head, narrowed his eyes and knelt down in the weeds. A few seconds later he came up with what looked like a rope, a foot and a half long, that had tangled itself onto his foot. The rope glimmered in the halogen reflection.

Callie recognized it. "That's Briana's." She caught up to him and took the braided leather necklace with the broken clasp, wiping off the accumulation of mud until the gold strand shone from end to end. "My God. How did it..." The answer seemed obvious. "Briana was killed right here. In this field."

There was rustle of twigs in the grasses behind them.

"She wasn't killed here." It was Keagan Blackburn, stepping from the road into the vacant lot, his face thrown into silhouette by the street lamp's glare. "When he dumped her, she was already cold. I checked."

"Keagan." Buddy's tone was matter-of-fact. "I hope you brought the Glenfiddich. I think we could all use a touch right now."

"Sorry. Short phone call. I came back and got fascinated by the view, if you know what I mean." He spoke and moved deliberately, inhaling deeply, as if trying to speed up the sobering process.

"That damn view," said Buddy sympathetically. "Source of all our woes."

"You're telling me?"

"It must have been quite the shock," Buddy said.

"Unbelievable." The CEO shook his head. "Stopped his car right here, pulled her out and dragged her onto my property. I was negotiating with my fellas 'round the world, hundreds of millions of bucks, and I see this guy dumping a corpse not a hundred yards away. I'm sure something must've showed on my face. Maybe got me a better deal, huh?" He pointed to the necklace in Callie's hand. "I figured she'd lost something when I pulled her back to the road. Wasn't easy. Not as young as I used to be."

"I don't get it," Callie said. "She was dead and you just moved her? You didn't call the cops? You drove a mile away and dumped her in another field?"

"Seemed like the easiest thing to do," Blackwell said.

"I hate being a Monday morning quarterback, Keagan boy, but it would've been smarter not to bring a shovel." Buddy made a face. "You didn't need to give her a good burial, just dump her."

"I didn't know." Blackburn sounded angry with himself. "I'd touched her. There were probably fibers on her from me and my truck, all that stuff. I didn't know what the cops could do with their forensic shit, so I decided on burial. What the hell? I was wired and could use the exercise. If it wasn't for that damn patrol car…"

Callie still hadn't pieced it together. "Why didn't you just say that? Why did you have to stonewall everyone and risk a murder charge?"

"He was never in real danger." Buddy fixed his eyes on the black silhouette of the CEO's face. "The real danger would've come from the police combing through this field for days on end with their dogs and their metal detectors and their whatnot."

The silhouette nodded slowly. "Buddy, my buddy. How did you know?"

"I should've known months ago, the night you killed them. The night you came blubbering over to the ranch. 'Oh, my Ingrid's screwing this lowlife wetback. Ungrateful bitch. Making a fool of me.' You sweating like a pig, which wasn't the least bit like you, which should've clued me in. Bad on me. I assume they were both already dead?"

The silhouette kept nodding, almost rhythmically. "I flew in a day early. Caught 'em in bed." He grinned at the memory. "Ingrid could see me going for my daddy's old Colt Python in the dresser. Her eyes went all wild, staring at the dresser and me, then trying to shield her worthless stud. One shot each. Clean – except for the blood.

"Afterwards, when things were such a mess – in the bedroom and in my mind – I came crawling to you. If ever I needed some-one to deal with the cops and the prosecutor and the press…" Blackburn's voice turned cold and snide. "Before I could say a word, you were consoling me: Things weren't so bad. The ice-cold bitch had no friends, you said. No one would miss her. I was in your study, drinking your whisky and I happened to think, 'God-damn, the man's perfectly right. Things ain't so bad.' I came up with the running-off story right there on the spot. Thank you."

"I should've felt it," Buddy muttered. "Something was off. I should've known."

"Time was on my side. I buried them right here. Not a deep burial, but deep enough to avoid the coyotes. I repainted the bedroom myself. The jewelry and whatever else she would've taken with her, all burned or buried. And the wetback Raul – that was his name, I learned from her phone, Raul Cabrera – was even easier. He owned a tiny, shitty trailer by the polo club up off 130. You know the place?"

"Yeah," said Buddy. "I remember it under the old management. State took a riding lesson or two before he discovered football."

"Raul was an illegal, turns out. No one came asking for his forwarding address. There were a couple of close calls with Ingrid, some communication from her parents in Norway, but nothing I couldn't divert. It was like a fun, new hobby, cleaning up my own mess. Every day got easier."

Blackburn took two more steps into the field, revealing more of his face. "And then that body got dumped." Callie noticed something at his side, like a walking stick but bulkier.

Buddy saw it, too. "That's not your daddy's Colt Python."

Blackburn glanced down casually at the shotgun. "It's from the front closet, by the powder room. I'm not sure exactly what to do here," he said, as if asking the fixer for advice. "This can't be suicide, I suppose. A double suicide with a shotgun? Even your dumb-ass son would question that."

"Hey," Buddy warned. "Let's keep family out of this."

"You're right, my friend. I apologize. And now…" The shotgun swung up, the stock sliding under his shoulder. Callie recognized it as a double barrel over-under, an old school weapon, hardly meant for assassination but lethal enough at close range.

Buddy countered by swinging up his empty hands, showing his palms. "Keagan, what the hell? How the hell do you see this ending? Two shotgun blasts in an open field? Someone's going to hear."

"No one heard last time. And let's face it, I can't ever sell this lot. Might as well make the most of it. Like a goddamn graveyard." His sighted down the barrels, training them on Buddy's chest.

Callie glanced around, left then right. She hadn't seen a car go by since she got here. The lights from the surrounding estates were few and far between, no houses at all on this section of the road.

"What's the best result?" Buddy blurted out, breaking the silence. Blackburn smiled, recognizing the phrase. "Let's talk. What do you want out of this?"

"The best result..." Blackburn kept his aim but gave the question a respectful moment. "Are you seriously asking? The best result is for me to shoot you here and now. Over and done."

Buddy didn't flinch. "Nah. I hate to disagree, but this'll be much louder than a revolver in a bedroom. People will hear. Even if no one calls the police, Callie and I would be missing and someone who knows my connection to you – Gil or my dumb-ass son – would make local inquiries and find out about the gunshots. By that time, of course, you could run off and leave the country and your life and most of your money. But you'd still get caught." He let this sink in. "One possibility..."

Blackburn was interested. "Yes?"

"One possibility is for you to drop the shotgun and give up."

"Screw you, McFee."

"No. Hear me out," Buddy said, his hands still raised. "I'll do what I can. We can spin this. I know we can."

Blackburn shook his head. "I don't see how."

"You found your wife and her buck in flagrante delicto," Buddy explained. "You acted out of passion. We'll find evidence to back that up. This being Texas, that will be an extenuating circumstance and we can sway public opinion.

You'll wind up doing time, yes. But watch your health and you'll be out and about and getting yourself another wife, if any woman will have you after that."

Blackburn shook his head through the whole proposal. "I know you're a talented man, Bud, but that's a non-starter. Want to know the best result? It's for you to just forget about this."

"Forget you killed your wife and her lover? In exchange for our lives?"

Even Blackburn knew better. "Yeah, that's not going to happen, is it? The second I let you go, you'll be calling your boy and having him dig up my property."

"Yes, we probably would make that call." Buddy used one of his raised hands to scratch his head. "Unless…" The word sounded long and inviting.

"Unless what?"

"Unless you have something on us as well."

"What could I have on you?" Blackburn asked.

"It's like something I arranged in the past," Buddy said. "Not for myself. And not murder. But if you put some money, say half a million apiece, from your personal account into each of our bank accounts – do it tonight, before we leave – then our hands would be tied. We wouldn't be able to tell the authorities about your – what to call it – domestic episode."

"What?" Callie couldn't believe what she was hearing. "You're blackmailing him? That's your solution?"

"Daddy's negotiating, sweetheart. Don't interrupt."

Blackburn seemed amused. "You're blackmailing me, McFee?"

"Oh, please, Keagan. I don't need the money. But if my daughter and I had a change of heart and went to the police, you would have the bank info to show we'd been extorting you. It wouldn't be in our interest to tell. In the meantime, I would recommend finding a better resting place for Ingrid and whatever-his-name-was. Some spot better than a field next to your own house, for God's sake."

Blackburn furrowed his brow. "Worth considering."

Callie was appalled. "You want a public record of us blackmailing a killer?"

Buddy waved her away. "Ignore my girl. What do you say?"

"Is this how you work?" It was as if Callie were seeing him for the first time. "Is this what you've been doing your whole life, in the study with your pals, while we played upstairs and loved the hell out of you? Letting people get away with murder?"

"No," Buddy said calmly. "I am trying to prevent two more murders, which I'm sure none of us wants." He stared his daughter down. "Am I right, sweetheart? Am I right, Keagan, old pal?"

His old pal thought it over. "Half a million for the two of you?"

"God, no," Buddy scoffed. "We want something believable. Half a million apiece."

"And you get to keep it?"

"Well, you want the blackmail to look real, don't you?"

Blackburn chortled at the idea. He seemed genuinely amused. "I gotta hand it to you, Bud. Only you. Only you could take a situation where I'm standing here with a shotgun and turn it into something where I pay you a million bucks."

Buddy adjusted his arms. He was tired of keeping them

up. "Okay, what are your alternatives? Shoot us and you'll get caught. Let us go and you're going to jail. But if some money goes into our banks, Callie and I won't ever be able to turn you in. Makes plain sense."

Callie was aghast. How could he do this to his own daughter? There had to be some other way. But the genius of Buddy McFee was that when he said it was the only choice, he made it feel true. On the one hand, death. On the other hand, abetting a killer plus half a million just for her.

Blackburn's head bobbed cautiously. "Makes some sense. In theory." The effects of the fifty-year-old Glenfiddich were still apparent.

It was the moment Buddy had been waiting for. "Good, we're all agreed. In theory. The instant you put down that gun, we have a deal."

The CEO hesitated, the shotgun wobbling then returning to its target. "No. The instant we do the bank transfer. If that's my leverage, I want it in place."

"Well, then," Buddy said, finally lowering his hands, "we all need to go inside and do a little banking."

"Maybe. Maybe." Blackburn adjusted the shotgun. It was no longer pointed at Buddy but at his daughter. "How about it? Are you on board?"

Callie felt a cold spot over her heart, as if the gun was no longer a few yards away across a patch of brush but pressed up against her bare skin. "Dad?"

"Give him your word, Callie. This will all be over."

She had always considered herself as practical as any McFee. She certainly didn't want to die. And yet making this promise…? These four little words, 'you have my word' were a ludicrously small price to pay for her life. Her father's, too. But the words seemed like an incantation, some evil spell that would make her just like the worst part of her father, like Keagan Blackburn and all the other dealmakers. She moved her mouth to say it, but it felt like a phrase from an unpronounceable foreign language. "I can't."

"Callie, honey," Buddy moaned. "You really mean that, don't you?"

"I'm so sorry, Dad."

"Well then, you are leaving me no choice. Damn!"

The attack was quick and reckless, with almost no thought behind it. The shotgun was still trained on his daughter's heart when Buddy McFee stumbled through the last of the underbrush separating them from Blackburn. The CEO had been viewing Callie as the threat, and it took him a full two seconds to realize it and turn. When he did, Buddy was already traveling the final three feet, leaping for the other man's legs, below the range of the barrel. Then the shot went off.

Callie was deafened. It was the noise, followed instantly by the shock and finally the pain, searing into her left arm. She looked down, almost curiously, at the three tiny holes in the upper arm of her thin cashmere sweater. Her first inclination was to touch them, but she knew that would only make the pain more excruciating.

The shotgun was in the brambles now, with probably another cartridge ready in the over-under. Her father and Keagan Blackburn were just a few feet away, two older men rolling in the brush, moving away from the weapon then toward it again. Both were bellowing – just sounds, no words, full of grunts and testosterone-filled howls. As the sonic concussion eased in her ears, Callie could hear a large dog barking in the distance. A house light went on somewhere through the woods on the other side of the road, and she was strangely, calmly pleased that Buddy had been right, someone would have heard their deaths.

"Cal, Cal, Cal . . ." Through the pain and the shock and reverberation of the gunshot, she could make out her father groaning her name over and over. That was enough to snap her back.

She knew shotguns. From the age of twelve she had handled smaller versions while hunting rabbits in the woods behind the ranch with her brother. She stepped around the wrestling men, giving them a wide berth and found the weapon lodged among the thorny patch of blackbrush. She barely felt the thorns, mere pricks on her hands, producing more little drops of blood. By the time she extracted the shotgun from the bush, Buddy had managed to push himself free and she had a clear shot at Blackburn's head. She switched barrels and aimed.

"Callie, don't. Callie, darling, listen to me."

She had never pointed a firearm at a human being before, but for a moment, a long moment, she could understand how people did it – how people could pull a trigger and end someone's life.

She hesitated just long enough for her father to get to feet and stumble through the briars and brambles. "Give me that," he wheezed, grabbing the weapon but keeping it aimed. "Good job." Blackburn stayed frozen in the brush, just staring at them, breathing heavily, not saying a word.

"I should have shot you both," Callie erupted.

"What? Don't even joke about that." Buddy sounded more than a little hurt. "Shoot your own daddy?"

"Blackmail?" she shouted. "You wanted me to blackmail a murderer?"

"Hell, no. What gave you that idea?"

"Because that's what you were doing."

"Jeez, I was stalling," Buddy declared. "That bank thing never would've worked. Half a million popping up? We would've been flagged in a minute. Keagan would've realized it too, had he not been so drunk and scared."

"Then you didn't mean it? Really?" Callie exhaled in a long, loud sigh.

"Course I didn't mean it. It was the only thing I could think of." Buddy stopped and gave it another moment's thought. "And like I said, it wouldn't have worked."

CHAPTER 32

"A Death In Westlake, Part 4, by Callie McFee and Oliver Chesney."

She kept staring at her screen, the slightest of smiles crinkling her eyes. It might not look like much, just the online version of an article from a free weekly paper – a headline, a sub-head and several pages of scrollable text. What made it unique was the never-before-seen photo she'd taken of her brother placing the mighty Keagan Blackburn in handcuffs just steps away from his mansion. At the top was a counter, tallying up the hundreds of thousands of readers who'd clicked through since they'd gone online just this morning. Two weeks had passed since that night in the field, and the public was still hungry for any leftover crumbs.

The rest of the media had followed the story, of course. How could they not? The CEO of a major company arrested on two counts of murder and two counts of attempted murder. Callie suspected that her father could have made the attempted murder charges disappear, but at some point, even for a political animal like Buddy, things got too personal.

As soon as she heard the knock on her wall, she clicked back to her homepage, but not soon enough. Oliver stood in the doorway. "If it isn't Wonder Woman with press credentials and a shotgun."

She lifted a single eyebrow. "How long have you been thinking that one up?"

"Good, isn't it?" He didn't wait for an answer. "Come on. You need to savor these moments. They don't come often. Whenever things go shitty, you can look back on this."

"If I savor them too much, I think it's like a curse, like walking under a ladder."

"Like I said, they don't come often." She expected him to walk on, to continue on his end-of-the-day circuit of the cubicles, but he stepped inside and lowered his voice. "Are things still okay with State? No repercussions from the department? I know he wasn't happy when you outed him as your source. The last time you said anything…"

"It's better," she said. "Turns out my brother is untouchable. It was his collar, a huge one. Plus the department is dealing with Blackburn's vanishing arrest record. No one wants to add fuel to the fire."

"Good." The young publisher took two more steps into her cubicle, pulled up her single guest chair and sat down. If she'd had a door, he probably would have closed it. "I know you don't want to talk about a book deal, but we got another offer."

"No thanks."

"You know, if you answered your phone, they wouldn't call me and I wouldn't have to bug you." He took a beat. "There's also a movie offer. Well, Netflix. This New York agent has a client, some big TV writer. They want to option the rights.

You wouldn't have to write anything, just talk to them and be a consultant. They mentioned Jennifer Lawrence for you. Can you believe? Don't you think that would be cool? She'd have to go red, of course, and she's really hot as a redhead."

"I hope you told them no."

"Hey!" He leaned in. "What did I say about savoring?"

For Callie it wasn't about savoring her fifteen minutes. It was about protecting her father, about keeping the cameras away, about leaving certain questions unanswered and letting the story die a natural death. And there were the Crawleys. She doubted if Briana's parents would savor seeing their little girl depicted on their home screen as a sugar baby.

"They could do it without your cooperation," Oliver warned. "The agent made sure to mention that. The public record."

"I know," Callie said. "And I checked the copyright laws. They can use any public information in their movie – arrest records, police statements, trial documents. But a lot of the details were first revealed in our story, revealed exclusively, which is copyrighted by the *Austin Free Press*. I doubt they'd want to do it without us. I wouldn't cooperate, State wouldn't, the Crawleys wouldn't, my dad wouldn't."

"Really?" Oliver seemed skeptical. "I don't know him well, but I'd think Buddy McFee would relish the attention."

"Well, he wouldn't," she lied. "How about you?"

"Me neither," he assured her. "I just want to see Jennifer Lawrence with red hair and a Texas accent. Is that too much to ask?"

Callie switched off her laptop and began packing up for the day. "By the way, I'm taking a personal day tomorrow.

It shouldn't be a problem with deadlines." Her phone rang before she could explain further. She checked the screen, rolled her eyes and hit the ignore button.

"Another movie offer?" Oliver guessed. "Maybe with Bradley Cooper playing me?"

"In your dreams. No, it's a friend. Nicole. She calls all the time. I'll call her back."

"Nicole from the TV station?" Oliver's brows formed two straight little lines. "Where you used to work? I hope Nicole and her people aren't trying to poach you." He said it half as a joke and half not.

Callie didn't have the energy to lie. "They want me to come on as on-air talent and as a producer. I told them no, but she keeps calling."

"Good." He looked like he wanted to rush over and hug her. "I mean, good for me. I know we can't pay you as much, but I could come up with a little raise. We just doubled our ad rates."

"Don't worry – although a raise would be welcome, don't get me wrong. I had my chance over at KXAN. It's not for me."

"Good," he repeated and instinctively reached out to touch her upper left arm. At the last instant, he pulled back. "Sorry. I keep forgetting."

Callie smiled. "Don't worry. It doesn't hurt. Probably the easiest gunshot wound I'll ever go through."

"I hope so. I mean, I hope you never get shot again." He leaned in, as if to tell a secret. "I gotta say this, Callie, hiring you was the best thing I ever let myself get talked into."

She tilted her head. "Interesting way to put it. Who talked you into it?"

"Who did?" he said with a trace of a stammer. "You did. I mean, when you came in to interview. Anyway, I'm babbling. Feel free to take your personal day. Take two."

"I am taking two, one for me and one for Jennie. She's helping me move."

"That's tomorrow? So soon?"

"A vacancy opened up in Sherry Ann's building. There are scads of U.T. students there, so maybe I'll get to relive my college days. They could use some reliving."

"Why didn't you ask me?" He seemed disappointed. "If you postpone it to Saturday, I can help."

Callie slipped her laptop into her bag. "That's very sweet, but the van is coming tomorrow from my storage locker in Dallas and, to be honest, there's not all that much. I'm thinking of it more as a girls' day than a moving day."

"Understood. Have fun." He offered a timid half-wave as she headed out of her cubicle. "Thanks for not quitting."

*

The first thing Callie saw as she turned off Hacienda Road was the unmistakable figure of Gil Morales, limping along the gravel path leading up to the main house. A week ago, he'd been released from the burn unit and part of his physical therapy was to walk, half a mile or more three times a day. As with everything, Gil took the regimen seriously, almost zealously, doing a circuit from the house to the road and back, morning noon and night, whatever the weather. Callie was surprised to see him on his phone, in clear violation of his instructions to concentrate and stretch the area around his thighs where they'd taken the skin grafts for his arms.

As she approached, Callie slowed down to wave hello. Gil had just gotten off his call and waved back. "Calista."

"Don't want to interrupt your therapy," she shouted out the window, slowing her truck to a crawl.

"No, no. This is an extra. Why don't you stop for a minute and talk?"

Callie knew what this was going to be about, but good manners demanded that she stop. "Who was that on the phone?" She put her truck into Park and leaned out.

"Our old pal, Felix Gibson." Gil's face had healed, turning from a post-fire red to a kind of orangey gray. There was a shiny tightness to his skin that would probably never go away, and he was clean-shaven for the first time since Callie had known him. She could see that he wanted to lean up against the truck, the typical posture of a Texas stop-and-chat, and had to prevent himself.

"What did Felix want?" she asked. "Or what did you want from Felix?"

"You assume it wasn't just friendly."

"Nothing is just friendly."

Gil's orange-gray mouth tightened into a skeletal grin. "Felix wants to drop over to discuss his primary coming up. I told him your dad was too busy. That's what I tell pretty much everyone. It only makes them want him more. I thought arresting one of the biggest shakers might make him a political pariah, but just the opposite. Now he's looking clean and smart and strong. Hell, he could run against Felix for attorney general and win."

"Please tell me that's not happening."

"Course not. My heart couldn't take it."

"Good to hear." Callie looked over her steering wheel at the house. There were still some repairs to do, but it had been restored to a semblance of its perfection in record time, as if nothing had happened – nothing but a fire and Angus's death and Gil's disfigurement. They'd been back in the house for only a week, and tomorrow she would be leaving.

Gil was also staring at the house, looking pensive. "You think Felix Gibson was responsible?" Callie asked.

Gil mulled it over. "Hell, I don't know. At first… I mean, happening right after that disastrous dinner. I was in pain and pretty paranoid."

"And later on. He was so anxious to get into the study, to see if everything was destroyed."

"I was anxious, too," Gil admitted. "No one, from the governor down, wanted the arson squad finding something that might open some long-closed door. When I ran back into the fire, I could tell it was all gone."

A suspicion teased at the edges of Callie's mind. "Was that the real reason you ran back in? I thought you went back to save Angus."

"Of course I went back for Angus." His outrage seemed genuine. "That doesn't mean I didn't see everything else. Dammit, Callie, what kind of ass do you think I am?"

"I'm sorry, Uncle Gil."

"That's okay," he said, still sounding upset. "Anyway, no arson's gonna happen now. We have this security system. State of the art. And I'll be cutting back his work load."

"Dad's not going to like that."

"We'll take it day by day." Gil shifted his weight from one

aching leg to the other. "You sure I can't persuade you to stay? It would add years to his life."

"And take years off mine." She turned, her eyes catching his. "That was your plan from the start, wasn't it? To get me to move back home."

Gil's skull-face grin faded. "What do you mean?"

"I mean it was you." He didn't answer. "You called the *Morning News* and had me fired. Then you called Oliver Chesney and asked him to give me a job. Anything in your power to bring me home."

"Is that what Oliver told you?"

"He said he let himself be talked into hiring me. I knew right away it was you."

She had expected Gil to deny it, but he seemed proud. "It wasn't easy, you know. They didn't want to let you go."

"Well, that's nice." For a second, she felt flattered. "Wait a minute, three other people were fired that day. You had them all fired?"

Gil shrugged. "Couldn't be helped. We had to make it look like a layoff. The paper was over-staffed anyway."

"You… It didn't matter that you were hurting people? Their families? It didn't matter that you were uprooting my life? Oh, no. Not an issue."

Gil shifted his legs again. "Was I so wrong? Was that the wrong choice, digging up your shallow new roots and bringing you home? How many friends did you have there? Tell me. How much family did you have? Your daddy needs you, Callie."

"I'll still be around."

"It's not the same. He needs consistency. In whatever

world he wakes up, the man needs the familiar. People and things from before."

"Is that what I am, some kind of prop? Part of his daily surroundings?" Callie shook her head and bit her lower lip. "Like Sarah? Like Angus?"

"Don't be maudlin. You're a McFee. Being part of this family is a gift. Honestly, I think it would be sad just living for yourself, not being a part of something bigger."

Callie knew what he meant. "I used to feel that way. Hell, I was bred that way. But now… You're more his family than I am. I'm sorry, Uncle Gil." Without another word or a moment more of hesitation, she slipped the truck into Drive and continued up to the house.

Her last evening at the ranch was a subdued one. Gil ate in his own part of the house, leaving Callie and Sarah to deal with Buddy. At dinner, he was in a quiet mood, barely saying a word as he worked his way through the sweet and sour pork chops, mashed potatoes and green beans. She never knew where he was during these quiet spells. Every now and then she would try to ask questions and bring him out, but he would respond only reluctantly, mumbling as few words as possible.

Afterwards, Callie helped Sarah in the kitchen, just to give herself something to do. The last few weeks had felt strange in a way she couldn't put into words. It was both comforting and uncomfortable, both nostalgic and sad, to sleep in her old bedroom and have Sarah once again in the house, to keep her company and gossip with, just like the old days.

From the kitchen, Sarah went back to her own little suite. Angus didn't follow. He had been on his bed by the pantry, waiting for any scraps that might fall from the counters. Angus had been with them less than a week, a rescue that State and Yolanda had picked up from the shelter. He was an Irish setter several years younger than old Angus but sharing the same gray face and laid-back ways. When Buddy was in the present, he realized it was a different animal. When he was in a fog or visiting the past, he didn't seem to notice.

Angus padded his way from the kitchen to the front study and his favorite dog bed. Callie followed, rapping lightly on the doorjamb before intruding. Her father was in his usual spot, a brown leather armchair almost identical to his previous one, with a little pillow acting as a bolster for his lower back. He was dozing, his head back and to one side. On the arm of his chair was his wooden Cohiba, artfully balanced, its long wooden ash poised over a duplicate of his old wicker wastebasket.

Callie was about to retreat. They would say their goodbyes in the morning, when he might be in a more receptive space. Then she smelled the air and noted the wisp of smoke spiraling up from the cigar. A second later and the burning ash fell into the wastebasket.

At first, she was puzzled. Had the little sculpture come to life? But the cigar was indeed real, as was the ash, now smoldering on the hardwood bottom of the wastebasket. She was just picking it up when her father roused himself back into consciousness.

"Daughter of mine." He grunted, shifted in his chair and threw her a lazy smile. His gaze lowered to the cigar in her hand. "I didn't have my morning one, so… As long as I finish it before midnight, I'm good with your mother." He reached out and she handed it back.

"Cohibas," she said. "Where do you keep them?"

Buddy frowned. "I can't remember. I found this one… I don't know where. I think your mother's been hiding them from me."

Callie made a mental note to tell Gil. He would draw the same conclusion that she was drawing now. A lit cigar falling into a wastebasket full of paper… How funny.

After all their worry and paranoia about the fire, all their suspicions of the ruthless Texas elite, the solution would prove to be something as simple as this. Buddy had promised Anita on her deathbed never to smoke again, and he was a man of his word – except, of course, when he was in the past and she was still alive. Callie and Gil would sweep the house in the morning, looking for whatever stash he'd left behind.

Buddy took a long, satisfied puff, releasing it through his nostrils. "Why don't you sit with me?" he asked, pointing to the chair opposite his own. "Till I finish this little piece of heaven." She nodded. She would sit by him until it was safely extinguished. "How about a little whisky?" he asked. "Want me to get you a little drop of whisky?"

She chuckled. "I'll get you a little drop of whisky." At the bar, she took two cut crystal rocks glasses. Just as she was reaching for the bottle of brown water, she realized that her father, in his current state, would raise holy hell at the taste. She located the real stuff, the bottle of Buchanan's at the back of the cabinet above the bar, and poured him two fingers neat. For her own glass, she poured the same amount, two fingers neat, but from the bottle of brown water on the bar. Like her father on a good day, she had grown used to the taste.

Settling down in the new leather armchair opposite his, Callie McFee toasted into the smoky air. "To family," said Buddy, toasting back.

"To family."

THE END

ABOUT THE BOOK

The Fixer's Daughter has been a long time coming. I had proposed a kernel of this idea in the *Monk* writers' room well over a decade ago. Like most kernels, it was a simple *what if*. What if a powerful politician, the holder of a dozen explosive secrets, begins to suffer from dementia? At the time, the other writers and I were unable to "find the funny" in the situation and still treat the character with respect. The kernel remained on an index card pinned to our cork board, along with a dozen other half-born ideas until the very end of our run. Had the show gone on for nine seasons instead of eight, who knows, we might have cracked it.

But the idea stayed with me. How do you protect someone like this? How do you deal with those dangerous secrets, now held in an erratic, failing mind? And can you even trust those memories to be true? This became the centerpiece of a TV pilot that I wrote a few years later. Unfortunately, the premise of a sympathetic character, the title character no less, with progressive dementia proved to be too disturbing for a basic cable network.

Years after that, a publisher called and asked if I had any ideas for a new novel. The old index card came immediately to mind. It took me less than a day to rough out an outline. In hindsight, I probably should have taken longer. As before, it was a tough nut to crack and, despite the publisher's initial enthusiasm, the book didn't happen.

But I felt I was on the right track. An estranged daughter forced to deal with her ailing powerhouse of a dad. The two of them on opposing sides of a murder investigation. It felt like a great story. And great stories are everything. In my experience, writers on their deathbeds, at least some, don't regret not having spent more time with their families. They regret not having finished all the stories they imagined but never got to bring to life.

In *The Fixer's Daughter*, I also got to use a pretty terrific plot twist. Old-school mystery writers tend to collect plot twists the way some people collect door knobs. Occasionally we craft them on our own, from our own designs. Other times we discover them in some classic structure from the 1930s, steal them, polish them up and make them fit. I have no memory of how this twist, the man in the field, came into my collection, but it's one of my favorites.

In the years following that index card and the various rejections, the saga of Buddy McFee and his daughter took shape, going through several iterations, each one happily separated from its predecessor by a TV gig or some other paid engagement. In an early, misguided attempt to make the story edgier, I wrote approximately a third of it from the viewpoint of a deranged killer, a predecessor to the Gavin Hollister character. I don't know what made me do this. Perhaps it was a

Stephen King fixation. The result was a diffused focus and a story that was much creepier than I had intended. Friends who were forced to read this version still hold it against me.

In a way, after all these years, finally publishing this book feels anticlimactic. Buddy, Callie, State, Gil and the others will no longer be my private property. They will no longer be the go-to response to the cocktail party question, "What are you working on now that your show got cancelled?" They are out in the world for everyone to love or hate, to believe or disbelieve, to want to see more of, or to quickly forget.

And because they're out there, they exist. They have a life now that's free of me. And that's all a proud parent can hope for.

ABOUT THE AUTHOR

HY CONRAD has made a career out murder, earning a Scribe Award for best novel and garnering three Edgar nominations from the Mystery Writers of America. Along the way, he has developed a horde of popular games and interactive films, hundreds of short stories and a dozen books of solvable mysteries, published in over a dozen languages. In the world of TV, he is best known for his eight seasons as a writer and co-executive producer for the ground-breaking series *Monk*. Other shows include *White Collar* and *The Good Cop*.

As a novelist, Hy has authored the final four books in the Monk series as well as the series, *Amy's Travel Mysteries*.

When he looks up from his keyboard, Hy sees either the hills of Vermont or the palm trees of Key West, depending on the time of year. When he steps away from his keyboard, he sees Jeff Johnson, his partner of 41 years, now his husband, plus Nelson and Stella, the latest in a dynasty of mini-schnauzers dating back to the 1980s.

www.hyconrad.com
Facebook: hyconrad
Instagram: hyconrad1

Made in the USA
Las Vegas, NV
17 June 2021

24932178R00187